GREG MUTTON

Chronicle of the Twelfth Realm

BOOK 1

REUNION

Cover design: Gail Rust.

Image: Shutterstock

ISBN: 978-0-646-81750-7 (paperback)

978-1-876409-44-9 (Ebook)

Third Edition 2020

Font Calibri 11.5 pt

Do the difficult things while they are easy and do the great things while they are small. A journey of a thousand miles must begin with a single step.

Lao Tzu

CAST of CHARACTERS

Abraham Family

Jason: Patriarch & father of Jeffery & Aaron
Amanda: Matriarch & mother of Jeffery & Aaron
Jeffery: CEO Abracorp & father of JT, Salina & David
Sonia: Professor of Horticulture, mother of JT, Salina & David
John (JT): Captain CSV Valiant

Salina: Marine Biologist
David: Financial controller Abracorp
Aaron: Freebooter Trader, estranged brother of Jeffery

Coalition Space Corps

Skye Wilson: Fleet Admiral
Simon Morris: Rear Admiral, Deputy to Wilson
Sam Grogan: Admiral – Commander Space Corps
Alan Dean: Captain – Adjutant to Admiral Morris
Sol Radchak: Captain – Commander Space Corps training

Crew ECS Valiant

JT Abraham: Captain
Jarad Cross: First Officer
Greg Holgate: Tactical Officer
Amy Rodregas: Chief Engineer
Colin Bryant: Sensor sensor/defence officer *Sharon Holm:*
Communication officer & linguist *Helen Tradeski:* Weapons
Officer

Dave Carmelli: Second Weapons Officer
Holly Morgan: Navigation Officer

Freebooter Characters
Freebooter Trade Ship (FTS) Condor

Aaron Abraham: Captain and CEO AA Trading *Petra Mannix:*
First Officer

Kate Albrecht: Second Officer

Simon Holm: Navigator

David Cross: Tactical Officer

Dianna Holland: Chief Engineer

Colin Anderson: Engineer

William Croker: Sensor Officer

Phillip Harper: Cadet

FTS Albatross

Steve Harris: Captain

Greg Lewis: First Officer

Other Freebooter Characters

Henry N'Gabo: Proctor AA Trading

Jacinta N'Gabo: Henry's Wife and Medical Technician

Allen Grainger: Freebooter Prime

Other Characters

Salim Malik: President Earth Coalition of Planets

Silas Greenbach: CEO Greenbach Technology

Kratc Dokad: Admiral – Krell Imperial Navy

Damien Albrecht: CEO Vision Cruise Lines

Eugene Sarclan: Former CEO of Sarcorp (liquidated) – dissident

Anthony Crompton: Dir. Coalition Intelligence Directorate (CID)

Ivan Klastok: General – Commander Coalition Army

Inter Realm Characters

Eldrac-Tar: Senior Eldoran Councillor

Jok-Tar: Son of Eldrac-Tar

Zal-Tar: Daughter of Eldrac-Tar

Mondrac: Eldoran Council Member – half-brother to Eldrac-Tar

Zarof: Leader of Galdor

Nefaris: Queen Regent of Nileros

Tocmal: Admiral – Commander Reglaos armed Forces

Acknowledgements

It's been said that writing is a solitary endeavour. That's partially correct, the actual writing, I've found is solitary but the final production of a book is far from that. I've been fortunate to have a group of people helping along the way.

The North Arm Cove Fellowship of Australian Writers' group has been always ready to encourage and assist, with advice from people who've been there and done this.

Peta Spear, who was the first to critically look at my work, set me on a much better path. I sent her the original manuscript, all 900+ pages and her advice has resulted in the trilogy—her critique and advice was invaluable.

Olly Griffin, one of the most wonderful people I've ever met has been an inspiration, a muse and a hard task master. But she has always helped me develop my stories.

Gail Rust, designed the cover capturing exactly what I had imagined and, helped greatly with editing my work. Her patience and skill made things happen.

My stepson Tim, whose study backs onto mine, is always there to listen, suggest and help. He's also a great sounding board.

My advance team—a small group of readers who make suggestions and let me know what they think about the stories. These people are invaluable and I am very grateful for their efforts.

And last, but probably most importantly, my wife Debbie; she has given me the opportunity to do this. She has encouraged, cajoled and put up with me in those times when it all seemed to be a disaster. She has listened, proof read and helped me develop parts of my stories that needed a "female" touch. Together we have embarked on the self-publishing journey, a saga in itself. Without her support, the books I am releasing would still be just a dream.

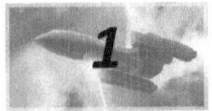

Wed Feb 5, 2921 Earth Standard Calendar

*T*he docking bay was depressingly empty.

Tall and solidly built, he moved with an economy of effort as he ran his long fingers through his short black hair. Johnathon Thomas Abraham 4th wore the uniform of Captain 2nd grade, Earth Coalition Space Corps and, at just sixty-two, was young for the rank. During his Academy years his name shortened and to most of his peers he became JT, a name that had stood the test of time.

Strange, he thought, *no shuttles, or work tugs, no vessel of any type.* He remembered a saying his grandfather used, 'sign of the times.' Was this another sign of Earth's increasing irrelevance?

JT replaced his cover and adjusted it to the correct angle, his dark eyes scanning the dock again, as if hoping he had missed some activity.

He continued to ponder the situation; this dock was one of eight in the complex. Even though it was the oldest and smallest, it was capable of housing and servicing twenty medium-sized spacecraft simultaneously. At one time there were five of these massive, manmade complexes orbiting Earth, now only this one was still operational. Two had been re-tasked as part of the, now mothballed, Orbital Defence system and one was the Corps' main hangar and maintenance station. The other two had been decommissioned and scrapped. He sighed; *Earth is no longer the centre of the Human race.*

As he watched, the dock entry force-field glowed red,

indicating a vessel was approaching. The field changed to green and a sleek silver ship turned for final approach. It was a tight manoeuvre, given the entry trajectory, but expertly executed. The dock entry flared bright white as the two force fields matched harmonics and the shuttle entered.

It was an *Askari* patrol ship. A beautiful vessel—sleek, fast and formidably armed; not what he was expecting, given that this was a routine inspection of the conversion project. The ship stopped, lowered its landing struts and settled effortlessly to the deck. The gangway extended to the port hatch and three people exited.

He recognised one immediately, Captain, third grade, Alan Dean. *Damn, I hoped I'd seen the last of him!* The history between JT and Dean was complicated. The incident at Zyralin 4 over twelve months previously, and the subsequent Court of Inquiry resulted in Dean being reassigned as Adjutant to Admiral Morris. It was no secret that he blamed John Abraham for the stalling of his career.

Admiral Sam Grogan exited the ship next. The Admiral was expected, in fact he was the only one JT knew was coming, as he had been overseeing this project from the beginning; but the third man, Rear Admiral Simon Morris was another surprise. JT moved to the airlock and snapped his best parade ground salute as it opened.

'No need for formalities, Captain. Please, let's keep things low key.' Admiral Morris's voice was deep and well-modulated. He was taller than JT, athletically built with dark curly hair and deceptively soft blue eyes. These eyes had been the downfall of many officers as they didn't give any hint of what was *really* going on inside his head.

Admiral Grogan stepped forward. 'How's it going, John?'

'Very well, Admiral,' JT replied. 'Initial testing is complete and we are ready for our final operational evaluation.'

'It better be,' sneered Dean, the shortest of the group. 'If you ask me, this is all a waste of time and money.' From the outset he had been a vocal opponent of the project.

'Thankfully, we're not asking you,' Morris retorted as he nodded to John. 'Lead on Captain Abraham.'

JT turned and walked to the waiting ground car. 'Not as elegant as your shuttle,' he admitted, 'but it'll get us there.' He stood aside as the two Admirals climbed into the rear seat; Dean walked to the other side and took the front passenger spot.

It only took a few minutes to reach their destination as JT stopped the car outside Hangar 7. The door to the observation lounge slid silently back as the group left the car and approached it.

'Is this the old *Valiant*?' Morris asked.

'Yes Sir,' JT responded. 'As you recall she had some damage from her last encounter...so we made a few modifications.'

'A few,' Morris said. 'It looks nothing like a "Vigilant" class ship.'

'As I said, a waste of time and money, just so Abraham can resurrect that old ship!' Dean added scathingly.

'Considering that he has paid for all the work himself, I would say the Corps is getting damn good value!' Jeff Abraham, John's father and president of Abracorp entered the room as Dean was complaining. 'If you recall Captain Dean, the Corps had written the old girl off. John bought her as scrap, so to return her in this condition is a bargain.

'Jeff, good to see you,' Morris extended his hand, showing Dean that further comment was not warranted.

'Simon,' Abraham senior returned, 'shall we have a closer look?' He turned to lead the way to the dock entrance. 'Silas is already on board,' he called over his shoulder as they fell in behind him.

The ship had indeed been transformed. Gone were the old Hyzene tanks and power nacelles that protruded from the rear of the engineering section. Now this section was smaller and blended purposefully into the main hull. The overall impression was one of grace and power.

'The new shape looks vaguely familiar,' Admiral Grogan mused. 'Can't quite put a handle on it though, it's been bugging me for months.'

'Sal calls it the *Manta* as she believes it looks like a Manta Ray,' Jeff explained.

Salina Abraham, John's younger sister, was an authority on things aquatic, having just submitted her thesis for her PhD in Marine Biology. Most of her free time was spent on various marine research and breeding facilities trying to re-populate the oceans of Earth. The effort of Sal and the teams she worked with was starting to attract attention; species once thought extinct were approaching a level where sustainable fishing was again possible.

'Overall, the ship is slightly larger than the original, but needs only two hundred and fifty crew members instead of four hundred; and crew accommodation has been dramatically improved...everyone now has cabin space, no more bunk rooms. We installed a new modular hold system, making it easy to change mission profile by simply installing a customised module...personnel transport, ground support; even a field hospital can be set up in less than half an hour.

'Thankfully this old ship had already been converted from solid state hardware to bio-chemical data systems, making the modifications much easier. All we needed to do was to inject the Bio system with a new catalyst to speed up communication and memory capacity...but I should let Silas explain all that, it's his baby after all.'

The group entered the ship via the starboard forward airlock—one of four airlocks, two on each side of the ship—the doors remained open as the dock was still at full atmospheric condition.

Silas Greenbach was waiting inside. 'Gentlemen, welcome aboard,' he said to the group as they entered.

Morris nodded to Silas, noting that he still looked much younger than anyone else in the room. 'Looking good, Silas,' he added.

'Thank you, Admiral.' Silas Greenbach's features defied age profiling. He could have been anywhere from mid-fifties, to well over two hundred. His hair was the colour of sand, his eyes a striking translucent blue. In all the recorded photos of Silas he never changed, which had given rise to much speculation on his age. Even though the genetic secret to longevity had been discovered long ago, aging still happened, albeit on a much slower scale. Silas Greenback though, never seemed to change.

The group walked to the end of the corridor and entered a transport pod.

'Bridge,' John commanded as a thin red light beam washed over him. The doors closed and the pod travelled the short distance to the bridge.

'Part of the enhanced security system,' Silas explained. 'Access to sensitive areas of the ship is only available to authorised personnel. Authorisation is by way of vocal and biometric scanning. Any unauthorised entry, or attempted entry, will be immediately stopped.'

'And just how is it stopped?' Dean asked sarcastically.

'You really don't want to find out.' The tone in Silas's voice cut any further discussion short, as the bridge door opened,

'Gentlemen, the new bridge,' John announced.

The bridge layout was conventional for a ship this size. The command chair was flanked by various operational stations, but the Bubble pad that held centre stage of the bridge caught everyone's attention. The Bubble or, more accurately, *Real Time Navigational and Operational Holographic Projection,* was a major component in the navigation, defence and fighting ability of many of Space Corps' ships.

Real time, three dimensional images of the ship and, more importantly, the space around it, were displayed in a holographic sphere or Bubble. The size of the Bubble was constant but the area it represented could be changed to suit different operations. All sensor, operational and navigation data displayed both in real time and in proportion to their operating area—the only limiting factor was the range of the ship's sensors. In a battle situation, this one instrument had accounted for more successful outcomes than any other. However, one had never been installed in a Vigilant Class ship before.

There was something else unexpected on the bridge— the occupant of the command chair—Fleet Admiral Skye Wilson. It took a few seconds for this fact to sink in and, as one, all officers snapped to attention and saluted.

'At ease, gentlemen,' Admiral Wilson ordered. 'Officially, I'm not here; I am in fact trout fishing with Stewart in Tasmania and will be till zero eight hundred Monday morning.' Skye Wilson, the most senior officer in the fleet was a small woman who commanded respect through personality, intensity and determination. But it was her piercing eyes that quelled any thoughts of weakness.

Throughout her career she had been a brilliant Star Ship captain and had rewritten a large part of space warfare theory. 'I have been fortunate in having Silas here to show me this ship; I'm looking forward to seeing her in action. Captain, your chair?' she stood up and indicated to JT to take the command position. 'I believe you have a live fire test arranged for today. Would you allow an old desk jockey to accompany you, purely as an observer?'

'My pleasure, Ma'am,' John replied.

JT took up his seat and ran through the normal system confirmations. Engineering, weapons, defence—with all systems checked, he turned to the navigator. 'As the Admiral is in a slight hurry, set course for the range at maximum displacement...pilot, prepare to leave the dock. Comms, give me an open channel.

The pilot called the dock master, obtained clearance to leave and commenced disconnecting from the dock umbilicals as John started his ship-wide broadcast.

'This is the Captain,' he began. 'As you all know, today is the final trial for our ship. Today we test the new systems in a battle scenario and, the enemy will shoot back. We all know what our ship can do, so let's prove it! That is all.' He cut the transmission. While he was talking, the ship had left the dock and was just clearing the controlled area.

'Coming up on the outer mark' the navigator called.

'Engage displacement drive,' John commanded. The pilot obeyed his captain's order and energised the drive's field emitters. There was a fraction of a second where everything seemed to waver, almost out of focus, as the displacement field energised and the ship entered its worm hole.

'Worm hole stable, displacement factor fifteen' was the call from the engineer. While this was not the highest displacement that Valiant could achieve, it was the maximum that could be used for this journey.

'Time to re-insertion, seventeen minutes twenty eight seconds,' the navigator reported.

JT turned to the tactical officer. 'At five minutes to reinsertion, sound battle stations and go to red alert. What's our shield status?'

The defence officer consulted the screen and replied, 'Shield generators are spun up and on standby, absorption bank is empty and the deflector array is functioning at optimum cruise setting.'

JT turned to the weapons officer. 'Guns, are we ready?'

Tall, blonde and athletic, the weapons officer, Lt Commander Helen Tradeski cut an impressive figure. While the handle *Guns* had been used for centuries for those who, technically, fought the ship, in this case it was more personal. Helen Tradeski was an expert on ancient weaponry and an avid collector of all types of antique projectile weapons.

'All weapon systems nominal Sir,' she replied.

'Then we have a couple of minutes for a quick bridge tour.' JT offered to his guests. They jumped at the offer and dispersed to various stations for a closer look at the operations. The bridge was larger than the original with the Bubble pad taking the centre. Immediately behind this was the forward view screen that stretched across the front of the bridge and gave a panoramic view of the space ahead of the ship.

The Command chair was to the rear of the bridge with weapons, tactical and defence control to the right, engineering, communications and sensor control to the left. Both groups curved towards the front of the bridge so all could have a clear view of the Bubble. Behind each station was the redundant, or back up, station, currently unmanned, but an essential part of the operation in any battle scenario. JT was admiring the simplicity and functionality of the design when Admiral Wilson interrupted his thoughts.

'May I have a minute with you; in your ready room?' she

asked. John led the way.

'I will make this quick,' Wilson said, as the door closed. 'While I can't go into detail here, we now know that the incident at Zyralin Four was not what it seemed, initially. The board of enquiry ascertained that your actions were correct, in fact if you hadn't acted as you did, the losses would have been total. It was also found that your commander at the time made some very serious errors and, consequently, will never be in a command situation again. The board made several recommendations and one of them is this.' She held out a small leather box.

John took it and lifted the lid. Inside were the twin sets of four sun symbols, the insignia of a full Captain—Grade 4.

'Congratulations Captain, you really earned these.'

John was about to speak when the distinctive sound of a Klaxon horn sounded three times and then the First Officer's voice spoke, *Red alert! All crew to battle stations! This is not a drill, red alert!* Three more blasts of the Klaxon followed.

'A Klaxon...?' Admiral Wilson asked.

'Very effective, it really galvanises the crew into action, you'll see.'

'Well, put on those pips and let's see if it worked.'

JT removed his old rank insignia and replaced them with the new ones as they exited the ready room. Already, the ship status display was glowing mostly red. The six redundant stations were now active, with four of them physically manned.

'With the new system, each station can be manned remotely if needed,' Silas was explaining to the others. 'While we think of ourselves as very advanced beings, we are still basically one step from the animal world and there are times when we simply cannot respond in person...

we still have bodily functions that rule us.' This brought a couple of knowing smiles from the admirals. 'Now each crew member can log onto their station remotely...all biometrically controlled and secured.'

The status display was now totally red and showed all stations as battle ready. John took his seat in the command chair. He turned to the assembled admirals.

'Thirty-eight seconds to battle readiness; not our best response, but acceptable.'

It was a calm, businesslike transition from cruise mode to battle stations; the only sign of urgency was the sounding of the Klaxon. Thirty eight seconds was an extremely good response time.

'This is the Captain speaking;' John began a ship-wide broadcast. 'Well done everyone. We are about to reinsert into normal space and commence our final exercise; time to show what we can do!' He switched off the comm system and looked at the defence officer.

'Lock her down, Lieutenant.'

The lock down procedure commenced with all external view ports closing and armour doors sliding across to cover them. All air locks sealed and the bridge lowered into its battle position. Now, in less than twenty seconds, the ship was one smooth, homogenous shape, with no visible protrusions or access points to the inside. The view screen changed from visual to sensor mode with an almost imperceptible flicker.

'Raise the Bubble,' JT commanded and the tactical officer switched on the holographic display. Immediately, the forward section of the bridge, until now empty, filled with a translucent blue glow—the Bubble. At its centre was the ship, but as they were still in hyperspace, the rest was just a constantly changing fog.

'Twenty seconds to reinsertion,' navigation officer, Lieutenant Holly Morgan announced. As if on cue, twenty seconds later, the Bubble cleared and displayed normal space in a sphere of one million kilometres diameter around the ship. Automatically, all shields were raised and the weapon systems initialised. Valiant was now ready to fight.

'Ahead...slow,' JT ordered. 'Tactical?'

At his console, the Tactical Officer, Greg Holgate, worked his magic and the tactical information began to show in the Bubble. Directly ahead and at a distance of three hundred and twenty five thousand kilometres was the target— an old converted freighter that had been enhanced and strengthened for the job. Not only built to take a blow, this target could hit back with a complete array of weapons: blasters, disrupters, torpedos and more—a squadron of Dart attack ships were also at its disposal. All that was of no consequence, the goal of this test was simply to prove the effectiveness of a totally new weapons system. They would face some deterrents, but they had already passed all other battle scenarios.

'Skipper, check this out?' Holgate pointed to the twelve drone gunships that seemed to form a funnel to the target. Outside this funnel was a myriad of constantly moving red dots.

'The red dots are mines. There's no other way to approach the target, except to run that gauntlet...strange set up,' Holgate muttered, trying to make sense of this strategy.

'Who is the range officer today?' JT directed his question to Admiral Grogan.

'Captain Radchak I believe,' he replied.

'Solomon Radchak?' JT raised an eyebrow. 'Sol and I were at the Academy together...he's a brilliant tactician, if somewhat unorthodox.' He returned his attention to the

Bubble.

'Tactical, what is the forward sensor array aperture?'

'Standard two metres, why?' Greg Holgate responded.

'Change it to fifty millimetres and sweep across our path,' JT responded. 'Display it in the Bubble.'

In seconds, the Bubble changed, showing a myriad of tiny black objects in the ship's path and extending out almost to the gunships. Everyone looked at these tiny objects, trying to ascertain just what they were. Sensor readings indicated they were solid and, with no power source being detected, the system classified them as space rock.

It was Holly Morgan who broke the silence. 'Pin mines, Sir...they're pin mines, but not activated as yet.'

'Well done, Lieutenant,' JT nodded approvingly to the young officer, 'Sol, you sneaky bastard!'

Their options were limited, they couldn't go around these because of the active mine field and the gunships. All the range officer had to do was wait until they were in range of the pin mines, arm them and sit back and watch the show.

This dilemma brought a smug smile to Dean's face. 'So, what do you intend to do about **this**, Abraham?' he gloated.

JT ignored him and looked back at his tactical specialist.

'Tactical...options?'

Greg Holgate smiled slightly. The bridge crew knew that this was a good sign. Not the sort of person who stood out in a crowd and with a physical presence that was best described as ordinary, Commander Holgate's mind was the proverbial *steel trap*, constantly working and able to come up with numerous options to most situations. His mouth curled very slightly now, but those who worked with him knew he had an answer.

'Corkscrew?' he suggested with a glint in his eye.

'Do it,' JT answered, a smile crossing his face.

'What's *corkscrew?*" questioned Admiral Morris who was standing just behind the primary tactical position.

'A little trick our chief engineer worked out...now, watch the fun,' Greg replied as he initiated the program.

Immediately the Bubble display changed and the shape of the ship seemed to change with it. The forward section appeared to elongate into a cone shape which looked as if it was starting to rotate.

Amy Rodregas, the Chief Engineer, responded. 'Really quite simple, Admiral, we just extend the deflector screen and start a rotating ripple that travels round the ship, it works like a funnel, but in reverse. Anything that the deflector moves out of the way is channelled along the tapered field and then flung out of the ship's path by the ripple.'

Greg interrupted. 'Deflector is at full rotation...we can proceed.'

'Ahead, dead slow,' came JT's command. In the engineering section, the latest Greenbach Gravitron Drive urged the ship slowly forward. 'Guns, any of those gunships draw a bead, take them out. Main armament, concentrate on the target. Is *Sling Shot* ready?'

Helen handed over the secondary targets—the gunships—to the redundant weapons Officer Dave Carmelli. 'Yes sir,' she replied.

Admiral Wilson looked to Silas. 'What's Sling Shot?'

Silas smiled. 'An experimental weapons system; it's the focus of today's exercise. Just watch...we'll explain it all later.'

Holly Morgan was monitoring the clearing of the pin mines. 'We're starting to move into the mine field.'

The ship slowly penetrated the first layer of mines, the

deflector starting to move them aside. Gradually a path was being forced through. Time dragged by, minutes seemed like hours, nobody spoke. It was as if they were afraid that even a slight sound might trigger the mines.

'Number one layer the screens...absorption outermost, we may need to soak up some energy,' JT ordered. Slowly, the mines in the distance began to change colour in the Bubble. 'Looks like Sol's twigged to our trick...He's initialising the mines...increase speed, ahead two thirds.'

The next few minutes were the most critical in the exercise, as using the corkscrew made evasive manoeuvring almost impossible. And they were still only a third of the way through the mines.

'We're being targeted...three gunships have us locked on!' Helen called.

The Bubble changed as it showed which of the gunships had them locked. As one they fired and three plasma balls sped towards Valiant.

'Don't wait for an invitation, take them out!' JT commanded. Valiant returned fire with a spread of torpedos. Two of the gunships fired a second burst, this time finding their mark. Valiant lurched and yawed, alarms screaming through the bridge.

'Hit, sir. Rear port quarter...no damage,' Amy called as she changed the emergency crew status from stand-by to active.

Valiant opened up on the defenders. Another spread of torpedos flew from their cradles, drive trails marking their progress. The port blaster array was now firing continuously, intense streams of pure energy assailing the targets. Two of the gunships exploded as the torpedos slammed into them, the third turned and tried to evade the onslaught from Valiants blasters, but to no avail. Turning had been the worst blunder as the energy beam snaked down the length of the ship and sliced through the hull, disabling its engines. It drifted helplessly.

Now others were entering the battle. Another plasma ball slammed into the rear port quarter and more alarms screamed—Valiant wasn't having everything its own way.

'Amy, how are we doing with these pin mines?' JT called.

'Nearly there, Skipper...another few seconds. It seems the pin mines are a problem for the gunships, more than they are for us.'

The scene in the Bubble told the story—three more of the gunships were disabled. The pin mines that had been deflected by the corkscrew effect had been flung out toward the defending ships. Once armed, their proximity detectors had found the gunships and detonated with devastating results. The target's own weapons were now attacking its defences.

'We're through the mines.' Holgate called.

'Guns, you're up.' John barked.

'Target selected...torpedos away,' Helen responded.

Three sleek torpedos leapt from their cradles, their drive units leaving a faint but visible trail. Two seconds later they impacted the shield wall of the target as Helen frantically worked at her console.

'Shield parameters caught...programming containment field harmonics...Sling Shot fired.'

There was nothing to see. Unlike the torpedos, which had a drive system that left a visible track, Sling Shot projectiles left no visible trace—the only visible evidence was the end result, which was usually spectacular. This time was no different. All three shots found the target: a mock-up main reactor cooling tower at the rear of the target ship. The

15

result was a brilliant white eruption as the target vaporised; but the battle wasn't over yet. The remaining gunships had changed position and were attempting to attack the obvious weakness in Valiant's rear port shields.

'Helm, evasive action,' JT called, and the ship swung away from the target.

'Guns?'

There was no need to ask. Tradeski had already selected targets for the ship's weapons. Three torpedos shot out of the starboard bank, and the forward disruptor spat raw energy toward the other two gunships. Those two didn't stand a chance. The lead ship was hit with the full force and its hull was torn open, slewing it off course and then smashing into the second, ending that run as well.

'Good shooting, two for one.' Admiral Wilson cried, obviously enjoying the action. The last three split up and headed away from the torpedos rushing toward them; too late for one, which was hit on the rear starboard quarter as it turned—the entire engineering section collapsed by the force of the explosion—the other two escaped.

Admiral Morris smiled. 'Well, I think this ship has just passed her final trial. Well done everyone. Captain, hail the target and offer assistance'

'Comms...open hailing channels,' JT requested. 'Captain Radchak. This is Captain Abraham of ECS Valiant. I believe we have completed the exercise. Do you require any assistance?'

The comm system sounded a return hail and the voice of Solomon Radchak boomed into the bridge. *I would concur; seems you have learned a few new tricks JT.*

'Someone once told me to never stop learning,' JT chuckled. 'Nice trick with the pin mines, by the way.'

I think I borrowed that. As for assistance, well, we were told to expect damage. We have a heavy repair ship behind the asteroid belt. Someone was obviously confident in your little boat.

'Ok Sol, thanks for the shake down; we need to return to base ASAP. Call me next time you're back home,' JT replied.

'Not so quickly,' Simon Morris interjected. 'Captain Radchak, this is Admiral Morris. We would like you to return with us, so we can have a full debrief ready for next week. Can you leave the repairs to your crew?'

There was a brief pause, no doubt for Radchak to confer with his second in command. *I'll need about fifteen minutes to get all the data ready.*

'No problem, we'll send a shuttle.' Morris finished.

John turned to the navigator. 'Set course for Earth and proceed as soon as Captain Radchak is aboard.' He diverted his attention to his weapons officer, 'Helen, I think the admirals would like an update on Sling Shot.'

Helen nodded to her captain. 'Yes sir we've set up a display in the ward room.' She looked to Admiral Wilson. 'Ma'am, if you and the other Admirals would like to follow me.' As she reached the pod, Allan Dean was behind her. She paused, not knowing what to do.

Silas came to her aid. 'Sorry, Captain, but you don't have clearance for this.'

'Rubbish, I have level 2 Red...top secret clearance.' Dean spluttered.

Silas's eyes narrowed and his stare was intense. 'Maybe for Space Corps, but this ship isn't part of Space Corps, it's the property of Captain Abraham and he has allowed us to use it as a test bed for our new systems. Those systems are proprietary designs and hardware of Abracorp and

Greenbach Technologies, and you have no clearance for either company.'

Dean spluttered something in indignation then returned to his previous place at the far rear corner of the bridge.

2

*T*he speaker on the command chair buzzed and announced, *Shuttle bay here, Captain Radchak's shuttle has docked*.

JT answered. 'Thank you; please bring Captain Radchak to the Ward Room.' He paused for a second. 'You have the con number one. Take us home, but I think the Admirals will need a little more time to go through the systems, delay our arrival for thirty minutes,' he added as he entered the pod.

Valiant's first officer, Jarad Cross, turned to the Navigator, his nod all that was needed.

'Course laid in, Sir.'

'Execute.'

With that one word things happened. The Displacement field was initiated and the pilot executed the insertion into the artificial worm hole. Watching this well-oiled operation, Jarad reflected on how far space travel had come. In a few centuries, humans had gone from being almost imprisoned in their tiny solar system, to reaching the edge of the galaxy. Where to next? These thoughts brought a smile to his lips as he sat in the command chair.

JT entered the ward room and saw the three admirals, his father and Silas in deep conversation; they were all grouped around a long table in the centre of the room. He approached the dispenser and ordered a coffee. Taking the offered mug he turned just as Solomon Radchak entered. He raised his mug questioningly. Radchak nodded and JT requested another and handed it to the new arrival.

'Sol, good to see you.'

'I really should salute you, congratulations old boy,'

Solomon replied tapping the four suns his friend's collar.

Admiral Grogan beckoned them over. The ward room was always neutral ground and usual military protocols suspended, so they both joined the group without fuss. A few strange items were on the table. Directly in front was a model of a Mark 9 torpedo, behind that was what looked like an ancient artillery shell and the third item resembled an ancient projectile weapon. Sol was perplexed.

'Please don't tell me you blew up our target with **that** old thing?' he asked as he pointed to the shell.

JT laughed. 'Actually we did, sort of. But this is a hell of a lot more than it looks...Helen, maybe you and Amy should explain.'

'Thank you Sir' Helen motioned to the table. 'If everyone would take a seat, we'll begin.' The scraping of chairs and soft murmuring followed. She started at the end of the table that held the ancient weapon.

'This is the weapon that gave us the idea for Sling Shot. It used an old form of magnetic propulsion instead of an explosive charge to fire the projectile. Back in the latter part of the Twenty First century, these weapons became very effective. One naval vessel was built for the Oceanic Navy and its only offensive weapons were two huge magnetic propulsion tubes. A projectile, similar to that one on the table, was loaded into the weapon where a moving magnetic field was established and that propelled the projectile forward at incredible velocity. This was far in excess of anything that could be obtained with conventional ballistic or missile technology. The downside was it had to be aimed manually as it had no guidance system.

'What *we* have done is take the concept of magnetic linear acceleration and apply gravimetric technology to do the same. Our long tube actually is circular and runs round the entire ship. The projectile we fire is a lot different but is still hampered by accuracy...it still needs good aim.'

'Are you saying you somehow used Greenbach's Gravitron drive system in this?' Wilson asked.

'Yes, a highly modified system.'

'Why? What's wrong with torpedos?' Grogan chipped in.

Silas answered. 'Cost...it simply costs way too much to build and destroy torpedos. Every time one is built, there is the cost and complexity of the drive system, the guidance system and then we blow it up. This will be far more effective and efficient; the projectile on the table is the standard unit for this weapon. Weighing less than a tenth of a torpedo; it takes up less than that to store and costs far less. We estimate these units will cost around five to ten percent of a torpedo and it will be faster; what is the maximum speed of a torpedo?' He didn't wait for an answer, pressing on regardless. 'I'll tell you: point five light. Amy, what was the speed of those three units fired today?'

Amy Rodregas smiled. 'Point six light; we didn't need any more.' She could see the questions forming on the Admirals lips. 'We can fire this weapon at various speeds, depending on the situation. So far, our max is point nine five light. The only issue is with the need to aim the unit. We are currently testing a modified projectile design that has a guidance system to see if it can do what we want.'

'But the energy it released on the target...surely no solid lump of metal can do that?' Sol asked.

'You're right captain,' Amy replied 'However, this is not a solid lump of metal. Only the outer case is made of metal.' She moved to the projectile and removed one side. 'Inside is a hybrid of Barainium and composites to contain a charge of antimatter. It's the antimatter inside that causes the damage. Matter collides with antimatter, Physics 101 mutual annihilation. That's why this weapon is so impressive.'

She tapped an icon on the data pad in front of her and the view screen came to life. It ran a short presentation showing the working of the system, the design of the projectile and a brief history of the ancient technology, including both the old ship and the other weapon on the table. At the conclusion of the presentation, everyone in the room was impressed with the potential of the resurrected weapon system.

'Did I see correctly...the name of that old naval ship...was it Valiant?' Wilson asked.

'Yes Ma'am, she was commissioned for the old Oceania Navy, the Long Axis Gunship Valiant, launched in twenty ninety six,' JT answered with some pride.

Admiral Wilson stood. 'Gentlemen, we currently have fifty of these old vigilant class ships mothballed at Jupiter Station. Silas, Jeff...I want you to come up with an action plan to convert them to the new...what did Salina call them... ah yes, Manta Class. This is to be of the upmost priority and outside of this room, the project is to be considered classified top secret. Nobody, I repeat *nobody* is to discuss this with anyone else. I'll convene a preliminary meeting for next Tuesday at ten hundred hours, at Headquarters. All of you are to be there and we will then work on the conversion timetable and training program. Thank you for a most enlightening morning.' She turned to Amy and Helen and shook their hands. 'This is a fantastic achievement, well done. Now, as officially I'm not here, I better get ready to go fishing.' With that she rose and left the room.

Amy moved across the room to speak to Sol. 'So, Captain, you're the one who banged my ship?' The chief engineer offered her hand to congratulate him. 'Good shooting.' Sol took her hand, noticing the firmness of her grip.

'I may have banged your ship,' Sol quipped, 'but I think *we* came off second best. Not only did you totally destroy the target, but you blew a twenty metre hole in the side of the base ship!'

'And we only used a *small* antimatter charge,' Helen chipped in.

Sol looked to JT as the latter cocked his head in the direction of the door. The two stood and exited the ward room, walking in silence to the transport pod.

'Bridge,' John commanded and the doors closed behind them. Ten seconds later the doors opened and the bridge lay out before them.

'Captain on the bridge,' an Ensign announced as John and his guest stepped out of the pod. He realised that the ship was technically still at red alert status. 'As you were,' he replied. 'Jarad, cancel red alert and stand down battle stations.'

The crew was extremely proud of their compact work area—no wasted space; every piece of equipment was functional and critical to operations. Every one of the bridge crew had been involved in the redesign process and this was evident in the efficiency of the layout.

'Can I have your attention?' The bridge crew stopped and looked to their captain. 'This is Captain Radchak,' he said, placing his hand on Sol's shoulder 'the enemy who just tried to take us down.' JT announced. He looked to his first officer, 'We'll be in the ready room.'

'Aye sir,' Jarad replied as his captain led his guest to the rear left of the bridge and through the door to the ready room. It wasn't a large space, measuring approximately five metres by four metres with the curve of the hull giving an illusion of more area, the large view ports on this wall adding to the illusion. Under the view ports was the captain's desk with a couple of comfortable looking guest chairs. The centre of the room held a low table and two curved leather lounges where six people could sit comfortably. On the wall behind this was a food and beverage dispenser.

JT headed for the lounge. 'Take a load off, Sol; we'll be back at Earth station in about ten minutes, time to catch up on the last five years.'

Eight minutes later their conversation was interrupted by Jarad's voice.' *Captain, can you come to the bridge?*

They stood and moved quickly to the bridge door. As they entered, the first officer moved to exit the command chair. 'Sir, the dock commander has requested we delay our arrival for another ten minutes.'

Changing or terminating any parameter of a ship's course once it has entered a worm hole wasn't done easily or casually. The calculations were complex; it was only ever considered in extreme situations. Their return had been given the highest priority—thanks to Admiral Wilson—so the request was totally unexpected.

'Navigator, do we have a reinsertion option?'

'Possibly, but it'll put us very close to commercial flight paths,' Lieutenant Morgan replied. 'It will give us the time that the dock commander requested.'

'OK, make it happen,' JT replied. He turned to the comms officer. 'Open a channel to the dock.'

The Dock was actually one of Abracorps' construction facilities and housed both commercial and military construction operations. There must be a good reason for this delay, given the security classification of the flight.

ECS Valiant, this is Orion dock command, the voice on the communicator was Elron Mansfield, dock commander.

'This is Captain Abraham, what's the problem Elron?' JT

asked.

Sorry captain, but we have some issues with media coverage and need the extra time to contain the situation. He sounded strangely embarrassed as he made this revelation.

'What media coverage?' JT was puzzled. Their flight was not worthy of any media coverage; in fact, the media outlets had been deliberately kept in the dark.

Again my apologies; Friday is departure day for Rhapsody and unfortunately, Albrecht has arranged for a media day prior to the launch.

Elron didn't need to elaborate. Damien Albrecht, CEO and majority share-holder of *Vision Cruise Lines,* had commissioned *Rhapsody of the Stars,* the largest cruise vessel ever built. With very good political connections, he usually got what he wanted—their current situation being the case in point.

'No problem, we'll deviate and avoid any encounters until you give the all clear; Valiant out.' The comms officer cut the connection.

'Comms, please inform Admiral Wilson of the delay and number one, make sure we are well away from any commercial traffic.'

'Aye, Captain,' Jarad replied.

'I better go and discuss the situation with the Admiral. Why don't you have a good look around the bridge?' JT suggested to Sol, who replied with a nod, then turned to his weapons officer. 'Guns, can you show Captain Radchak around? Just make sure he keeps out of trouble...and don't let him touch anything!' JT chuckled as he headed for the pod.

'Yes Captain,' Helen responded.

The pod door slid open and the three Admirals entered

the bridge. Before the traditional announcement could be made, Admiral Wilson spoke.

'As you were. John, can we use your ready room?'

JT shrugged and led them across the bridge and into the room.

'What is bloody Elron up to?' Wilson was agitated to say the least.

JT replied. 'It appears Albrecht has arranged a media circus for Rhapsody today; Elron wants us to stay clear for a while until he can clear a flight path for us.'

Admiral Wilson just shook her head. 'Well if we have to wait, I don't suppose you have a bottle of that single malt your father always keeps back on the dock?' The mood lightened as JT moved to his desk and came back with glasses and a bottle.

'I wouldn't be an Abraham if I didn't have some of this...I'd probably be disowned.'

'Why anyone would build a ship as big as *Rhapsody* is beyond me.' Sam Grogan mused.

Morris answered. 'Simple...greed; Albrecht seems to think that it will pay for itself in five voyages. If that's so, he says he'll build more; only problem I had with the decision was the lack of security. It appears that some political pressure was exerted and the design was approved with only a minimal security presence on board. Thankfully, its first trip is nowhere near the bad-lands.'

Everyone took the offered drinks and drank in silence, the thought of the massive cruise ship probably foremost in their minds.

Captain, the first officer's voice came over the communicator, *the dock commander has secured a flight path for us for the next twenty minutes.*

'Proceed number one,' JT replied. 'Looks as if you'll get some fishing in after all, Admiral.' This brought a smile to Admiral Wilson's face. Everyone was a little more relaxed now and the normal buzz of conversation resumed.

Valliant's new course kept the moon between her and the dock, well away from prying eyes and the media. Although still technically a vigilant class vessel, Space Corps wanted her mods kept quiet.

'What happens to that dock now?' Sol asked, still looking at the huge facility, now vacant.

Silas answered. '*Project Galileo*; funding has been authorised by the Council and construction should begin in a couple of weeks.'

Valiant slid effortlessly into dock 7 and all umbilicals silently attached. Once atmospheric conditions were stabilised, the air locks opened and the three Admirals disembarked and headed for their patrol ship, now berthed at the opposite side of the dock. Within minutes it had departed for Earth.

JT & Sol stood and watched as it disappeared from view.

'What now?' Sol asked.

'I have been summoned to the Station,' JT replied referring to his father's request that he spend his next few days at the family property in central New South Wales. One of his father's passions was the raising of pure-bred Hereford cattle and their company held vast tracts of land for that, as well as many other agricultural operations.

'Seems that there is a family dinner tomorrow night and I have been shanghaied into it. I think you should join me...I need some cover from the *"join the company"* attack that'll surely come.

It was no secret that JT's father was expecting his eldest son to join the company and take the reins. But it was his mother who was the main protagonist. She was like a dog with a bone over the issue. So far, JT had avoided the inevitable confrontation—mainly by staying away—but this time he had no excuse, so he had to go home.

It was an Abraham family tradition that the first born son inherited the CEO position, and JT was no different. All his predecessors had gained their education, done military service, as JT was doing, and then returned to run the company. Whether he liked it or not, this was his eventual fate. The best he could do was delay that day for as long as possible.

Sol chuckled. 'A seat at the family feud, no way I can pass *that* up.'

'Thanks, I think,' JT replied. 'Now go and have a good snoop around...I know you're just dying to. I've got to finalise things and organise the crew leave with Jarad. We should be ready to leave around sixteen thirty hours.' With that he walked back onto the bridge.

It took longer than he thought to arrange things. There were issues that he needed to finalise: paperwork from the dock supply section; requisitions for parts and equipment for the repairs and finally a long discussion with his father about the weekend.

It was just after 17:00 when JT finally made it back to the ship. Sol was waiting for him in the shuttle bay.

'Sorry, got a bit caught up,' John apologised. 'Let's get going.'

They walked towards the rear of the bay where John stored his personal transport: a prototype *AC185 Hawk* two-seater fighter—Abracorp's latest addition to the company's armament catalogue. Designed to operate in both space and atmosphere, it was equipped with a standard Gravitron drive and a small displacement unit. Fast in both arenas, it could hold a displacement factor of 20 for short periods. The design brief was for a fighter and ground support vehicle and, so far, this prototype had excelled in both.

'Seems it pays to be an Abraham,' Sol smiled with this taunt.

'You mean costs!' John replied. 'The "powers that be" couldn't make a decision on building this prototype...they just kept stuffing around, as bureaucrats do. Abracorp paid for this one...everyone else will get them at the Corps cost. The best part is I've been designated as test pilot. Come on; let's see if you still remember how to fly.'

3

Aaron woke slowly, his head taking longer than normal to clear.

He opened his eyes, but couldn't make anything out—it was still too dark.

'Lights, fifty percent,' he commanded and the lights slowly increased until his surroundings became clear; he was in his room at the Morgan Hotel—the only place he stayed when he was in Central City. He sat up.

'Curtains open.' The heavy drapes covering the windows began to slide back, revealing the vista of the city skyline.

His room was on the 105th floor and gave him what he considered the best view of the city. He climbed out of bed and stood at the window, enjoying the scene before him; tall elegant buildings some topped with gardens and pools, others with roof top restaurants—already busy with the breakfast crowd. His head was still full of cotton wool, probably due to the third bottle of Altarian Claret they had enjoyed with their meal.

The previous evening Aaron had arranged to meet a friend at the Flame Grill, his favourite restaurant in the city, perhaps in the galaxy. As he was about to enter the establishment he had received a call, his date had an urgent matter to attend to and couldn't make it. As a new trader, she was working hard to build her business, something Aaron remembered from his early years. He accepted the fact and arranged to complete their date next time they were both back on Argos.

The lure of a good dinner was too great so he decided

to dine alone, if he had to. He remembered walking in the door and noticing a stunning redhead sitting at the bar, talking on her communicator. He sat at the next seat just as she finished her call, visibly unhappy with the outcome. Up close, she was even more stunning, flame red hair, green eyes, small upturned nose and lips that could only be described as luscious.

His throat suddenly dried up as he tried to introduce himself. 'Hi,' was all he could manage to say as she turned toward him. The effect was immediate; he felt his heart quicken and the room suddenly felt hotter, as if the atmospheric controls had malfunctioned.

She looked at him, studying him before she spoke. 'Hello,' she finally replied.

Aaron's mind was blank; he couldn't think of anything to say—at least anything that would sound even remotely intelligent. 'Care for another?' he asked, noticing she had drained her glass.

'Thank you,' she turned to the bartender. 'Same again, please.'

Aaron's composure had returned. 'I'll have the same.' He watched as the bartender measured out two fingers in each glass and then put in two ice cubes, swirled them for a couple of seconds, then poured each drink into a fresh glass, minus the ice.

'I don't like my scotch watered down.'

Aaron smiled. 'Good call, Glenfiddich...30-year-old...why spoil it with water? I'm Aaron,' he said as he held his glass up in salute to her taste.

'Petra,' the woman replied.

'Seems we both have the same problem.'

'What's that?' she asked.

'No date,' Aaron confessed. 'Sorry, I couldn't help but overhear the end of your call. Mine came just as I reached the door.'

'Ah well, I believe that things happen for a reason. Maybe we were destined to meet? Two sad cases...both stood up.' Her eyes seemed to sparkle, almost challenging him as she spoke.

'Well, the evening doesn't have to be a complete bust. I don't get here as often as I would like but, believe me, their carnivore plate is something else. Maybe we could have dinner together; no point in wasting a reservation.' Aaron tried desperately to sound suave and casual, but inwardly he felt like a silly school boy trying desperately to impress some young girl.

'Well, as I'm a real meat lover, I can't refuse. Thank you; but I must admit it's been a long time,' she said.

'A long time, I don't understand.'

She laughed—the sound at once being both lilting and subtly sexy; 'since I've been picked up in a bar.'

Aaron shook his head, having absolutely no come back. Fortunately, the waiter came over to tell him his table was ready.

The rest of the evening went much smoother as Aaron's nervousness finally vanished. They talked about things he never talked about, small talk, mostly, and nothing in depth; as if they were sounding each other out. The meal, though, was another matter—the Flame Grill Carnivore Plate lived up to its reputation. Slow cooked ribs, pork and beef coupled with sixteen hour smoked Brisket, all old school and done to perfection. Thankfully neither had dressed formally. This was a meal that must be eaten by hand, and could be messy.

Aaron recounted a story of when he brought some friends here and one of the women had, only that day, spent a huge amount on a new dress. Unfortunately for her, she couldn't bring herself to wear one of the bibs the waiter offered and ended up with a large sauce stain down the front of the very expensive outfit. Petra had no such problem—she readily donned the protective offering and attacked the meal with gusto. By this time, the second bottle of wine was gone and a third was ordered. Aaron didn't want the evening to finish—he couldn't remember when he had enjoyed someone's company as much.

Petra solved this dilemma: she had an important meeting the next day and didn't want to be at anything but her best for it. At a little after midnight, she asked if they could call it a night. Aaron reluctantly agreed, but asked for her details so he could call her next time he was in the city; Petra agreed and they synced their communicators. He watched as she left the restaurant, a feeling in his stomach that he hadn't experienced before. At that moment he made himself a promise to call her the next day.

His thoughts ended and he remembered where he was now: in his hotel room standing, naked, at the huge picture window gazing out over the city with breakfast diners on the roof opposite gazing back. He left the window and consulted the room service menu, called the concierge, placed his order and went to the bathroom. He turned the shower on and let the water reach the correct temperature while he relieved the pressure in his bladder.

The shower was exactly what he needed. He groaned in perverse pleasure as the hot, needle-like spray danced off his body, awakening his senses and clearing his sluggish mind. He changed the shower setting and stood under the large, flood-type outlet in the centre of the cubicle. This was like being in a tropical downpour and it reminded him of earlier times when, as a boy, he and his brother, Jeff, had accompanied their grandfather on an annual pilgrimage to

Northern Australia to fish, catch mud crabs, hunt and live very simply for two weeks. He also remembered the fight he had had with Jeff more than thirty years ago. A touch of sadness accompanied the memory of the argument that had descended into violence and resulted in Aaron leaving, swearing he would never set foot on Earth again. To this day he had kept his vow—in over thirty years he had never returned. But lately, different thoughts had begun to insinuate themselves into his mind, and he found himself reviewing that decision.

He had kept himself informed on some things. Being so successful, the family company, Abracorp, was easy to track. He had also kept up to date with the adventures of his favourite nephew, Johnathon Thomas Abraham[4th], now a Captain in the Earth Coalition of Planets Space Corps. There had even been some contact with his sister-in-law, Sonia, after she had finally tracked him down twenty years ago. Sonia always sent him invitations to family events, but he never attended. Now, his thoughts were heading in a different direction; maybe he should give family a second chance?

The sound of the door-bell interrupted his thoughts—breakfast had arrived.

Bacon and eggs accompanied by sautéed mushrooms and fresh toast, Aaron was surprised how hungry he was, considering the size of the meal the previous evening. He finished eating, cleaned his teeth and left for the foyer, with scant minutes to spare. He was being collected for a meeting with Allen Grainger, friend and business partner, but also the leader of Freebooters. His position, Freebooter Prime, was equivalent of President and held the responsibility of governing Argos. The elevator deposited him in the foyer and a young, official looking man approached him.

'Captain Abraham?' the official enquired.

'Yes, I hope I didn't keep you waiting,' Aaron replied.

'No, you are right on time, I have a shuttle waiting; if you would follow me,' he said, moving toward the elevators. 'My name is James by the way.'

'James...thanks,' Aaron followed the official into the lift. It delivered them to the roof and they boarded the blue and silver shuttle.

'We will be going to the residence for the meeting; about a ten minute flight.' James took the pilot's seat and began the lift-off procedure.

Aaron sank down into one of the large plush leather seats and gazed vacantly out the window. He reflected on the last thirty odd years since he had come to Argos. After leaving Earth he had just floated around for a couple of years, taking temporary jobs as flight crew on any vessel he could. The last one had gone south in a huge way, the Captain of the vessel had tried to smuggle contraband but was caught. The vessel had been impounded and Aaron—with the rest of the crew—was left stranded on Varga. A small M class planet, Varga was not on regular trade routes, making the prospect of leaving in the near future, highly improbable.

As happened, fate had stepped in, in the form of Allen Grainger, Freebooter Trader. They had met in a small bar behind the space port, had a few drinks and soon realised they had mutual needs—Aaron needed a way off the planet, and Grainger needed a flight officer. A deal was struck and the next day Aaron joined his first Freebooter ship.

Freebooter society is unlike any other branch of the Human race, being the only one where all people, regardless of race, religion or colour, lived in harmony, each respecting and accepting all others. The main reason—the total absence of politics. Unlike every other human colony, Freebooters had shunned all forms of politics and this had appealed to Aaron.

For the next ten years he had worked with Grainger, first as a flight officer, then as a partner in, and Captain of, one of Grainger's trade ships. Eventually, he had purchased his own ship and started his own trading operation. The friendship and business connection with Grainger remained and, to this day, they were still partners in a number of ventures. Things had changed, however, a few years previously, when Grainger was elected Prime; a post that carried a 50 year term of office.

Captain Abraham, we are about to land. James's voice emanated from the lounge speakers, breaking Aaron's train of thought. James brought the shuttle down towards the landing field and with a great flourish, flared at the last moment to execute a perfect touchdown.

'Nice landing,' Aaron remarked as James came through the flight deck door.

'Thank you, Sir,' he replied, accepting the praise without further comment. 'Follow me please.'

Built into the hillside overlooking Freedom Park in Central City, the capital of Argos, the Prime's residence boasted some of the best views of the city and the park. The landing pad was on top of the underground hangar complex and, except for times when shuttles were operating, was hidden from the residence and offices. The complex was only accessed from the hangar via a subterranean walkway and transport pod, with security stations at both ends.

Aaron and James exited the walkway through a security portal in the west wall, and continued down the tree-fringed path to the main building. There were ten buildings that made up the complex with the central one the private quarters—totally off limits except to those who the Prime personally invited. As they walked up the front steps to the wide veranda, two of the Prime's security officers approached them and moved them through another security scan into the front reception vestibule.

'Thank you gentlemen,' one of the officers said. 'Please wait in the next room.'

The entry was through dark, wooden doors to a wide room with a marble mosaic floor. Tapestries hung from the very high walls and the ceiling was domed with an oculus in the centre, creating a spotlight effect on the centre of the floor enhancing the mosaics.

'Please take a seat and I'll announce you,' James said and went through the next pair of doors.

Aaron allowed his gaze to wander round the room. He had always admired fine art and the tapestries on display were some of the best he had ever seen. He was so engrossed with them he didn't hear the doors behind him open.

'Beautiful, aren't they,' the voice of Allen Grainger, Freebooter Prime echoed round the room. 'That one you are looking at actually came on the Drake with Joseph Jones himself. It's supposed to be from an ancient Scottish castle the Jones family had once owned...well, that's the story anyway.'

The voice dragged Aaron back to the present. 'Sorry, Allen, I was totally engrossed in your tapestries.'

'No need to apologise. It's always gratifying to see someone appreciating them. Unfortunately we don't get many visitors to the house, so they aren't appreciated like they should be. Come through here and we can relax and have a chat.' They headed through a small door to the right of the main entrance and into a well-appointed office. 'I thought this might be a good place, better than the hustle in the main office. Would you like some coffee? James makes an excellent brew.' Without waiting for an answer he started to pour two mugs of the steaming coffee, before continuing. 'How is the new Eldoran jump drive conversion coming? Is it ready for service yet?'

Aaron had converted his newest ship, Condor, to the newly acquired technology, something only known to a select few, Grainger being one.

'We have concluded trials of the drive, and are giving Condor a final inspection, so she should be ready later today.' Aaron was puzzled. Surely Grainger didn't need a meeting to learn this? After all, he was an equal partner in the drive project.

'And the maximum duration issue?' Allen Grainger seemed to be angling towards something that Aaron could not quite get a handle on.

'So far no problems; we have limited the maximum time we spend under drive conditions to forty minutes, with no side effects. I firmly believe we'll be able to increase this as we progress the trial, but you know this already...I sent you a full report and specification three days ago.'

'You're right, I do know,' the Prime admitted.

Aaron studied Grainger's face. His hair was greyer and his face had a few more wrinkles, but those eyes were still the same. Behind them was a mind that had taught Aaron so well and had enabled him to start his own trading company, to become one of the most successful Freebooters in existence.

'I have a favour to ask!' Grainger looked intently at Aaron and took a sip from his mug. 'But before you say anything, hear me out; you may not want to grant it.'

'Ask away.' Aaron replied, with a quizzical frown, it was a rare occurrence for the Prime to ask a favour.

'You are aware of the incident near Zyralin Four just over a year ago?' Grainger asked.

'Yes, my nephew was involved. There were some deaths and he faced a court martial which I believe exonerated him.' Aaron was intrigued, and he gave Allen his full attention.

'Yes, a huge loss of life, and your nephew was fully exonerated...in fact he is somewhat of a hero...even if Space Corps hasn't admitted it yet. The rumour of a Krell attack was false and there have been, shall we say, developments?' Grainger always loved a bit of drama. 'What I need is for you to transport someone to Space Corps Headquarters on Earth. This person has vital information and has already been targeted with one attempt on his life. Problem is, we don't know for sure who made the attempt. It could even be his own people, so this may not be a simple job...there may be complications.'

Aaron gave the Prime a long, hard look of concern.

'Sounds like we're getting involved in politics,' Aaron said, his voice showing his concern. 'If so, it goes against everything we stand for. We have always been neutral and kept out of any political issues; it's even enshrined in our constitution. Hell, we deal with all sides of any conflict equally! So why the change?'

'I have wrestled with this issue for the last three days, and I know every argument for, and against,' Grainger replied. 'When Joseph Jones and his group settled our world and drew up the constitution one main theme was the lack of politics...the very reason they left Earth and the new coalition was the politics.'

'The petty clawing for power and the intrigue, all led to a total lack of progress and massive restrictions on the freedom of individuals. Jones was determined that Freebooters would always be free of these machinations;

but even he could foresee the day when we may need to take sides. You've read his books; you know his ideas, his vision. I think that the day may have come, the day where we need to take a stand may be at hand.'

Grainger sank into his chair. 'I don't ask this lightly, Aaron. The risks to you are grave and if you agree, this must be totally off the books. The less you know the better, for you and your crew. All I ask is that you meet him… and then we can talk further.'

Aaron thought for a few moments. He had known this man for over a third of his life and he had never seen him do anything against the society he now presided over. 'OK, I'll meet with him,' Aaron's said.

Grainger activated the intercom. 'James, will you please bring our guest in,' Grainger asked.

The door opened and James ushered in the mystery guest. Aaron rose and turned toward the door and stopped suddenly; his jaw dropped as he saw the guest.

'Admiral Dokad?' His voice was almost a whisper.

Aaron hadn't seen the man standing before him for a number of years. Admiral Kratc Dokad, Senior Commander of the Krell Imperial Navy; a man Aaron held in very high regard.

After Freebooters had brokered the peace between the Empire and the Coalition that ended the most destructive war in human history, they were granted an exchange program with the Empire. Every year for centuries now, five Freebooter flight officers were chosen to be trained at the Krell Space Academy; Aaron was one of the lucky ones. He had spent three years studying, and achieving, his Captain qualification. It was also where he had met, the then Captain Dokad. The two had become firm friends and Aaron had been billeted with Dokad's family for part of his stay.

After he left the Krell home world, they had kept in touch, often meeting in far flung places of the galaxy. As Aaron's business and Dokad's career had flourished however, this contact became less and less.

Aaron looked at his old mentor and noted the sling on his left arm, the Nano skin across half of his face and the left eye-patch he wore. 'What happened?' he asked concern etched in his voice.

'Someone took a shot at me,' the reply was accompanied by a slight chuckle. 'Knocked me down, it did. But when he came to finish me off, Golac got to him, almost took a leg off. Sadly Golac was killed and the assassin fled.'

The sadness in his voice was strong. Golac was a Jardoc, a creature similar to a very large canine and Dokad's constant companion. Aaron remembered the animal and the history of their association with Krell warriors.

Throughout all Krell's recorded history, the Jardoc had been companion animals and were often mentioned in ancient literature. They were long-lived and loyal to the end; usually if the master died so too did the Jardoc. Saving the life of their master was something also mentioned in the texts.

Aaron could see this had been a terrible blow for Dokad. 'I'm sorry Admiral.'

Dokad straightened and looked at Aaron. 'If he had not defended me, I would surely be dead. He did me, and many others, a great service; but he will be missed.' True to Krell form the old Admiral quickly shrugged off his grief. 'But now to business,' he announced. 'Allen has explained my request?'

'Yes he has. But you're a fleet admiral...why not just use one of your own ships? Why all this cloak and dagger stuff?' Aaron asked.

Dokad explained, 'In reality, my rank is now more honorary; I have very little connection with the navy. For the last five years I have been acting as ambassador to the Coalition and, as this attack on me was probably an internal operation, using a navy ship could be suicidal.'

He paused for a few seconds, 'You two are the only ones I can trust; so my fate is in your hands. This information could have far reaching effects on both human and Krell futures. All I ask is that you consider it.'

'When do you need to be there?' Aaron questioned.

'Next Tuesday...Earth time...at the latest,' the Admiral replied.

Aaron thought for a few moments, and then smiled as he remembered something. 'There is a family celebration this weekend on Earth. My sister in law has been trying to get me back there for a number of years and always sends me invitations to any family events. It might be time for me to go to one and, as you are well known to my brother, perhaps I should bring a friend?'

'Are you wanting to end the feud with your brother?' Dokad asked.

'Feuds must end sometime and I suppose this is as good a time as any,' Aaron shrugged.

'Excellent! Family is everything. It would be an honour to accompany you.'

'It's settled then,' Grainger spoke and turned to his aide. 'James, can you assist the Admiral to gather his luggage? Captain Abraham and I have a few details to sort out.'

With that, the Admiral rose and walked to the door. 'Make no mistake, old friends...there are forces out there that will do anything to stop me.' He looked at both men, smiled weakly and left the room.

'Thank you Aaron. I have some idea of the information, so believe me when I tell you that his getting to Earth is critical to the future...theirs and ours.' Grainger paused to allow this to sink in. 'While there can be no official recognition of this venture, I do have some leeway and some funds available.'

'Don't worry...this will be a private trip,' Aaron said with absolute conviction. 'No contract, no payment. I owe that man a lot, so this will help repay some of the debt. I'll ensure he gets there in one piece. By the way,' he added, 'how is Grace?' Aaron changed the subject.

Grace, the Prime's wife, had taken a great interest in Aaron when he first arrived on Argos. As a newbie, he had needed assistance coming to grips with the differences in culture and in Freebooter society. Grace had been there to help—arranging for Aaron to be billeted at their house and helping him learn Freebooter social etiquette. Aaron also believed, fondly, that Grace had been working with Sonia Abraham to try and bring the two brothers back together.

'She's fine...gone to Caprica to visit friends,' Grainger replied. 'I'll pass on your greeting. Oh, and just one more thing,' he asked. 'I believe you are now short a first officer?'

'Yes, almost forgot that with all these other developments. Steve has just started his own operation and will be heading off tonight...damn!'

Aaron had come to rely on his second in command a great deal and they had been a good team. When Steve Harris had come to him with his proposal, Aaron had agreed immediately and together they had formed another company with Steve as the major shareholder and CEO. Now, with Condor flight-ready, Steve had left the ship and was setting out on his first trip as an independent Freebooter trader.

Grainger looked up from his desk. 'Well, I might have a

candidate for you. First rate pilot, degrees in engineering and quantum physics; top of the class in astrogation, currently working as a trainer at our new academy and...has capital too! Interested?'

'Sounds good...when can I meet him,' Aaron asked?

Grainger chuckled and emphasised, '*She* is in the outer office.' With that he pressed a button on his ancient intercom. 'Commander, will you please come in.'

Aaron stood and turned towards the door as the Commander entered—and was visibly shocked at who stood before them.

'Commander,' he greeted the newcomer, hesitantly.

'Captain,' she replied, momentarily off guard when she saw who she was meeting.

Grainger, baffled by this curious exchange, asked. 'Do you two know each other?'

It was the Commander who answered. 'Yes and no. We ran into each other last night and got talking...though we haven't even been formally introduced.' Her green eyes flashed Aaron an amused look.

'Well, let me rectify that,' Grainger continued, 'Captain Aaron Abraham this is Commander Petra Mannix.'

Aaron moved forward and extended his hand. 'Pleased to formally meet you, Commander; the Prime tells me you are interested in a berth on Condor.'

'A berth is one way of putting it.' She smiled cheekily, raised one eyebrow and turned back to the Prime. 'Thank you for the introduction Sir.'

Grainger nodded and gestured for them to sit. 'Aaron, James has transmitted the commander's CV to you but if you want, I can have him bring it in here.'

'No need Allen...your recommendation is good enough

for me.' He turned to Petra. 'Why my little operation, surely there are a number of more prestigious commissions available?'

Before she could answer James interrupted. 'Captain, your guest is ready to leave. He will travel in a different shuttle, one with less conspicuous markings,' his reference being to the blue and silver markings of the official vehicles. 'He will wait on Zephyr.' He turned and left the room.

'Captain,' the Prime stood and walked to the large window on the south wall of the room and beckoned Aaron to follow. 'I think you could use the Commander on this trip. Anyhow, it gives you a good cover for being here today. Why not use this as a sort of job interview. See how she performs and then decide?'

'Yeah, not a bad idea,' Aaron replied. His smile was broad and not unnoticed by Grainger.

'Well,' Grainger started, 'maybe you two should get back to the ship, sort of familiarise the Commander with the umm...intricacies of your operation?'

'Yes. I agree,' he turned towards Mannix, 'Ready Commander?'

He took the Prime's hand. Grainger suddenly grew serious. 'Be careful. I cannot emphasise the gravity of the situation strongly enough...be *very* careful.'

He turned toward Petra. 'Looks like you have a trial trip. Congratulations Commander, I cannot thank you enough for the time you have devoted to the academy. It will be hard to replace you, but I have a feeling this will prove to be an excellent move. Good luck.'

The door opened and James beckoned them to follow him.

'Your shuttle is ready, Captain.' James looked at Petra.

'Do you need to collect your gear from the academy, Commander?'

'Thank you, but no, she replied, 'I'll have it sent over tonight.'

'Packed already?' Aaron asked, 'Very confident.'

'Not really Sir,' there was an assured note to her voice. 'I travel light and always have a go bag ready, just in case.' Petra led the way up the steps into the shuttle where they settled into the soft leather seats, facing each other. James went to the flight deck, took the pilot's position and closed the door.

'By the way, I really enjoyed dinner last night,' Aaron said.

'So did I...thank you,' she replied. 'Maybe it was fate?' She smiled and sat back in the seat. 'By the way, how do you know the Prime? You seem to be on very good terms.'

Aaron thought before replying. 'I have known Allen Grainger for nearly forty years. He took me under his wing when I arrived. I may be an Abraham but I was a *new born* in Freebooter terms. He gave me a job...even gave me a place to stay at his home till I got settled. After his son was killed his wife, Grace, sort of took me on as a project and has been looking after me ever since. I owe them a great deal and am probably closer to them than I am to my own family. But this situation is really testing all I believe in. How much did he tell you about why I was here?'

'Not much,' Petra admitted, 'just that you are taking some *off world* official on an unofficial trip. No more than that and the fact that you need a new first officer.'

'Well, let's handle the second bit first. Yes I do need a new first officer. Steve Harris and Greg Lewis, my previous number two, have just bought into their own ship; actually, we have formed a new partnership with my old ship, *Albatross*. They are already prepping for their first trip and should leave tonight. My third officer will be a good number two, but she's not ready for a number one ticket, just yet, so the need is real. As for our guest...well...let's just say he is an old friend who is accompanying me to an Abraham family function.'

'But I thought that you were estranged from your family?' she asked. The feud between the two Abraham brothers was well known and everyone made sure they kept a good distance from any involvement.

'It may be time to mend things. Besides, it should make for an interesting trip in any case.' Then Aaron lightened the mood a bit. 'I could do with a drink...let's see what's in the bar.'

He poured two stiff measures of scotch and returned, handing one to Petra. Both settled back into their seat to enjoy their drink. They sat in silence for a few minutes. Aaron's throat was dry and he had knots in his stomach, but he decided silence was a virtue; at least until he figured out what was wrong with him.

Petra held her glass up. 'Captain, thank you for giving me this opportunity, I'll do my best to make sure you don't regret it.'

Those green eyes seemed to bore into Aaron's soul, seeing right through him as he raised his glass. 'Welcome aboard, Number One.' He smiled as they touched glasses. Petra returned his smile.

*T*he shuttle landed on the external apron of the dock complex. Aaron and Petra bid James farewell and walked through the open door.

Waiting just inside was Katherine Albrecht, currently third officer on Condor—she smiled and greeted them. 'Welcome back, Captain.'

'Thanks, Kate,' he responded, 'this is Commander Mannix, she will be joining us as First Officer for this trip. Petra, meet Kate Albrecht, our new Second Officer.'

Kate was slightly taken aback. 'Thank you sir,' she said, and she turned to Petra, extending her hand in greeting. 'Welcome aboard, ma'am. Do you have any luggage?'

'It'll be coming over later today,' Petra replied.

Aaron had that distant look that signified his communicator was working. 'Kate...we have a special guest coming on this trip and discretion must be high, if you get my drift?'

Kate smiled. 'No worries Captain.'

Aaron looked at both of his officers, 'I think it'd be good if you could show our new Number One how the yacht operates, check her piloting skills and bring her up to speed on our way of doing things.'

While all trade ships carried a number of shuttle craft to handle crew transfers and planetary operations, Aaron had his personal yacht for official duties.

'An excellent idea, let's go!' Kate was always ready to have a run in Aaron's favourite toy. 'I think you'll enjoy this Commander.

The three entered a transport pod, selected their dock

number and settled into the seats. Two minutes later the pod stopped at the dock assigned to Condor. They left the pod and walked over to the viewing window. What greeted them was not what Petra expected. Sitting in the dock space was, she thought, one of the ugliest ships she had ever seen. There before her was Condor, eight hundred and twenty metres long and almost as wide from wing tip to wing tip. Extending in front was the bridge and command area attached to the main body by a short tubular section that moulded itself into the central bulbous body—Petra assumed this was the main living and working quarters.

The *wings* drooped down towards the centre of the body line, curving back until they returned to the main structure; from here a delta shaped, horizontal tail extended aft, where usually the engineering and drive sections were housed, based on current starship design.

Condor was nothing like current design—from a structural or architectural view. Petra's initial thoughts were fairly correct except that most of the body was a large modular hold area that could be restructured into many different configurations simply by changing modules.

The bridge was where she thought, as was main accommodation: engineering was immediately behind this and took up the front of the main body; drive systems were housed in the top of the body; displacement field generators in the wings. Power generation was by antimatter reactors, with secondary energy harvesting of stellar sources— such as solar radiation—handled by the skin of the ship. This could supply all of the energy needed for life support and essentially made Condor one large life boat. Weapon systems were housed in various locations in the main body and wing area, each having its own power supply and control system.

'Not so fast.' Aaron knew how much Kate loved to take the yacht out. 'We need to file a flight plan first...come to the office.'

He turned and led them towards the administration section of the dock; as he entered the receptionist addressed him. 'Captain Abraham, welcome back. The *Proctor* asked if you could give him a few minutes.'

'Of course, can you tell him I'll see him in thirty minutes?' Aaron asked.

The receptionist nodded and entered the information to The Proctor's message board. 'All arranged, Sir,' she confirmed.

Aaron's office was not overly large, considering he was the major shareholder and CEO of the company. He rarely used it—preferring to spend his time trading—hence The Proctor, whose job it was to actually run the company administration. A myriad of responsibilities fell on the Proctor, Henry N'Gabo, including all day to day details, legal and H.R., and the thousand and one other duties it took to run a multi-planetary organisation.

'Lieutenant,' Aaron turned back to Albrecht. 'You will need to file a flight plan for all the usual atmospheric checks plus orbital assessments. Also, you need to clear the Commander for docking, so arrange to dock with Zephyr... she is still in orbit. Personnel will need all the records in order to clear her for our shuttles. When you dock with Zephyr, you will collect our guest and bring him directly to the Condor. Understood?'

'Understood Sir,' Albrecht replied.

Aaron looked from Petra to Kate and gave them his sternest Captain look. 'Discretion is of the utmost importance from now on, is that clear?'

'Yes Sir.' Both replied almost in unison.

'Good, you two better get going, you have a good three hours flying to get all that done,' he added. They both saluted and left the office as Henry walked in.

Henry turned and watched them head down the passageway. 'Steve's replacement, definitely better looking than him; is she any good?'

'You can see for yourself...her CV is now on your message board,' Aaron answered. While they were close friends, the duties of work meant that they had little time together these days. 'How are Jacinta and the girls?'

'Good thanks, wondering when they'll see you again.'

Henry sat down opposite Aaron's desk. He was a big man—200cm tall and heavily built—some could think he was running to fat but that would be their mistake. Henry was one of the fittest men Aaron had ever met and a desk job hadn't changed that.

Henry was of ancient African descent and carried his heritage with great pride. His hair was a mass of black curls and his dark eyes always conveyed happiness. In all, Aaron thought Henry to be the happiest person he had ever met; but this wasn't evident today.

'What's going on Aaron?' He fixed his gaze on his friend. 'First I get some cryptic message about a trip to earth, with a request for *discretion*, then I start getting strange requests about what you are doing with Grainger. Now, Condor is being fast tracked to launch.'

'Nothing that you need to worry about...I'm going to Earth for an Abraham family function. My crew could do with a bit of R&R; they've been running pretty hard lately, so I thought this was a good opportunity.' Aaron went to the sideboard, produced two glasses and poured them each a scotch.

'Bullshit. Why this sudden need to go home? You have refused invitations for twenty years, to my knowledge.

What are you up to?' Henry never pulled any punches.

Aaron handed him the glass and settled down behind his desk. He hoped that it would not be necessary to pull rank, but he was the boss.

'There's nothing to be concerned about...look, I've been thinking about the rift in my family for a long while. Every time I see you and your family, your brother and sister, your parents and your kids...I get to thinking about what I may have missed. Maybe I'm getting old. Hell I don't know...I just think it may be time. Anyhow, Sonia sent the invite and I thought, why not?' He stopped and took a swig of his drink.

Henry considered what he had just heard. 'I still say bullshit, but I know you too well to pry further...just don't do anything foolish.'

'Yes Father,' Aaron retorted. 'I'll try and be good.' Both men laughed.

They finished their drinks and spent the next hour going over company business before Henry left. Aaron still had another hour of work before he looked up from his monitors. It was getting dark, so he closed his console and headed for Condor.

***

After leaving Aaron's office, Kate and Petra went to Personnel to collect the documentation needed for a flight appraisal—a prerequisite for any new flight officer—and the documentation also vital for company records and insurance; this is where things stopped.

Personnel officers can be a breed to themselves and these were no different. It took over half an hour to complete all the other documentation they required prior to authorising the flight evaluation. The delay continued as Petra was scanned for her uniforms and arrangements made for all her records to be sent from the academy. They also sent a stern message addressed to Captain Abraham reminding him of the *correct* procedure for starting a new employee.

Finally, Petra and Kate managed to extricate themselves and headed double time for Condor. As they stood on the walkway to the upper entrance port, Petra stopped to evaluate the vessel before her.

'This must be the ugliest thing I have ever seen,' she commented. 'What is that, just in front of the main body?' She pointed to the almost petal-like structure.

'That's the forward sensor array. Don't let the Captain hear you call his baby ugly, this is his pride and joy,' Kate retorted.

Petra shook her head. 'Well they say beauty is in the eye of the beholder.'

They boarded the ship and went directly to the hangar. The sign on the door read *Captain's Yacht authorised personnel only*. As they entered, a sharp gasp from Petra told the story. What stood before them was a small version of the Condor but at this scale, Petra could appreciate the beauty of it.

'Now I see....' she whispered. She stood awestruck, looking at the gleaming silver-grey vessel before her.

'We need to get going; we're way behind time, thanks to the bureaucrats!' Kate exclaimed, leading the way up the ramp. 'She has capacity for ten, but really only needs one to fly her. She can maintain displacement factor of twelve for extended periods and can manage fifteen for short bursts. In space, she can run all day at point nine five light...and she can bite!'

They entered the flight deck and Kate directed Petra to the command seat. 'Run through the systems and ask any questions you need.'

All Freebooter vessels were designed to a standard so that the main operations and controls were similar; meaning a minimum amount of time was needed to orientate any new flight officer. Although the Yacht had a number of different systems that she hadn't seen before, it took only ten minutes for Petra to announce she was ready to start the evaluation.

She initialised the guidance and drive systems, brought the main reactor on line and opened the hangar door. These were shaped like the Yacht and slid seamlessly back into the top of the hull. The yacht was no small shuttle at one hundred metres in length and almost the same wide, the hangar took up a large section of the upper hull of Condor.

Petra lifted the yacht off and brought it out to hover about one hundred metres above Condor. Now she could appreciate the true beauty of the larger ship. She smiled and turned to Kate 'First impressions can be a bitch.' Both laughed and Kate gave Petra the initial flight plan.

The assessment was comprised of a number of navigational changes, flight profiles and emergency drills. Once these were completed, they pointed the nose up and headed out of the atmosphere. Here was more work, and a little fun—a short displacement hop and a couple of runs over the weapons range only took forty five minutes. Kate was constantly recording Petra's operation of the ship, quietly impressed with her new boss's skills.

'That wraps up the main test, now let's see you dock with Zephyr.'

Petra quickly located the transponder and locked onto it. They approached from the planet-side and manoeuvred to within twenty metres when suddenly alarms started going crazy. Quickly and efficiently, Petra cleared the alarms, held her position and interrogated the ship's systems, clearing the dock control failure simulation that Kate had initiated, quickly and efficiently.

'Well done, Commander.' Kate congratulated her. 'I don't think even the Captain could have sorted that out so well.'

Petra nodded and again contacted Zephyr for docking authority. Once this was given, she expertly mated with the docking ring on the underside of the freighter. Although docking was a standard manoeuvre for certification, in this case it made an excellent cover to bring their guest aboard.

Two people came through the airlock, the mysterious guest and the docking officer who needed to confirm the docking record. Once he was finished he left, secured the airlock and gave them permission to depart. The return to Argos was much quicker and fifteen minutes later they were back in the hangar.

'It's amazing the way this ship handles the atmosphere,' Petra began, 'There was no flare, no heating...nothing. It's as if the atmosphere doesn't exist.' Every other ship she had piloted before had to be carefully manoeuvred into the atmosphere—too steep and it could burn up, too shallow and it could bounce off. Petra had deliberately used a steep entry angle but there had been no heat problems on this ship's skin.

Kate smiled. 'We have an absorption field. On re-entry approach, the sensors automatically set up a field just a few millimetres off the hull surface. It responds exactly to any surface changes such as when we manoeuvre but it absorbs the heat from atmospheric friction and converts it into energy which is then fed into a storage battery. Hence no heat problems and no need for expensive and bulky ablative skin coating. Our engineering company has already licenced it to Abracorp, and I believe they have built it into one of their newest ships.'

Petra and Kate stayed on the bridge to complete the

shutdown procedure and flight evaluation. At the same time, Aaron came aboard, collected his guest and left, almost unnoticed. With the formalities complete, they left the yacht and headed for the wardroom; Aaron was already there when they arrived.

'How was the flight?' he asked as they entered.

Kate was the first to answer. 'Excellent, she passed with flying colours; should be a great addition to the flight crew.'

Petra was a bit more reserved. 'It was a good flight but I would like more time to get accustomed to her; she certainly is an interesting yacht. You collected your guest, I see.' She looked at Aaron.

'Yes. He's had a couple of taxing weeks and wanted to rest up. He asked me to thank you two for collecting him. By the way, your new uniforms and your go-bag have arrived; they were put in your cabin.' Aaron was interrupted by an Ensign.

'Captain, you have a call on the secure system.' He saluted and waited for directions.

'Good, I'll take it in the ready room.' He turned to Kate. 'Can you show the Commander to her quarters? I'll check back with both of you later.' He didn't wait for an answer as he followed the Ensign into the passageway.

Aaron entered the Ready Room from the passageway and moved quickly to his desk, accessing his console. He looked directly at the screen as a thin blue light scanned his right eye. His biometrics confirmed; the console came to life; looking back at him was Allen Grainger.

Captain, I have some information for you. The following conversation was both enlightening and concerning; Grainger's parting comment strangely cryptic. *Don't jump unless absolutely essential. Good luck!* And then the connection terminated. Aaron could only assume he meant the new jump drive, which was going to cut things fine if he couldn't use it. He stood and stepped onto the bridge. Ensign Anderson was at his engineering station.

'How soon can we get underway Ensign?' Aaron asked.

'Now, Sir, if you wish,' he answered.

Colin Anderson was the duty engineering officer and had been overseeing the preparation of Condor for space. He was fairly young at thirty five standard years and was one of the company's better recruits. A brilliant engineer, he continually surprised his chief—Lieutenant Dianna Holland—with his ideas, many of which had been incorporated into Condor's systems.

'Good. Can you contact the senior officers and ask them to meet me in the ready room in ten minutes?' Aaron didn't wait for an answer as he left the bridge. *Time to get into uniform and become the Captain again,* he thought as he entered the pod and addressed the control panel. 'Accommodation, Deck One.' The pod doors closed and it quickly transported him to his destination.

Accommodation Deck One only had three berths: the Captain's suite; two guest suites; and the private observation lounge. He walked to his door, and was scanned again before he could enter the room.

Welcome back, Captain. The voice seemed to have a sarcastic edge to it. *You seem to have disconnected your link.*

Shit! Aaron consciously re-established the connection. One of the technologies Freebooters had gained from their association with the Eldoran Federation was the origin of the voice he now heard. While all starships ran bio-chemical computers, the Eldorans had traded a new technology—a bio-chemical computer very similar to a human brain. Condor was the first ship to have the system actively installed and Aaron was the first Freebooter connected to it; giving him an edge in most things. The ship could now think; it could constantly monitor its own health as well as being able to communicate directly with the Captain. Aaron had been deemed as suitable and an interface had been installed into his cerebral cortex; now he was, in effect, part of the ship and it was part of him.

Being the first 'lab rat' was interesting as he was constantly breaking new ground, but so far it had proved very worthwhile. Initially, he had found some difficulty with the operation but on the advice of one of the Med Techs who were overseeing his integration, he had decided to give the brain an identity, naming it *George*.

So George, what's the goss? His thoughts instantly transmitted to the brain.

You seem on edge, George started, *even though your endorphin levels are somewhat elevated. I take it your trip ashore was eventful*? the voice still had a sarcastic edge.

Now to business, our guest is resting comfortably and I have taken the liberty of monitoring his medical requirements. He was in a degree of pain and distress so I adjusted the atmospheric mix to encourage sleep.

Our new First Officer has completed her assessment, a very interesting addition to the crew.

The senior officers have gathered in the ready room so I have arranged for the usual refreshments. And your uniform is ready. At those words, the wardrobe door opened and the uniform slid out on its rack. Aaron quickly dressed and headed for the door.

'Keep an eye on our guest and inform me when he wakes,' he said as he left.

Aaron entered the ready room and the assembled officers stood and saluted.

'As you were,' he moved to the coffee pot and poured

himself a mug. Taking a sip of the steaming liquid he continued. 'First order of business is to introduce our new first officer, Commander Petra Mannix. Welcome to the team, Petra.' He paused as the assembled crew introduced themselves to her.

'Next, I have a guest on board...an old friend who I'm taking to Earth for a family function.' There were a few stifled gasps at this; to hear that Aaron was going to an Abraham family function was astonishing. 'Yes I know, this is a surprise but let's get this put to bed. I am finally going home to hopefully mend the rift between my brother and myself. Now, as this is a private trip, there will be little or no opportunity for trade so we will treat this as a company R&R exercise. There will be shore leave for everyone, accommodation will be arranged and the tab picked up by the company.' This time the smiles were very broad and open.

'One issue is time. I need to be on Earth in three standard days so we will have to pick the pace up a bit. Dianna, is the old girl ready for three days at a displacement of 15 plus?'

'Why so slow?' her answer was filled with confidence.

'Good. Navigator, please plot our course and file the flight plan. Oh, almost forgot, as both Steve and Greg have left we also need a new second officer,' he stood and beckoned to Kate. 'Lieutenant please stand.' She stood, facing her captain. 'Katherine Albrecht, I hereby remove the rank of Lieutenant from you and offer the rank of Lieutenant Commander as replacement, with all the responsibilities of said rank and that of second officer on Condor. That includes any benefits that accompany the position. Do you accept?'

Kate stood to attention before the group and replied in the traditional manner. 'Sir, I, Katherine Albrecht, accept the position and rank as described and will carry out any and all responsibilities required to the best of my abilities.'

Then she added light heartedly, 'and any benefits will also be enthusiastically accepted.'

Aaron moved in front of her and removed the Lieutenant insignia and replaced them with the one-winged eagle, the insignia of a Lieutenant Commander, to the cheers and applause of the senior officers.

'Congratulations, Kate, you've earned this, and I'll update personnel immediately.' He smiled and moved back to let the rest come and offer their congratulations. 'Ok people, we have work to do; I want to de-planet within the next two hours. Commander Albrecht, as our new second officer you're now responsible for supplies. Do we have enough on board for this trip?'

'Yes Sir, we have the standard three months of supplies, which are being loaded as we speak; we will be fully stocked and ready on time.' She turned and followed the others to the door, walking with purpose.

As the assembled officers left, Aaron beckoned Petra, 'Commander Mannix, a moment please?'

He went back to the coffee pot and asked 'Another?'

'No thank you Sir.'

Aaron returned to the sitting area.

'Please sit down. The formal stuff is over for now.' He sat and she did likewise, opposite him. 'As second in command you need a little more info on what we are doing.' Aaron paused as he drank a little more coffee.

'My guest is Admiral Dokad of the Krell Imperial Navy and he's injured...there was an attempt on his life. The Prime has requested that I take him to Earth as he has certain information that he believes may be critical to the survival of the Coalition, the Empire and possibly even us. I've absolutely no idea what the information is but, as he's an old friend, I've agreed to do this. Grainger also intimated that there could be certain dangers...unspecified...as the source of the attempt on the Admiral is unknown. It's even possible that it was Krell in origin, so we need to be on our toes.' He paused to let this sink in.

'Also, as First Officer, you are my right hand and backstop. There are a number of things about this ship that are not generally known. We are equipped with much Eldoran technology including a new drive system. I won't go into this now...better if you talk with Dianna...she and Colin know it backwards. We are also a fully functioning brain ship. Our standard neural network has been significantly upgraded and is connected to an artificial bio-chemical version of a human brain, to which I am also connected. I'll release specific details to your personal console; please read the information, then we can discuss it.'

He sat back and drained his mug.

'Interesting, how deep does the connection go? Can the brain take you over?' she asked, curious as to the implications.

Aaron thought for a moment. 'How deep, as deep as I allow it. I have control and can disconnect when I need to. Can it take over? I don't actually know. There is a function where if I am incapacitated, it can actually assume certain command functions and it can defend the ship. In fact, that's one of the prime functions, to protect the ship and those on her.

'It's still very early days with this technology and we'll be testing for at least two years before we have anything like the data we need to decide what, if anything, we can do with it. At worst, we can hand it back to the Eldorans if we feel we can't utilise it, or they can take it back if they feel we're not ready for it. For now, look at the information; we can discuss it later; we have a ship to get moving.' Aaron put his mug down and led Petra onto the bridge.

5

*B*ack on Earth, JT and Sol spent a good three hours putting the new Hawke through its paces.

They did some incredible atmospheric passes, pushing Mach 15, for extended periods and even at these speeds manoeuvrability was quick and precise. Sol was impressed. 'This thing is bloody fantastic! Handles like nothing I have ever flown and with no heat problems.'

'Yeah, it's a new protection shield...an absorption field from an Argosan engineering operation. Abracorp has just signed a licence agreement and it's going to be huge!' JT replied excitedly. 'Its function's simple: it absorbs energy. In atmospheric configuration, as it is now, it separates the ship from the air around it at the molecular level. Just a few millimetres thick, but it allows all control surfaces to work normally and no friction issues. Even better, any heat generated is converted to energy which is stored on board; works the same with energy weapons.' He was animated in a way Sol had never seen before.

'Sounds like an ad for Abracorp,' Sol needled. He smiled and handed control back to John who programmed the auto pilot so they could both sit back and relax. They descended to one hundred metres and flew nap of the Earth at just over three hundred kilometres per hour, allowing them to take in the scenery below. Their track took them south over the old inland city of Dubbo, once one of the most important rural centres in New South Wales, now it was almost totally gone. The countryside was looking particularly green and productive however, due mainly to intensive reclamation work carried out by Abracorp.

Ahead, they could see the lights from the Orange complex.

Orange had once been another of the major rural centres like Dubbo. Now, it was the premier university for agricultural studies on Earth and also close to the family compound at Lucknow. They flew over the university and turned east to the compound. They arrived at the landing field and the auto pilot executed a perfect landing. JT carried out the shutdown procedure, and secured the ship.

'Come on Sol, we may as well get this over with.' JT sounded resigned—he was dreading what may transpire this weekend.

'Not looking forward to tonight?' Sol questioned. 'I thought you'd be happy to get home at last.'

'I am...I suppose,' JT's voice carried no conviction. 'Just have my back, when my mother starts...OK?'

'What? A big boy like you; a hero, a Four-Sun Captain no less, scared of his mummy?' Sol teased.

'You know my mother,' JT retorted.

'OK, point taken...I shall be your ever-vigilant wingman,' he announced, slapping his friend on the back as they walked down the boarding ramp. 'Just so long as you have some of that good Scotch you keep telling me about.'

It's going to be a very long weekend, JT thought.

The Abraham compound was set on a hill overlooking the countryside. The house had been designed so that the main entrance was at the rear of the building with the front facing a one-hundred-hectare lake. The hangar/garage complex, where they were now, was further to the north at the rear, with a two hundred metre transport pod and walkway access to the main entrance. There were two other houses, one each side of the main building. To the west was Salina's house, while David's occupied the eastern side of the lake.

After being trussed into the fighter for a few hours a walk was just what they needed, to straighten out the kinks in their bodies. They deposited Sol's kit into the transport pod and sent it to the house. As they came to the top of the hangar/garage building, the main house shone like a jewel on the horizon, the ground and upper ground floors ablaze with light. The other two floors were different; the closer they got to the building the more eerie it looked with most of the upper windows dark and brooding.

'This place always amazes me,' Sol announced, 'must have been fun growing up here.'

Sol and JT had met when they attended the academy and while Sol had visited the house on many occasions, he still derived some perverse pleasure ribbing his friend about his family's wealth.

'Not as much as you might think,' JT answered. 'It's so fucking big it's easy to lose yourself.'

'By the way,' Sol started, 'where is your house...I can see David and Salina's...are you hiding it?'

'You're looking at it. One of the joys of being the eldest, I get to live in that monstrosity. When the second bought the property he originally built a modest home for his family... he was really more interested in his folly. But he decided that it should be the seat of the Abraham family and set it up so that every first-born inherited it.

'Each subsequent owner has added on to it, Dad's contribution being the two other houses. Prior to that, everyone lived under the one roof. I also have another place...we flew over it...near the old Dubbo site. I might turn this into a research facility or something when it's my turn. In reality it's now more a company site than a family home.'

They walked the last few metres to the front steps in silence. As they opened the front door, John's mother walked into the vestibule and smiled as she greeted them.

'I thought I heard a shuttle land...thought it might be Jeffrey.' She walked over to her son and hugged him. She moved to Sol and planted a gentle kiss on his cheek.

'So good to see you again, Solomon, how did you get Johnathan to bring you here? He hardly comes home anymore and never brings any guests; you would think he's ashamed of us.' She took both men's arms and guided them through to the Library.

Sonia Abraham was a tall, elegant woman with a well-rounded face and flashing blue eyes. Her hair was naturally blonde but tonight it was jet black. Her lips were full and her skin a golden brown. Her figure was best described as curvy and she had always been a head-turner. For all her perceived beauty, she was a humble person and exceedingly proud that she and her husband had raised three children together, in a traditional family. She also held a doctorate in Horticulture and headed up the horticultural research department at the University.

John thought his mother was unusually agitated tonight and turned to her.

'Slow down mum, you're running round like a dog chasing its tail.' He moved over to the sideboard and produced a decanter of amber liquid. As he started to pour, his mother spoke again.

'It's just that I was expecting Jeffrey and I have some unbelievable news for him.' She always used everyone's full name, no abbreviations; her philosophy being if parents gave their child a name, then it should be used as given.

'What news?' JT asked.

'I should wait for your father,' Sonia replied.

'Come on, you started this.'

'Alright...it's your Uncle Aaron. He's coming here this weekend.' Her voice was almost a whisper, her words hanging in the air and stopping everyone in their tracks.

'Aaron here...for the party,' John couldn't believe his ears. His uncle had been a great childhood favourite, always seeming larger than life. It devastated a young JT when he came home from the academy one day to learn that his father and uncle had had a huge row and Aaron had left, vowing never to return. To this date he'd kept his word.

His mother held the glass that JT handed her and took a slow sip. 'I don't know,' Sonia said in a quiet voice. 'I have been trying to get those two pig-headed fools to talk for years, but they're both as bad as each other.

'Your father won't talk about it and I still don't know what they fought over. Anyway, I managed to track Aaron down, on Argos, and every time there is a significant event I always send him an invitation. He has never accepted before this.'

She turned to Sol. 'I don't know if Johnathan told you, but this celebration is for Salina's latest marine triumph; she successfully released the first Giant Manta Rays back into the ocean. She's been working really hard for years on this project and it's finally paid off.'

Turning back to JT she continued. 'I couldn't believe it when I received Aaron's reply today saying he was leaving Argos tonight and would love to attend. He also added that he was bringing some old friend and thought it was about time that he and Jeffery buried the hatchet.'

She sat back and drained her glass. Sol stood, taking Sonia's glass and refilling it for her. JT just sat there as if lost in thought.

'Sounds like I came to the right party,' Sol said under his breath and sat down again. It felt like an eternity before anyone spoke or moved until JT rose to refill his glass.

Sonia had regained her composure and looked at them both. 'David and Salina are out by the lake; why don't you two go and join them. Don't say anything, I haven't told them yet.'

Both men stood and moved towards the door into the entry vestibule when Sonia took John's elbow. 'Go easy on your father; this will be a huge shock for him.' Her eyes were pleading and John could never refuse his mother, also he knew how hard the separation had been on his father.

Like his mother, JT had never learned what happened; every time he broached the subject his father would either clam up and walk away or, if he was in a more contemplative mood, he would just say, 'a stupid fight between brothers' usually accompanied by advice that he should always keep communication channels open with his siblings. For all this, JT could always see the sadness in his father's eyes whenever the subject came up.

'Sure, I'll be good,' he answered and his mother patted his arm in gratitude. They walked to the front of the house and down the twenty steps to the pathway that wound round a central fountain and down to the lake about one hundred metres away.

The front garden was his grandmother's domain and, although she and his grandfather had moved off world, she still checked on its condition regularly. There were over five hundred individual plantings and about half were roses; old varieties, new hybrids, even some that had been bred off world. As a young child, this had always been John's favourite part of the compound and his grandmother had built it with children in mind. There were hidden paths, secret sitting areas—to a young child it was a place of wonder and adventure.

JT saw his brother and sister sitting on the jetty; he waved and they returned the greeting. Salina raced up and gave her brother a big hug.

'Hello big brother, care for a drink?' she giggled.

David stood and also hugged his brother.

'JT…it's been a while since we saw you here.'

There was some rivalry between the two brothers, mainly due to David being head of finance for Abracorp, while his big brother was still off adventuring around the galaxy and not settling down as everyone believed he should. Still, they were brothers and, despite the sibling rivalry, quite close. JT declined the drink and walked to the end of the jetty, another favourite spot in the compound.

The lake had been stocked with various breeds of fish and offered the chance of some solitude as well as a fresh fish dinner for a lucky angler. He especially loved balmy spring or autumn nights just floating around in the clear, cool water. His thoughts were interrupted by the distinctive hum of a shuttle overhead; he recognised his fathers' transport and turned back to his friend.

'Now things get interesting!' he muttered.

Sol stood beside him and they watched as the shuttle transitioned to vertical operation for landing and disappeared behind the house.

JT's thoughts were about his uncle as they walked back to the house, both excited and concerned at the same time. For over thirty years there had been little or no contact between the family and Aaron Abraham. He knew that his mother had been trying to bring about some resolution for many years, to no avail. His sixth sense was working overtime and although he would be glad to see his uncle again, warning bells were going off in his head.

6

*A*ccording to Argos time, Condor was finally cleared to de-planet at '26:25' hours—six hours after filing the flight plan. Even in a society that minimised officialdom, bureaucrats managed to find ways of complicating things.

Still, it was good to be away and Aaron started to relax a couple of hours later when they were heading to Earth at a comfortable displacement factor of 15. The worm hole was holding firm and the field generator *purring like a kitten,* according to Dianna. He handed the bridge to Simon Holm, the navigator and acting third officer and went to his quarters.

Meanwhile back on Argos, Allen Grainger called James to his office.

'Condor away, James?' he asked.

'Yes sir, as arranged; they were held for a few hours due to an administrative issue, but they were finally cleared at twenty six, twenty five hours. She initiated a worm hole just outside the exclusion zone and is finally away.'

'What time is it, anyway?' Grainger asked.

James consulted his console. 'Two ten am sir; time to retire?' he suggested.

To keep time relative to Earth, all human colonies had adopted a similar time system; sixty seconds to a minute and sixty minutes to an hour. This gave Argos a twenty eight hour day and, due to its proximity to—and orbit around its star—a three hundred and eighty five day year.

'Not yet, we still have a couple of things to do,' Grainger said as he reached out to his console. He brought up the document they had been working on; one of the reasons that Condor's departure had been delayed.

'Please transmit this to the Krell Emperor.' With one key stroke he sent the file to James. At the same time, he brought up another message, this time accessing the secure communication system. Silently he re-read the message, initiated transmission, and then sat back.

'The die is now cast,' he whispered to himself. 'I hope this doesn't come back and bite us on the arse.'

James looked up from his console.

'The message has been transmitted to the Krell Palace... now to wait.' They both knew that there would be no sleep this morning, and very little for the next few days.

Grainger looked over to his assistant—he and James had been working closely for many years and could almost read each other's mind.

'One more thing...can you contact President Malik and arrange a secure call urgently?'

James had anticipated this and the call was already being routed through to the Presidential residence at Maputo, in what used to be Mozambique on Earth, using the new sub space communication system—another Eldoran technological advance.

With most of the northern hemisphere of Earth still covered in ice and snow, continental borders and tribal separations had disappeared. The African continent was one country now; only some islands—like Australia—still held their own identities.

'President Malik is coming on line now, Sir,' James said as he left and sealed the room.

The new comm system had only been installed in the Presidential Palace and the Prime's complex. The beauty of it was negligible communication delay between Earth and Argos; conversations could now be held in real time with only a seven second delay. This one technology, if successful, could revolutionise communications throughout the galaxy.

'Prime Grainger, peace be upon you my friend,' Malik opened with his traditional greeting.

'And upon you, Mr President,' Grainger responded. 'I apologise for the hour, but I have something we must discuss as a matter of urgency. Is your room secure?' He saw Malik gesture to someone else at his end of the connection, followed by a brief silence then the sound of a door closing.

'It is now. What is the problem?' Malik asked.

Grainger started to brief his Coalition counterpart. At the end of the conversation, Malik sat back in his chair, his face solemn. He and Grainger were about the same age but whereas Grainger was clean shaven, the President of the Earth Coalition sported a full and lush beard, as was the tradition of his people.

'This is very concerning but thank for you bringing it to my attention. Be assured, I will act accordingly. Again, thank you. I know this must have been difficult; farewell my friend,' and the connection was terminated.

The time on Argos was now four forty-five am. Grainger decided that sleep was not an option, so he stood and opened the door. James was just outside.

'Well, it's done. I think I'll head down to the pool...a few laps might just be the best medicine at the moment.'

***

On Condor, Aaron had just entered his quarters when the secure message came through. He sat down and read it, then re-read it to make sure he understood it correctly. He shook his head.

'Politics, fucking politics! Now we're back in that game.' He spoke out loud and swore again for good measure. He tapped the comm button on his intercom. 'Commander Mannix,' he growled.

Petra's voice came back almost immediately, *Yes Captain?*

'Meet me in the private deck observation lounge in ten minutes?' Aaron barked.

Yes, Captain...ten minutes.

Aaron walked out his door and across the passageway to the cabin opposite and pressed the annunciator button.

The door slid open and Aaron saw Dokad sitting on a lounge at the far side of the room.

'I hope you are comfortable, Sir?' he asked.

'Perfectly, this is much better than on any Krell cruiser I have served on. You do look after yourself, and your guests; I thank you.' Admiral Dokad stood and walked over to Aaron. 'My arm is much better now, thanks to your doctor. No need for the sling and he tells me I will have my old face back before we get to earth. Might have been better if he could have given me a new one,' he chuckled.

'Admiral, would you come with me? We have a lounge forward that gives much better views than the cabins, and there are some developments we need to discuss. I have asked my First Officer to join us.' Aaron stood aside and let the Admiral leave the room first. They headed forward to the double doors at the end of the passageway—these opened to reveal the lounge. It stretched fully across the ship and had an almost uninterrupted view port.

The sight was spectacular. The swirling patterns and colours that made up the extremities of the worm hole were in constant motion and passing bodies—be they planets, stars or asteroids—were ghosted in the background. It was a sight that never ceased to amaze Aaron, as possibly the most incredibly beautiful spectacle he had ever seen and one he never tired of looking at. The doors opened again and in walked Petra.

'Admiral, may I present my First Officer, Commander Mannix. Commander Mannix, our guest, Admiral Dokad of the Imperial Krell Navy,' Aaron said as he stood back.

Petra snapped to attention and saluted the Admiral who, in fine form, snapped the traditional Krell salute where he placed his left fist over his heart. Most Krell were left hand dominant with their primary heart—a two-piece organ for blood flow—being located under their right shoulder. The salute was a show of peaceful intent—weapon hand over the heart—analogous to the human handshake.

He then relaxed and moved forward to shake her hand. 'If you are as good an officer as you are beautiful,' Dokad said smoothly, 'I may be forced to try and poach you away from my friend.'

'Thank you Sir,' Petra replied shyly, looking to Aaron for some help. While a true gentleman, the Admiral did have a reputation as far as women were concerned, as did most Krell males.

Aaron rose to the occasion. 'Commander, can you get us all a drink? Admiral, please sit down, we have a lot to discuss.' He waited until they were all seated with a drink then began. 'Admiral, it appears that your suspicions of your injury being an inside job may be correct. I've had a communication from Argos which indicates that there is a huge increase in Krell presence in our sector. There have also been certain discrete enquiries regarding the incident when you were shot. So, this is how the Prime has handled it.'

Aaron took a sip from his glass before proceeding. 'He has

sent a communication to Gaddok Prime, stating that there was an incident on Argos involving a Krell subject, and the body...you're dead, by the way...was badly damaged and that we're investigating the matter. It won't hold them for long, but should give us enough time to get you to Earth. Admiral, I have to ask, what the hell is so important that we are now risking a confrontation with one of our best and most valued trading partners?'

Aaron realised he had raised his voice. 'Sorry, Sir, this is spiralling out of control. My ship and crew are at your disposal, *but*, I will not risk their safety on a fool's errand! I believe that you owe us at least some explanation.'

Dokad took a good sip of his wine before he sat forward and nodded conspiratorially. 'Aaron, I know the risks you face, but the information I have is vital to us all. Secrecy is of *utmost* importance. How secure is this room?'

Aaron stood and walked over to the view port. 'Sir this whole deck is totally secure, even the internal sensors can't see in here. It's been designed to be invisible to any sensor probe and I *know* it works. Anything said in here will stay in here. Now, what is so bloody important that our Prime would risk so much?' he asked grimly.

'Very well,' Dokad responded and began to explain why he was here. It took just over an hour for him to impart the information. At the end there was total silence for several minutes. It was a story of intrigue and subterfuge, of plots and rebellion—within both the Coalition and the Empire, a story that, if true, would spell doom for the entire galaxy.

'Are you sure? I mean, rebellions and coups on so many human colonies are bad enough, but political upheaval on Gaddok Prime at the same time?' Petra asked the Admiral.

'Totally certain my dear Commander. I also believe there is a common influence in all of these political manoeuvres, but more than that I do not know,' he replied. Another long silence followed.

Aaron shook his head. 'Thank you Admiral, if you are correct we must let the coalition know. Now I understand why it is so important we get to Earth. I apologise for my previous reservations.'

The Admiral stood and looked down at them. 'Aaron, we are old friends, but even friendship has limits. I know I have placed you in a very difficult position but you said no more than you needed, and I fully understand your frustration. Believe me; we are doing the right thing. Again, thank you,' Dokad resumed his seat and finished his wine.

They sat in silence, each processing the information just discussed, each trying to find a flaw in it. Aaron rose and offered refills for each, the offer gladly accepted.

The silence reigned until finally, Dokad spoke. 'This is very fine wine my friend but I do not want to continue with this gloom. Consider the histories of both our people. We have faced incredible obstacles in our evolution, yet we mastered them, both our races survived and flourished. This is just another obstacle we have yet to overcome. We...both Krell and Human civilisations have prevailed in the past and I am certain we will again.' He paused and took another sip of wine. 'For the moment we are safe in the worm hole. What is transpiring outside at this moment is immaterial...there is nothing we can do from here.

'Let's finish our wine and enjoy a brief respite from all this intrigue. Allow me to change the subject; there is something I have wanted to understand for a long time. I have known Freebooters for many, many years and still have no idea how that name came about. You are made up of many races and species, yet all assume the same mantle. Please, how did your society become known as Freebooters?'

Aaron smiled, the grim mood lifting from the room. 'Well I suppose it won't hurt to tell you that secret, but understand this is from memory, dates may be a bit off. It was back in the mid twenty sixth or seventh century, Earth Calendar. Jones had settled Argos and established a union, of sorts.

It was made up of independent traders so they could negotiate and compete with the large conglomerates. Back then travel time between colonies was shortening, but it was still much slower than it is today.

'Anyhow, the story goes like this: The conglomerates were getting tired of the Free Traders Guild clawing away some of their territory, so they came up with a plan to stop them.' Aaron stood and walked to the dispenser, filled a coffee mug and returned; Petra followed with a mug for both herself and the Admiral. When they were again seated, Aaron continued.

'What the conglomerates did was pressure the Coalition Council into a new planet tax. Every time a ship landed or took off, a tax was paid. President Abercrombie was in his final year in office and was...shall we say...*encouraged* to support the tax. This new law was brought in quietly with the rationale to raise funds to improve space ports. It was in the execution that things got messy.

'Every time a person set foot on a planet a tax was charged, and the same was done when a person left, but these taxes were only levied on people engaging in trade. Landing or leaving for any other reason was exempt, for example tourism, tour groups or individuals.

'What this meant was that each time they took a shuttle to the planet to land goods or brought it back, traders had to pay tax on every person on board. It became a huge cost impost for the Guild. The conglomerates, being part of the coalition, were able to use this tax as a write-off against profit, so the real cost to them was negligible. By the time it was introduced virtually all of the independent or 'Free Traders' had registered on Argos and, therefore, paid no tax to the Coalition.

'By imposing it, the conglomerates believed it would weaken the guild and eventually, eliminate it altogether. This went on for years and the tax became known as the Boot Tax...put a boot on the surface or take it off and you paid a tax. The guild petitioned the Coalition Council a number of times, Jones even met with the President more than once, all to no avail...the tax remained. What the politicians didn't factor in was the resolve of the Guild.

'Two colonies, Kandar and Milos, were more rigorous with their tax than others. They were heavily underwritten by the conglomerates and forced much higher payments onto Independents. But they were at the far reach of Coalition territory, for those times, and separated by a large, dangerous part of space known as the Stygian Black.'

Dokad interrupted, 'We know that place; very dangerous to navigate. The Krell avoid it at all costs.'

'So did the Coalition,' Aaron continued. 'The problem was the time it took to bypass this area. The fastest time between the two colonies, Kandar and Milos, was forty-five days, and that was in a Coalition Frigate. Trade ships typically took eighty days or more.

'In one of the meetings Jones had with the Council, President Chang was present. After listening to the petition, he made Jones an offer. Find a quicker route between the two planets and the Guild would be exempt from the tax. Fail and no more petitions would be heard. To cut this long story short, two years later Jones announced he could do what the President asked and a demonstration was arranged. President Chang left Kandar on the same Frigate that made the run in forty five days. Jones left in Freedom two days later.'

'When the Frigate arrived at Milos, Freedom had already been there for ten days. He had cut twelve days off the best time that a military vessel could make the trip in and more than halved the usual commercial time. Chang kept his promise and exempted the guild from the tax. Generically, this became known as the Freeboot amendment.' Aaron paused to finish his coffee.

'As you can imagine, the conglomerates were furious! Not only had Jones found a way through the Stygian Black, he kept the secret to himself. The heads of the conglomerates demanded he give them the secret, but that never happened. Evidently President Chang was tired of the corruption he found when dealing with the Trade Conglomerates.

So, Jones kept his route through the Stygian Black secret and, to this day, it is only known to members of the Council of Seniors. The term "Freebooter" came from the generic name of the tax amendment. It stuck, and was adopted, officially, one hundred years later.'

'How did he do it?' Dokad asked.

'We really don't know, but the myth is that he did a deal with some outcasts from Milos...pirates and thieves who lived inside the Black. But that has never been confirmed, although we do know there are a few colonies there.'

'This Jones sounds like the sort of person I'd like,' Dokad announced as he rose from the lounge. 'Thank you for sharing that story, Aaron, I think I shall retire now. Good night, my friends,' he said before he turned and left.

'Our history doesn't cover that. All it says is that President Chang exempted the Guild from the tax. I hadn't heard that story before. Is it true?' Petra asked.

'As far as I know, but do *you* know how to navigate the

Black?'

Petra considered her answer. 'No, according to what was taught at the academy, there's no known safe passage. But aren't you a member of the Council?'

Aaron smiled broadly, 'Yes, I am.'

'So if it's true, you know the way through?'

Aaron just kept smiling, and changed the subject. 'I think we can assume that there may be some interest in our trip,' he commented as he walked to the bar and deposited his glass in the cleaning unit. 'We can only hope that Grainger's ruse works for the next few days. Even so, I think we need to be extra cautious; one of us should be on the bridge at all times.' Petra looked at him, realising that he wasn't going to be drawn on the Black story further.

'I agree Sir,' she said as she joined him and placed the other two glasses beside his. Their hands touched for the briefest of moments—Aaron felt something akin to an electric shock. He quickly withdrew his hand and turned away.

'I believe this is my watch...see you in the morning Sir,' Petra turned and left the room.

Aaron returned to his cabin, and went straight to the head. He picked up the novel he was reading on the way, might as well finish the chapter while he was there. A short time later, the intercom in the other room burst into life.

Captain, could you come to the bridge? It was Petra's voice and she repeated the call.

His gloomy mood was not helped by the interruption. *Bloody typical*, he thought, *can't even take a dump in peace!* He initiated the cleaning cycle anyway—a jet of warm water flooding his nether regions with the blow dryer finishing the job. He exited the head and spoke to the intercom.

'On the way,' he said as he left his room again.

Kate was in the command seat as he entered and she indicated towards his Ready Room. Petra was sitting at his desk with Ensign Croker and a Cadet Officer before her. From the atmosphere, it was evident that there had been some type of altercation.

'What's up?' he asked as he walked over to the desk. He took one of the chairs in front of the desk, leaving the other two in no doubt that Petra was still in charge.

Ensign Croker turned to Aaron. 'Sir, Cadet Harper has reprogrammed the sensor arrays without proper authorisation.'

'I'd like to hear what Number One has to say,' he said, turning to Petra. 'Commander, if you please?'

Petra looked directly back at him. 'Sir, firstly, what the Ensign says is correct,' she said as she held up her hand to silence an obviously agitated Harper. 'But what Harper has been doing could be very useful...I think you should hear what he has to say.'

'Sir,' Harper snapped to attention. 'I believe we are being tracked by five D'Grak class cruisers.' He was obviously nervous, the slight warble in his voice gave that away, but his posture indicated he firmly believed what he said.

'Sir, this is all in his imagination,' Croker interrupted.

Petra held her hand up again. 'Ensign...Harper has the floor. Now, Cadet Harper, what leads you to believe this?'

'I've been tracking them, Ma'am,' he replied in a matter-of-fact tone. 'So I reprogrammed the sensor array to look for their heat signatures.'

Croker couldn't contain himself any longer. 'Sir! He did this without any authorization...it could have compromised the ship's security! And he *knows* that we can't track any ship in hyperspace; it's just not possible!'

Harper was about to speak when Aaron shut them both down.

'Stop!…Number one, what's your take?'

'Harper is assisting Professor Fraslok at the Academy,' Petra started, but Aaron interrupted.

'Loony Lennie,' he quipped.

Leonard Fraslok was the epitome of the mad scientist in every way. He was short and slightly hunched, with a mass of curly white hair; he wore thick horn rim glasses and was one of those edgy characters who constantly looked startled. For all this type-casting, he did have one of the most brilliant minds in the known Galaxy.

'The same,' Petra answered. 'I know, he's had some crazy ideas in the past. However, there are some that have proved to be of immense value. I also know that Harper is one of his best students, and that the Professor thinks very highly of his work. I think we should take a look at what he's doing.'

Aaron looked at each of them, considering his answer.

'Granted, some of the Professor's inventions have been extraordinary, but we just don't have the ability to track anything in hyperspace. Commander, this is your show… technically, I'm off duty…so it's your call. How do you want to handle it?'

Petra turned to the junior officers. 'Cadet Harper…firstly, never reprogram the sensor array without authorization; got it?' She paused for this to sink in. 'Secondly, what data do you have that we can verify?'

'Ma'am, I can show it to you right here, if I can use your console?'

Petra motioned for him to proceed and turned to Croker, beckoning him to follow. 'Ensign, your actions were technically correct, we can't have anyone just reprogramming things as they want, but, you should have handled it a little better.'

'You're correct, I can't track them in hyperspace, but look at this.' Harper pointed to the console screen. 'This is the track I recorded from when we left Argos till we reached the outer marker and initiated the displacement drive...you can see five distinct heat signatures on a parallel course...I believe they were ghosting us.'

'How do you know what ships they are...indeed even if they are ships at all?' Croker asked.

Harper brought up a matrix table on the screen. 'This details all the heat signature data we have recorded over the last three years...have a look at the readings from my recording and page thirty seven of that workbook,' he looked slightly triumphant as he said this.

Aaron shook his head. 'Bugger me.' The evidence in front of them was compelling—the latent heat signatures were almost identical. 'Ensign, can you set up to re-run our sensor recordings and these readings together?'

'Yes Sir, but we would need the Bubble to do it,' he answered.

'Ok, make it happen.' He turned to Petra, 'Number One, can you do without it for half an hour?'

'No trouble Sir, we aren't using it at the moment anyhow.' She smiled, 'Come on you two, you have work to do,' and she ushered them out the door. As they left, she turned back to Aaron. 'You know Captain, if this is accurate we need to ask the question; why are five ships of this size tracking us? One would be more than enough; unless they have something else on their minds!' She turned and entered the bridge.

Aaron felt his heart rate quicken, it seemed to happen whenever he was near the First Officer; he waited a few moments until it returned to normal then left the ready room. Once on the bridge they all watched the recorded sensor tracks intently.

The Bubble clearly showed Condor at the centre and five definite objects travelling on a perfectly parallel course, until Condor approached the outer marker and engaged her displacement field. Then the other five objects disappeared.

'Am I seeing things, or did the tracks show a change in intensity as we entered the worm hole?' Croker asked. They re-ran the recording again, and then a second time. While the Krell drive technology wasn't the same as Human, they did use a similar form of displacement drive for space travel.

'That's their displacement generators initialising...they *are* ghosting us!' Harper looked slightly bemused. 'Why would they want to do that?'

Aaron's composure was back to normal and he replied. 'Quite simple Cadet; you all know we work closely with the Empire...hell they're one of our major trading partners! Part of working together is training; and this used to happen even when I was at their Academy. Their ships would work closely with "friendlies" to train their crews, see just how close a Krell warship could get before being detected. With their cloaking technology it was usually very one sided, most of the time individual ships never knew a Krell vessel was anywhere close; and if a vessel was detected...well...that ship's commander was soon flying garbage scows. It seems that Mr Harper has put a dent in their training routine; now does anyone want to inform the Krell Navy? Or should we keep this our little secret, at least until we can conclusively prove the technology?'

Everyone looked relieved and one by one, shook hands with Harper or clapped him on the back.

'Ensign Croker and Cadet Harper, you are both now tasked

with writing the program to integrate this new sensor operation into our systems. Good work.' Aaron looked over at Petra, who gave just the barest shake of her head. When she walked over to Aaron, he felt again the strong impact of her close presence as she spoke quietly, almost conspiratorially.

'You'd be a great politician...you make bullshit so believable. Well done Sir.' She turned and stepped up to the command chair and sat down.

'Number two, I have the con, and I believe that both you and the Captain are off duty. Maybe you should get some sleep; I would like to be relieved on time.'

The rest of the bridge watch went back to their stations. Aaron turned to the Navigator who was also off duty and walking towards the pod.

'Commander, fancy a quick drink?' he didn't wait for an answer and they both entered the pod.

***

The ward room was very quiet when Kate Albrecht came in. Only the captain and Simon Holm, the navigation officer, were in the room, and they were huddled in one of the corner seats. They looked up as she collected her mug and walked toward them.

'Kate, care to join us?' It was an open secret that she and Simon were involved and they took every opportunity to get together. She sat down beside Simon and eyed both of them curiously.

'What are you up to? You look like two naughty boys caught with their hands in the cookie jar?' As an Empath, Kate's natural abilities gave her great insight into the actions of others. While she couldn't read minds, she was still extremely good at reading people, with uncanny accuracy.

'Captain, what was that *load* you just shovelled on the bridge?' The Ward Room was neutral ground and here free speech was encouraged. Aaron looked at Kate and then to Simon.

'You better watch yourself Simon...you'll never pull anything over her!' He looked back to Kate, 'It wasn't *all* bull. When I was at the academy, we did routinely ghost friendlies to test the cloaks, and it still goes on. But, five cruisers on one target; never! So, you are right, it is a concern. Simon's just told me that we will be at our reinsertion point in six hours. That's when we'll find out if anything is going on or not. I'm going to get some sleep and so should you two; we need to be on our best game in a couple of hours.' Aaron drained his tea cup and bid them goodnight.

As he stood, Kate followed him, catching him just before he exited. 'Sir, what's between you and Commander Mannix?' she asked.

'Nothing, she's just our new First Officer, why?'

'Oh, no reason...just an observation,' Katie replied with a sly smile. 'Goodnight sir.'

On returning to his quarters, Aaron headed directly to the bathroom. He removed his clothes and dumped them into the sanitizer. By the time he had finished his shower they would be cleaned and back in his wardrobe.

'Shower...fat rain!' he commanded as he entered the cubicle. Instantly, the shower responded with the ceiling depositing large drops of water onto him, at the correct temperature.

'Soap!' at this command, the water stopped and a soap dispenser came out of the wall. He soaped, scrubbed himself thoroughly, and then called again. 'Rinse!' the water again started, but this time it was harder and washed away all of the soap. 'Dry!' was his last command and the air dryer started. When he was dry he exited the cubicle.

He initialised his connection to the ship's computer. 'George,' he asked, 'what's your take on today?' Earlier he had asked the computer to analyse the information that Dokad had given to try and verify some of it.

The artificial voice replied. *If you take each piece in isolation, it seems just too circumstantial and there is not enough hard evidence to support his hypothesis. But if we analyse it, as he has done, then his conclusion, though seeming far-fetched, is very plausible. If correct, we could be looking at a new war scenario, but who will be at war with whom is still unclear. It is possible that it's all just Krell politics being played out on a larger field.*

'What I don't get,' Aaron surmised, 'is the oblique references to rebellions, supposedly on some coalition colonies and the possibility it's all organised by one person. There is no indication of who Dokad suspects, which is all very farfetched.'

Possibly, but the potential for disaster is too great to ignore.

'I concur...now I need some sleep. Can you wake me in four hours?'

Four hours it is, George replied, as Aaron lay down on the bed.

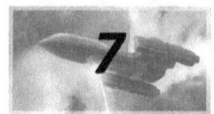

7

*J*T woke early, dressed and headed down to the kitchen where he made himself a mug of coffee; then he headed out to the lake house.

It was only 4:30 am—sunrise would be another half hour, and this was his favourite time of day here. With few clouds above he felt certain the sunrise would be spectacular.

He turned one of the deck chairs to the east and sat down to wait—his thoughts wandering back to last night and dinner. It had been an unusually quiet affair with his father not engaging in much conversation. After Salina excused herself early, his mother had suggested the four men have a port in the library while she supervised the clean-up. They obeyed and were soon ensconced in the large old leather chairs with a good snifter of vintage port.

JT opened the conversation. 'Mum told me about Aaron's visit, Dad,' those words seemed to breach Jeff's defence. For the rest of the evening they talked around the pending visit.

'Seems like a lifetime since he was here...I wonder, why now?' Jeff mused. 'I know we parted badly and all over nothing, as it turned out. I just hope we can sort this out once and for all...I've missed having him around and I know his absence has affected you.'

It had been a huge blow to JT when his uncle left without any explanation. He had just finished his third year at the Academy and came home to the news. It had been especially hard as it was *Uncle Aaron* who taught young JT most things: how to fish, instilling a fascination for exploring and sparking his interest in ancient automobiles—something he was still passionate about. So great had been his fascination with these ancient things that his father had converted the bedroom next to John's into a hobby room. In here, the young boy had stored and displayed his passion with cabinets full of models, drawers full of ancient drawings, photos and technical data. But most important of all, there were fully restored videos from that era showing everything from sales advertising to complete racing series. In time it became his sanctum when the world got too difficult for a young boy. Even today, as a grown man, he still maintained the relics whenever he was home.

The conversation carried on for the next hour before they all decided to retire—still no reason for the years lost—but with hope remaining that all could be put right this weekend.

JT's reverie was interrupted as the first rays of the sun broke through the light cloud base. The colours here were fabulous: purple; and pink; through to brilliant red exploded across the canvas of the sky, as the sun rose above the horizon.

'Thought I would find you here,' his mother's voice startled him. 'Ever since you were a little boy you would sneak out here to watch the sunrise.' She smiled and placed her hand on his shoulder, enjoying the morning vista with her son. They both stood in silence.

'I'm glad you're here this weekend, Johnathan' Sonia said at last. 'Your father will need our full support and you being here will help.' She paused, looking small and vulnerable. 'Your father has never told me what happened between them but it was so sudden...one minute Aaron was here, the next gone, with no reason or any indication as to why or where. It took me years to track him down but...I think your father knew where he was.' She straightened and tilted her head to one side; there was something else on her mind.

'And you, Johnathan Thomas Abraham…what excuse do you have for not coming home for so long, and I'm not counting the brief visit a year ago. Also what right did you have to scare twenty years of life out of your mother with that Zyralin Four thing?' Sonia was back to her full strength. 'Don't answer…you will only try to placate me. Just remember, no matter how old you are or how much brass you have hanging off your uniform; I am still your mother!'

JT smiled; he kissed her on the forehead. 'I'll try…next time someone attacks us, I'll tell them that they will have my mother to contend with if any harm comes to me,' he chuckled. 'That'll stop them.'

'Be serious. What sort of mother would I be if I didn't worry about my children…especially the one who deliberately look's for trouble?' She held on to her son, not wanting to break the contact.

'Ok Mum, I promise to be more careful.' There was no point in arguing, JT knew he would always loose.

She patted him on the back and turned towards the house, 'Make sure you do. When you're ready, we are going to have breakfast at Salina's this morning…she says she has something special for us.' JT groaned. *Special* to his sister usually meant raw seaweed or something equally green and unpalatable.

Salina's house was a total contrast to the grandeur of the main house. Some would have called it minimalist, but to JT it was empty. Furnishings were sparse, and strictly functional, no artworks or frivolous decorations, only practical stuff or images of fish and her work to re-populate the oceans.

Breakfast proved to be delicious with fruit juice, scrambled eggs, bacon and some edible green stuff followed by an excellent pot of coffee.

'Well done Sal. A great improvement on what you usually

serve. Have you finally decided to join the human race?' JT could never pass up a chance to niggle his sister.

'Not really,' she retorted, 'I did this for Solomon...at least *he's* a gentleman! If it was just you, I could always rustle up some hay.' The banter went back and forth for a while as they finished their coffee. Salina could be a huge flirt and it seemed that Sol had a target painted on his forehead when she turned to him. 'So, Solomon,' she purred 'what do *you* want to do today?'

'Well, I was hoping that I could have a look around the compound,' Sol answered. 'Looks like the place has changed a lot since I was last here, and in all the times I have been here, I haven't really seen that much of it. I bet there's some interesting history to tell, maybe even a skeleton or two.'

JT groaned. Sol had walked straight into the trap. *Talk about a spider and the fly*, he thought.

'Solomon, you're correct. There is a great deal of history.' One of Sal's other passions was family history and she never passed up an opportunity to talk about it. She moved her chair closer to him. JT and David were both smirking but not moving to Sol's aid.

Sal continued. 'Our ancestor, John Thomas the second, acquired this property over six hundred years ago, during the ecological disasters of the early twenty fourth century. The droughts of the late twenty third century finally finished western NSW, and land was virtually worthless. He saw an opportunity and purchased huge parcels of land for almost nothing; acquiring this one because of the old gold mine that occupied the site. If you remember your school history, you will know that times were extreme back then. With famine and violence ruling the world, he wanted to provide security for his family and employees.

'During excavations, they found two major things: a

very large vein of gold, which eventually paid for all the construction; and an underground aquifer, which is still a source of water for the compound today. After these discoveries, he enlarged the underground complex to be capable of housing all of the company's executive and administrative operations.' Salina paused and refilled her tea cup.

JT couldn't contain himself any longer. 'Come on, Sal, that's a bit thin, you should actually *read* his journals instead of looking at them as some sort of religious relic.'

'And I suppose you have?' she retorted.

It was her father who answered. 'Give your brother some credit, Sal, he has. In fact, I think John is the only person, other than Aaron, who actually *has* read them.' Jeff turned to his son, 'why don't you elaborate on what your sister has said so far.'

'No worries. The Second, as we know him, was no altruistic philanthropist but rather an astute and ruthless opportunist; in some ways a real skeleton in the closet. Why would he buy land here if he didn't have some evidence that it would pay off? At that stage, the company didn't have any agricultural interests or capability but to his credit, he *did* have the welfare of his employees and family utmost in his heart; but he didn't want to foot all the bills.

'As Sal said, things were different back then. Taxation was a massive impost, levied at over fifty percent on corporate earnings, plus companies were tasked with providing safe communities for their employees. Given how bad things were back then, this was a massive undertaking. Coincidentally this was the same time that the Coalition Council relinquished control of Earth to the local authorities; further aggravating the situation. But, the Second was shrewd: by buying all the land and constructing the bunker, he received huge tax concessions from the new Earth Terrestrial Government; and the gold find wasn't reported until many years later.'

'Ok, so he wasn't perfect,' interjected Salina, 'but he did look after anyone he employed. The bunker was an example of that, where everything they would need: fuel; food; and other logistics were all there. The only problem, by the time it was completed, things had settled down.' Salina paused, looking to her brother for any more interruptions. He said nothing, so she continued.

'That's not to say everything was ok...far from it. Five billion people had died in the ecological disasters and the Earth had changed. Most of the northern hemisphere was either covered by several metres of ice and snow or was sub-arctic, so something needed to be done. Fortunately, the exodus project was already under way. The only real obstacle was all the space junk making it almost impossible for the Exodus Ships to navigate out of the atmosphere. As they say though, one man's garbage is another's gold and the space junk was just that. The Second seized the opportunity and Abracorp Salvage began, charging a token fee per item removed.' She paused and looked at her brothers, as if challenging them to contradict her.

Again JT interrupted. 'Close, but not *entirely* accurate; yes, the fee was a token, but the real profit was in the salvage. The company kept the garbage and recycled it; do you have any idea of the value of the rare metals used in those old satellites? The story goes, there was some resistance from the military...secrets and all that...but it was short lived as the survival of the human race depended on completing this task with a degree of urgency. But it gets better. It was Abracorp Construction who was building the exodus ships, as they were called, and all the while The Second knew that they wouldn't get past the debris field. He said nothing until it was almost too late, then, true to form, he had the solution and Abracorp Salvage was born. With that one contract it became the most profitable arm of the company for many years.'

JT turned back to his sister. 'You got any more?'

She paused to take another sip of tea, glaring at her brother. 'I'll just fill in the last bits. Unfortunately, with the exodus under way the problems faced on Earth became less important. The violence stopped and a period of peace began. The huge underground bunker he had just completed was suddenly a bit of a white elephant. Nobody really wanted to live and work underground unless it was absolutely necessary. The bunker, or *The Second's Folly*, as we call it, was abandoned and the first part of the existing house was built. He did, however, incorporate the entrances to the bunker into the construction, just in case!' Sal paused to take a sip from her tea cup.

'The main house has been built over subsequent generations, each one adding something new. Part of the original construction, the ground floor, is now company offices, housing most of the on-world personnel. Our great grandfather, John Thomas the third, reopened the bunker and after more than two hundred years, people again trod its passageways. Our Grandfather started a restoration program so that history could be preserved and Dad has continued the process. The long term goal is to integrate some of these areas back into the company operations above and turn the rest into a museum.'

"Thanks for the history lesson, teach,' JT chuckled 'but I think Sol would rather see it for himself.' The three young men rose, Sol giving JT a look of gratitude at the reprieve from his sister.

Jeff stopped them, for a moment. 'OK, but remember,

there's construction happening on the first two levels and we still have to certify below level six. The site manager will meet you and ensure you don't go off exploring. I'm serious about this, we can't risk anyone haring about on their own... do you hear me? Stay above level six.'

JT knew that his father must have his reasons, so reluctantly he agreed.

Just then the face of Ajay, Jeff's PA, appeared on the comm screen on the far wall, *Mr Abraham...you have a call on your personal line.*

'Ok. I'll be about five minutes.' Jeff replied and rose from the table. 'Enjoy yourselves,' he said as he left the room.

***

The first stop for David, Sol and JT was the safety office. They needed hard hats, eye protection and overalls to enter the construction site. Once they had these, they entered the old elevator located in the centre of the administration office on the ground floor of the house. This had been here as long as the building but had been painstakingly restored and was now fully operational. As the doors closed, JT pointed to the panel of buttons on the wall.

'Notice the markings,' he said. The panel had two rows of buttons on one side and an emergency stop button and intercom on the other. The buttons on the two rows were marked B1, B2 and SB1 to SB12 in sequence.

'B1 and B2 are the basement levels just below us. The SB stands for *Security Bunker* and the level number, as I understand,' David explained. 'The normal basement levels are company administration and an ever decreasing area for us. Things like the wine cellar and storage are on B2 while B1 is now totally over to administration. The SB levels start thirty metres below B2, but you can't access them without one of these.' He paused while producing an old key. 'In the old days, there would also be other security measures and even armed guards...I can't imagine what it was like to live back then.'

He turned the key and pressed the button marked SB1 and the lift started to descend.

'We've retained the keys, for historic reasons...Dad wants to open this up to allow students to see, first-hand, what things were like back then...sort of like a *Time Capsule.*'

It took the old lift nearly a minute to reach the first bunker level where they donned their eye protection and helmets before exiting. What was before them was a large foyer that was in the throes of some major refurbishment—the goal being to reconstruct exactly what was originally there.

A figure approached them. 'Gentlemen, Graham Rogers, site supervisor. Mr Abraham senior called down and asked if I could show you around.' They shook hands and he pointed to the wall behind them. 'There are another five lifts like the one you came in. Unfortunately not all are working as yet, but we will get them back. If you follow me, I'll start the tour.'

He led the way to the far end of the room. Before them was a long ramp heading to the surface. 'We drove this drift so we could bring in equipment and material more easily; the original had caved in, but we will eventually reinstate it and fill this one in when we finish. Now, a quick view of what we know and what we think is here. Levels one and two are essentially common and assembly areas, levels three and four are marked as administration on the old maps we have. Levels five and six are living quarters and, up to this time, as far as we have certified.

'We have had some exploration of lower levels, but we can't be certain if the schematics are correct; eventually we will generate a complete plan. We think levels seven and eight were set up as a garage and hangar to store ground vehicles and aircraft; we haven't got to opening anything that far down, so we can't be certain. One major issue is level nine. Designated as armaments and ammunition, the schematic shows details of blast doors and a complex vent system. We assume this would operate in the event of an explosion, to minimise any damage, but we still don't know for sure. Unfortunately, we don't have any real detail of what is stored in there or what security measures are in place, it's totally off limits for now.'

JT spoke up. 'I might be able to help! I have all of the Second's journals and I'm sure I read some references to what you need. I'll have a look when we get back.'

Rogers smiled. 'That'd be great; we need any help we can get. If you think about it, the mansion above could be sitting on a huge time bomb, especially as we believe there's an old fusion reactor on level ten or eleven.'

The next three hours passed very quickly. Even David, who spent a lot of time on the project finances, was impressed by the scale of the complex, and he now fully grasped the work needed.

'There's nowhere on Earth that has all this, at least nowhere we can access. There would be some in the north but it is still under many metres of ice. We owe it to our children and their children to preserve it as it was.'

Rogers looked directly at JT and David, 'You two must continue the work your father has started here.' He stopped, thinking that maybe his passion had gone too far.

'Have no fear, we will,' JT answered. 'There's no alternative; it must be preserved.'

'Agreed,' David added.

That calmed Rogers—the heir apparent and the head of finance committing to the project was all he wanted to hear. He looked at his watch. 'I've arranged for lunch so we should head back.' They returned to the entry foyer and went into one of the meeting rooms for their lunch. Laid out all around the room were plans, models and sketches of the site and, more importantly, impressions of what it could look like.

JT fidgeted as the food was delivered, not even looking at the plates but quickly cornering Rogers instead. 'Have you heard about the Second's collecting obsession?'

'JT, for Pete's sake...let it go...' David interrupted, 'there's no old car collection!' All his life he had had to put up with JT's crazy notions and he'd heard it all before.

'Come on Dave,' JT sounded exasperated. 'It could be true, and down here would be an ideal place to hide it!'

Rogers shook his head. 'Mr Abraham, I have heard such stories and believe me, I would love to solve that mystery; but there is nothing indicated on any of the plans. So far, we haven't found anything to suggest they're down here. Sorry.'

'Yeah, let the poor guy alone...let it remain a myth,' Sol chipped in as he placed a generous helping of caramel pie on his plate. 'Come and get some of this, before I'm forced to eat it all.' JT shrugged and went back to the table, finishing his lunch in silence.

The rest of the afternoon was spent wandering around the compound above ground, including a quick tour of the ancient power farm. While the majority of the power for the complex was generated by the MAM reactors, the ancient solar and wind generation systems had been restored and were fully operational.

The house itself was also intriguing—it was huge and was said to have over seventy bedrooms. The family only really used six of these on the upper ground floor. The other two floors above were used to house visiting executives and their families, as well as visitors from *off-world* operations. At any time there could be as many as one hundred people in the house or as few as two. Further to the west was another village where most of the staff resided, all provided by the company as part of employee remuneration packages.

It was just before five in the afternoon when they returned to the house, where they were met by Ajay who addressed John.

'Sir, your father would like you to join him in his study. I'll take Captain Radchak and your brother to the library.' He turned and led them away. John knocked on the study door, memories of his youth flooding back. This was where his father spent most of his time and where he disciplined wayward children. John smiled as he entered.

'You want to see me?' His smile widened as he remembered entering his father's study so many years ago, with the same words...the moment was not lost on Jeff, either.

'Long time since you were sent to the study,' Jeff chuckled, the irony of the situation not lost on him.

'Can't think of what I have done wrong today.'

Jeff waved his son into a chair then moved over to a sideboard and poured two good measures of scotch. He handed one to John and sat opposite his son. The chairs were ancient Chesterfields and seemed to envelope them as they sat. They both took a long sip of the liquid, savouring the flavour.

'How was the tour today?' he asked.

John looked at his father, not believing for a moment that this was the real reason they were in here. 'Great...and we didn't go anywhere you didn't want us to.'

'I know, and thanks. I know you don't want to be seen as

one of the Abraham family, but unfortunately son, you are. Not going past where I asked sets a good example. You must remember that we've nearly 300 employees down there... if we don't obey the rules, how can we expect others to?'

John eyed his father warily. *Here it comes,* he thought, *the time to join the company speech...well I'm ready for that.* His jaw tightened, determination evident on his face.

'It seems as if we are going to have another surprise visitor this weekend,' Jeff continued. 'Probably a few...the President and some others will be here. Evidently, he has decided that the event your mother has planned would be a good time to honour your sister for all her work in the marine arena. He also expressed interest in having a look at the bunker while he's here, but I get the feeling there is much more to this than meets the eye.'

John interrupted his father. 'Hang on...how many has she invited?'

'Around one hundred and fifty,' Jeff smiled back, revelling at the effect of this news.

'What?' John exclaimed. 'She told me it was just a family affair!'

'Calm down,' Jeff commanded, 'you know your mother. All three of her unattached children in the house at the same time...did you honestly think she would pass up a chance for some match making?' He paused as John squirmed in his chair.

'Forget that,' Jeff resumed, 'I'm far more interested in the President's timing. Firstly; your uncle's coming with some mysterious old friend. Then there's the final exercise for your ship and Wilson's presence and now Malik invites himself to the party.' He paused and drained his glass. 'No John...there is something else going on...have you heard any scuttlebutt?'

JT shook his head. 'Nothing...I thought Malik would be going on Rhapsody...at least, that's what we were told.'

'Well apparently not; he's coming here directly from the launch and his security detail will be here first thing tomorrow morning.' Jeff smiled, evidently pleased at a new thought. 'I'll bet Albrecht will be pissed when he finds out; his media hype will fall a bit flat.'

8

*A*aron couldn't quite make out the distant sound—was it a bell? No, someone was speaking—now the bell again! Slowly he climbed through the darkness back to consciousness.

Finally...I thought you would never wake up! The voice sounded again in his head. *Four hours, as you requested.* The link with the ship's central brain was still new to him—sometimes he wished he hadn't been compatible.

'Thanks George,' he said as he moved to the shower.

The needle-like drops hitting him at well below body temperature soon had his senses back on line. Aaron shut off the water and grabbed a towel—a vigorous rubdown completed the awakening process. His uniform was waiting in his wardrobe and he quickly dressed.

Although he had a full kitchen in his cabin, he headed down to the ward room where he ordered a bacon and egg roll and a coffee from the dispenser. He sat at one of the tables to eat his roll, then, with coffee in hand, headed to his ready room. There he reviewed the last watch data and noted that there had been no change in the projected course of their five mysterious companions.

Still a bit over two hours till insertion, then we'll see if this thing works, he thought. He was interrupted by the sound of the chime, announcing that someone was at the bridge door to his ready room.

'Come in,' Aaron replied to the chime.

Petra entered the room. 'Good morning, Captain.' The door closed behind her.

'Care for a coffee?' he asked; his throat suddenly dry and

his heart beating a little faster.

'Sounds good,' she turned to the dispenser. 'Coffee, white, no sugar, fifty-five degrees,' and a mug of steaming coffee appeared on the pad. They moved to the lounge area and sat facing each other. 'Uneventful watch, no change and everything was quiet; next couple of hours could be interesting though.' She smiled her mischievous, challenging smile.

'What do you mean...interesting?' Aaron asked.

'Well, do you have a plan in mind for when we reinsert?' she asked.

'Not as such,' he answered. 'But I have asked Kate and Simon to meet me here in about fifteen minutes and then we will all work on a solution.'

'So...we have fifteen minutes to kill do we?' she smiled flirtatiously.

Aaron felt the strange fluttering in his stomach again, he was about to say something when the door chimed. Kate and Simon were a little early; they both ordered a cup of coffee and sat on the opposite lounge.

'Where are we up to Simon?' Aaron asked.

'In just under two hours, we reinsert into normal space; then a little over seventeen minutes before we reach our next insertion point; then next stop, Earth.'

Travelling through hyperspace was not just a set-and-forget process. Very rarely did any journey happen by engaging the displacement field and travelling directly to ones' final destination. For one thing, the energy needed for this was immense; for another, there was the fact that space, and everything in it, was in constant motion. To arrive at exactly the desired place and time usually meant a number of shorter operations, as was the case here. The trip to Earth needed two separate worm-hole insertions to arrive exactly where, and when, they had planned.

'So,' Aaron looked at the group. 'We have seventeen minutes...we could have five possibly-hostile ships to contend with...options, Number One?'

Petra put her coffee mug down and spoke. 'As this has been an uneventful watch, I have taken some time to study the engineering schematics; she really is one hell of a ship. As I see it, we have three options: one, we do nothing and reinsert as normal with only the deflector operational; two, we reinsert at full battle readiness; or three, we go in sneaky.' She paused, inviting comment; none came, so she continued.

'The design on this ship differs from most others I have served on; this one has a distributed power system, with each major system having its own generating capacity. At the moment, we're running in normal cruise mode with the main reactor providing the bulk of the ship's power requirements, so this is what I suggest; we run up all generating systems and initialise shield and weapon systems...initialise only...we don't bring them on line. Once we reinsert, we can have everything on line within seconds, if needed. Now, I haven't had a great deal of experience in combat but this would seem to be quite quick. If there's nothing there, no harm done, but if we do run into hostiles, it may give us an edge.'

Kate added, 'Basically, going to alert status amber... without the fuss...works for me.' Aaron and Simon nodded their approval.

'Still your watch Number One; it's your plan so you'd better get cracking,' Aaron urged.

The process was simple. All generating systems were slowly brought online, with the main reactor and generators adjusted to compensate. This would look like a normal power setting to any sensor scan and, with weapons and shields only initialised. They wouldn't be a recognisable threat to any vessel in the area.

Aaron let his crew do their job and stayed in his ready room, telling himself that this would be a good test of the new first officer. He checked the time, six minutes to reinsertion. He left his desk and strode onto the bridge. Simon looked up from his console. 'Five and a half minutes to reinsertion; do you want a count down?' he asked.

Petra vacated the command chair and took the number one's spot to the right of the chair, behind tactical. Kate was already at her console, left of the chair and behind comms.

Aaron looked over to Simon, 'Sounds good...do it.' He looked over to the sensor console toward Harper. 'Is everything ready Cadet?'

'Yes, sir.' Harper answered back. 'I've put the theoretical tracks into the Bubble so we can have an idea where they should emerge. As soon as we pick up their signature the system will make any corrections.'

The track in the Bubble showed the five amber dots on a slightly converging course that would intersect with Condor just prior to re-insertion. The hairs on the back of Aaron's neck stood up as he saw this—he knew what this could be the start of and he didn't like it one bit. He moved over to the nav console.

'Simon, if we miss this insertion point, how long to the next one?' he almost whispered. Simon's fingers flew over his console making calculations at lightning speed.

'Four hours,' he answered. Aaron nodded his thanks and returned to his chair, he beckoned Petra to join him.

'Number One, how much do you know about Krell battle tactics?' he asked quietly as she joined him.

She looked at the Bubble before answering. 'Not a great deal. I studied the basics of battle theory but not much else, why?'

Aaron thought for a moment. 'There's an old trap they use, it's called Katoc; loosely translated, it means fist. They place one cloaked ship in front of the target effectively blocking its path, while the others fan out around the target to form a flanking formation. If it all turns to shit, they have the advantage—they can concentrate fire and the target must divide any response. It can crush the target like a fist,' here he clenched his fist to demonstrate, 'hence the name. Aaron followed her gaze to the holographic scene in the Bubble. 'If Harper is correct and they reinsert where he says, things could get very interesting.'

Petra was surprised. 'You don't seem too worried...they could destroy this ship!'

'Ah, you forget!' Aaron smiled. 'I spent a couple of years at their academy. There is one way out of the trap; ballsy, but effective. If they carry it out, we can still get through. Probably with a bloody nose, but we can get out.' He turned back to the nav station.

'Simon...how long?'

'Thirty seconds.'

Aaron looked back at the weapons officer. 'David, get everything spun up as soon as we reinsert.'

'Everything?' David questioned.

'Yes, everything.'

Simon's voice intruded, 'ten, nine, eight, seven, six, five, four, three, two, one...reinsertion.' Again, that fraction of a second when everything seemed to shimmer out of phase, then they were back in normal space.

'Harper,' Aaron called.

'Coming up now sir,' Harper replied and he turned to the Bubble, 'just a couple of seconds.' He looked like an expectant father waiting on the birth of his first child.

The five amber dots changed to red, one by one.

'Yes!' Harper exclaimed and punched the air. 'It worked!'

Aaron watched the five red tracks as they divided and moved into new courses that would allow them to initiate the fist. He swore under his breath.

'Fuck!' he said again out loud. 'Sometimes it would be better to be wrong.' He turned to Tactical.

'Dave, those five red dots may be hostiles...don't ask now,' he said as he waived away the question that was forming on the Tactical Officers lips. 'Just get everything spun up and the ship prepared for a fight.' He turned back to the nav console.

'Navigator, can you insert a timer into the Bubble? I need to know where we are with respect to the insertion timing.' Simon's fingers again flew across his console and immediately a countdown clock came up on the view screen.

'I don't know about the Bubble, but will this do?' he asked, sensing that urgency was the key.

'Excellent.'

The seconds seemed to creep by and after about five minutes the comms officer spoke.

'Sir, there is a lot of chatter out there...can't understand it...it's encrypted, but there is a lot of it.'

Aaron turned to the tactical officer. 'Dave, if these are Krell cruisers, we could have some problems.'

David could not contain himself. '*Krell* cruisers...what the hell's going on Skipper? I thought we were all friends?'

'To be honest, I don't know it all myself, but this could just be a ghosting exercise, or we could be heading into a fist. If so we need everything ready and all the shields at max, ok?'

'Sure Skipper.' He looked a bit surprised and worried. 'You're thinking of hammerhead?' Aaron nodded and both smiled. 'Never a dull moment,' David said, quietly.

He went back to his tactical console, working feverishly to complete his captain's commands, the adrenalin level rising in his body, a few drops of perspiration forming on his brow.

'What's hammerhead?' Petra enquired.

Dave looked up. 'Hammerhead; the only way to break through this is to do just that...break through. We will set our shields to counter as much of the cross fire as we can but we throw everything at the front ship...crash or crash through...hammerhead!'

Petra was still confused. Aaron pointed to the Bubble.

'What's our objective? To go to our next worm hole insertion point...but what's stopping us? The front ship; it's trying to block us. We can't go round them; that'd change our insertion angle and we'd end up who knows where. So, we hold our course and hit the front ship with everything we have and crash through. We'll take a few licks but this old girl can handle it.' He turned and patted his chair as if to assure the ship he knew what he was doing.

Just then the voice in his head joined in. *Patting your chair won't do much.* George said, the sarcastic tone now gone, *as you said, ballsy...but there is no other choice.'*

Already the computer was calculating the most probable damage points and working on repair logistics. One of the huge advantages of having a *Brain* ship was that all the behind the scenes tasks just happened. Aaron watched both the counter and the Bubble while the tension on the bridge rose exponentially.

'Sir, there was a lot of chatter as we reinserted, but it

has just stopped,' the comms officer announced. They all waited and watched the red dots, knowing their entire future depended on the next ten minutes. Another minute ticked by, then another.

'Sir,' it was Harper. 'The lead ship is slowing.'

Aaron watched as the Bubble confirmed Harper's words. The lead ship had slowed. *This is wrong...they're too far from the insertion point* he thought.

'Chatter just started again, almost sounds like an argument.'

Aaron pressed a button on his chair and the chatter filled the bridge.

'One of the flankers is arming his weapons,' tactical called.

'Have any of them locked on to us?' Aaron asked.

'No Sir, they just started spinning up their weapons system,' Dave replied. 'Doesn't make sense; they must know that doing that allows us to see them!'

'Comms hail that ship; find out their intentions,' Aaron commanded.

The comms officer transmitted the hail.

'No response Sir.'

'Number One, bring the ship to full battle stations; make a lot of fuss about it.'

Aaron winked at Petra. She responded and the alarm bells sounded throughout the ship; bulkhead doors slammed shut and crew manned their battle stations.

'Bill...light them up!' Aaron called.

William Croker, the sensor officer, knew what his captain wanted—a big show. He turned on every active sensor that he could and the space between Condor and the target almost crackled.

Aaron smiled. 'That should wake things up.'

At the same time, Aaron mentally contacted George. *Get the admiral in our loop.*

Moments later, the sound of Admiral Dokad's voice sounded in Aaron's head.

What can I do? He was in his cabin speaking into the comms system with George relaying his words to Aaron via their subliminal link.

Sir, could you stay at the console and advise me through this contact? We have a situation with a Katoc of five. One has revealed itself but we are tracking the others. I may need some insight.

Aaron programmed his station to be mirrored in the Admiral's cabin.

'Sir, we're being hailed,' the comms officer spoke.

'Put it on the view screen...but my face only in return,' Aaron replied.

The view screen changed from the vista of space to the bridge of a Krell warship; its Commander's face filled the screen. 'My apologies Captain Abraham,' the voice was smooth and well-modulated.

The face that looked back at Aaron would be considered handsome, for a Krell. His forehead was high and his eyes solid black. His white hair was close cropped and his nose long and aquiline.

'Excuse my bad manners,' he turned to someone else and gave the order to de-cloak. 'We are conducting a training exercise, and one of our trainee officers got carried away; I hope we didn't cause you too much concern.'

Dokad's voice again sounded in Aaron's head. *Be careful... that is Ga'Dok; one I suspect was involved in my recent 'death.'*

Aaron looked at his counterpart and noticed that the

other four red dots were starting to move away from their original track, clearing the path to their insertion point.

'Not at all, Commander, I hope he has learned some good lessons.'

'Indeed he has…again, my apologies for any inconvenience.'

'No inconvenience Commander. It is actually fortunate that your subordinate made his mistake. I have a new First Officer and we were about to demonstrate our weapons system to her. I'm glad that we didn't accidentally fire on your ship.'

At the same time, Aaron programmed a track for a target drone to fly past the knuckle ship and approximately 100,000 kilometres behind it. He pressed another button on his chair console, and a target drone was transferred onto the launch rail.

'Your position is fine, Commander; you are welcome to watch this demonstration if you wish; who knows, you may see something you wish to obtain? After all, the Empire is one of our best trading partners.' He signalled for the communication to be terminated.

Aaron what are you doing? This man is dangerous! Dokad's voice sounded again in Aaron's head, this time with a great deal of alarm.

Aaron signalled his tactical officer to launch the drone and David complied.

So am I Admiral…so am I!

'Number One, man the weapons console. Dave make like you're instructing her.'

Petra took up the position and David stood beside her.

'Sir,' Croker spoke up. 'They scanned us pretty heavily while he was talking, like they were looking for something, and they received a sub space transmission from somewhere.'

Commander Albrecht moved back to the comms console. 'Captain, from the strength and frequency, I believe it came from Krell High Command.'

Aaron was watching the drone's track in the Bubble. The flight took it over the ship directly in front of the knuckle but once clear, it changed and settled into the pre-programmed location, placing the knuckle ship directly between Condor and itself.

'Comms get them back but allow the rear of the bridge into the field of view...*not* the Bubble.'

The view screen wavered and the Krell's bridge again filled it.

'Sorry Commander...as you see I also have some crew issues to work on,' he apologised.

'No apology needed. I see you have launched a drone?' There was a degree of concern in Ga'Dok's voice.

'As I said, Commander, your ship is perfectly safe and you are free to watch,' Aaron turned to David. 'Weapons, you may fire at will.'

'Captain, wait please,' Ga'Dok's voice was urgent.

Aaron held his hand up to David and Petra. 'Weapons hold. Is something wrong, Commander? As I said, you are in no danger.'

'Not at all Captain, while we are firm friends with Freebooters, we do not need to view your training methods. If you could give me a few minutes to clear the area, I will be out of your way.' Ga'Dok's voice was again smooth and measured. Simultaneously, the knuckle ship began to accelerate away.

'Of course Commander, I look forward to our next meeting; maybe we could share a glass or two,' Aaron smiled and cut the transmission, his relief obvious.

The Krell ship engaged its cloak and moved away.

'Keep tracking them, Mr Harper.' He looked back at the timer—two minutes till insertion.

'Number one, don't waste that drone. Let's give them a farewell show...hit it with the plasma cannon.'

'Aye, Sir,' Petra replied and she fired the forward plasma cannon.

A huge ball of highly charged energy sped from Condor to the target. It took less time than a blink of an eye and the drone was vaporised spectacularly.

'Good shooting...hope they got a good view.'

Aaron stood and looked at his crew; many questioning faces looking back.

'I know this has been an interesting event, to say the least. I thank you all for your trust and congratulate each of you for doing a great job. Mr Harper, continue to monitor those ships.'

He knew this wouldn't answer any questions, but it was all he could say at this time. He needed to keep his crew in the dark a little while longer, something Aaron hated doing.

Just as the timer reached zero, the Navigator initiated the displacement field and Condor slid quietly into the relative safety of her worm hole.

'Tactical, secure the ship from battle stations. Number Two, I believe you have this watch?'

'Aye Sir, I have the con,' Kate replied and moved to the command chair. 'Sir, shall I change the clocks?' Aaron looked at the time readout on the top of the view screen. It read *18:52;* still on Argos time.

'Good idea, notify the crew we will be operating on Earth time from now.' He turned as Kate changed the ship's internal timing system; the readout changed to 07:55,

Thursday, February 6, 2921. Condor was now operating at Earth standard time.

Aaron paused. 'We should also start acclimatisation as well.'

Kate nodded and issued the necessary instructions to change the gravity and atmospheric conditions to match those of Earth. She allowed two hours for the change, giving the crew time to gradually become accustomed to the new conditions.

Aaron smiled to himself—his choice of second officer was proving to be correct. He motioned for Petra to join him and they entered the pod. He selected his accommodation level and spoke as they set off. 'I want to get our guest's take on what just happened and see if he can decipher the sub space transmission—seems it's highly encrypted. You collect the Admiral and meet me in the observation lounge. After that, I might make us some dinner, or breakfast, or whatever we should be having at this time.'

Petra just smiled and headed for the Admirals cabin. Dokad was expecting the call; he was ready and followed Petra to the lounge.

'Good morning I believe,' he greeted Aaron as he entered the room.

'Ah yes, Earth time.' The clock on his console had changed, as had all on the ship. 'Admiral, can you take a look at this communication and see if you can decrypt it?'

The Admiral walked over to the console and sat down. 'You might want to get a drink; this could take a while.'

Petra was already at the dispenser and returning with three steaming mugs of coffee. They sat in silence while Dokad worked through the recording. Finally he sat back and smiled.

'Seems I am dead,' he said. 'The transmission was from Navy High Command informing all vessels that a report had come from Argos stating that an assassination of a Krell officer had taken place on Argos. It also said that, while it appeared the victim was a high-ranking officer, identification of the body was hindered by the extensive injuries sustained, and requested any information as to the possible identity of the officer be sent urgently. The high command believes that I was the only officer to be on Argos at the time. They have deduced that I must have perished.' He paused and took a sip of his coffee. 'Ga'Dok volunteered to go to Argos and retrieve the body.'

Aaron smiled. 'Looks like Grainger's ruse worked. It'll be interesting what he comes up with when they arrive to collect you.'

'Well, I'm awfully hungry for a dead person,' he chuckled.

'Admiral, how do you feel about one of my famous omelettes?' Aaron asked.

'Providing the good commander joins us. While I am fond of you Aaron, the company of a beautiful woman always makes a meal more palatable,' Dokad beamed at Petra.

Aaron simply nodded and Dokad offered his arm to Petra. 'I believe this is one of your human customs,' he said as they followed Aaron out of the lounge.

*A*aron led them into his private quarters, with Petra still holding the Admiral's arm.

As they entered, a plaintive cry greeted them. Petra looked toward the source to see a small brown nose appear in the doorway to the sleeping area, followed by the rest of the long cream body.

'You have a cat?' she cried.

'Shit! Yes...I forgot!' Aaron stammered. 'You aren't allergic or anything I hope?' he said to his guests.

The cat walked up to Petra with his long brown tail held vertically, with just a hint of a curve at the tip. He stopped at her feet and sat down, as if inspecting her. Next he reached up and stood on his rear legs as if asking to be picked up. Petra bent down and lifted the cat into her arms; immediately he settled and started purring.

'Looks like I am going to have to keep you; his highness seems to approve,' Aaron quipped.

Petra stroked the cat and it accepted the petting loudly. 'Well, does he have a name?' she enquired.

'Yes, sorry. Petra Mannix, Admiral Dokad, may I present Prince, the real commander of this vessel,' Aaron said with a flourish, as he made the formal introduction. 'He's a Siamese. I found him on Coltara three years ago. Well, he actually found me and just sort of decided to adopt me.'

Petra scratched the cat's head, the purring increasing in volume. 'I'm not allergic and I love cats. Does his acceptance give me an edge for the job?' She looked past Aaron. 'And you have a kitchen?' she added in surprise.

What was in front of her was a full kitchen; not just an alcove with a dispenser, but the real deal.

'Guilty, I love to cook,' Aaron admitted. 'The dispenser is all well and good but, there are times when reconstituted protein and vegetable matter just misses the spot. Don't get me wrong, we have the best dispensers available, but it's just not the same. So every now and then, I come in here and cook from scratch. We even have our own vegetable and herb garden. And I'm not alone. There are a number of kitchens on this ship, on all our ships, so the crew can make their own meals if they want. It's good for morale...not just for the stomach. Now, if you would both like to make yourselves comfortable, I'll cook us something.'

'As I remember, you once made your omelettes for us on Gaddok Prime, a most excellent meal,' Dokad added as he guided Petra to the sofa. Petra sat down, Prince curling up on her lap. 'Seems the cat has decided that you should stay,' said Dokad, smiling as he sat beside her. Aaron watched the scene, with a knot growing in his stomach. He turned back to the kitchen and started to prepare the meal.

Twenty minutes later, the delicious aromas emanating from the kitchen announced the meal was ready. Aaron walked to the table with a plate for each of them. 'Breakfast is served,' he simply stated. Petra stood and the cat slid onto the warm place she had left behind.

'Ham and Asparagus omelette,' said Aaron, 'with a mushroom, garlic and tarragon sauce.'

The Admiral held the chair for Petra as she sat. 'As usual, Captain, you have excelled. If you ever get tired of the Freebooter life, I could offer you a position in my kitchen.' He sat and started to eat with much enthusiasm. The meal was consumed in relative silence, hunger taking priority over conversation.

Finally Dokad moved his chair back and turned to Aaron. 'An excellent meal my friend, thank you.' He stood and took Petra's hand. 'It's been a pleasure; however, I've taken up enough of your time.' He winked at Aaron as he left.

Aaron sat, watching the door for a while.

'Ok sir, what's worrying you?' Petra asked.

Aaron looked back to her. 'This whole thing, Dokad, Ga'Dok, Grainger and all this political shit; nothing seems to fit.' He stood and started pacing. 'Do you know much about Krell society and history?' he asked.

'No, not really,' Petra answered.

'Ok then; Krell 101 for the uninitiated. Their society is patriarchal in nature; females are only for bearing children, pleasuring their males and keeping house. They have no inherent rights and, in effect, live at the pleasure of their male folk.

'They have a very strict social hierarchy based on the number thirteen. Each family unit strives to have thirteen adult males at any one time. A male can only leave and start his own family when a fourteenth male reaches adulthood.

'At any time there can be as many juvenile males as can be supported. Children can be borne by any number of females and the number of females also depends purely on the ability of the family unit to fund them.

'A family unit is called *L'aktor*, and the head of a L'aktor forms part of a kinship group called a *Pakol*, with thirteen-member families. These members are usually from the same family group...thirteen brothers can form a Pakol, but it is not uncommon for external L'aktors to join a particular Pakol, for strength or advantage.

'From each Pakol a leader emerges, usually by combat, and he then forms an alliance with twelve other Pakols.

From this thirteen, a *Todak*...or Warlord...is chosen.

'This makes up a basic Krell state. The Emperor and Imperial L'aktor succeed either by decree or by force; any challenge to an Emperor's authority is always by combat. The present Imperial L'aktor has been in power for nearly two hundred standard years...a monumental feat in Krell History. Most don't last more than a few decades and their families are dispersed when they fall.'

'Ok,' Petra was confused. 'What's all this got to do with our situation?'

Aaron thought for a moment. 'The Admiral is an imperial Todak. He's also a member of the imperial family. For years I've been close to the Empire. I spent time training at their academy. I lived in the imperial compound with Dokad and his family and it's one of my largest trading partners. In all this time though, I have never heard of Ga'Dok. Yet, here he is, commanding a fairly impressive battle group, and the Admiral said he was the one responsible for the assassination attempt.'

He paused and thought for a few seconds. 'George,' he called, deciding to use audible communication to include Petra, 'get all the information available on this Commander Ga'Dok.'

'For Ga'Dok to have command of a battle group either meant he was exceedingly good and had come to the attention of an opportunistic Todak or...' There was a nagging question mark in his head. It took George about ten minutes to reply and even then, only basic information was available.

As Aaron had suspected, the information confirmed what he thought. Ga'Dok *was* from the ranks of a minor Todak, one not known to Aaron and not close to the Imperial Family. Neither was Ga'Dok's family particularly well connected and didn't possess the wealth to purchase his command. Again, the same was true for his Todak; he didn't appear to have the necessary resources either. The mystery only grew.

Petra had been having a look at other information about Krell society.

'So, let me get this right,' she stopped and gathered her thoughts, 'a Krell can be promoted by combat, excelling at a function or by wealth.' She was not posing a question, just thinking aloud. 'Yet, from what I see, Ga'Dok doesn't qualify for any of those...he has no recorded combat victories, nothing exceptional in the little information on his academic record and he doesn't seem to have any great wealth. In all, he is exceedingly average.'

Aaron stopped pacing and noticed that Petra looked tired. He consulted the clock on the console, seeing it had been three hours since they had entered the worm hole.

'That's enough,' he said firmly. 'You're tired and we'll start jumping to wrong conclusions if we keep at it. You've just come off watch; go get some rest and we'll pick this up again later.'

'A good idea,' Petra replied, suddenly feeling the strain of the past few hours.

'Yes, sleep well,' Aaron stammered. Petra stood and left the cabin. Aaron cleared the table, putting everything in a sanitiser. He walked into the sleeping area where Prince was already on the bed. The cat seemed to look past Aaron back into the dining area, as if searching for something.

Aaron stopped. 'Don't start,' he spoke to the cat. 'I know what I'm doing.' Prince appeared to give a feline version of a shrug and curled up to sleep.

Inside Aaron was filled with questions and a strange feeling deep in his gut. He kept pacing, back and forth, trying to piece the puzzle together in his mind. It was like the solution was there, just out of reach, but no matter how hard he tried to stretch his mind, he just couldn't grasp it.

Then, finally he remembered an old Zandian meditation trick one of his crew had taught him many years ago. He dimmed the lights and lay on the bed and started the ritual. He focussed all his mental energy on a single spot, letting all his questions float out of that spot. Slowly, very slowly, he began to descend into the meditative trance, allowing his mind to free itself of any questions or concerns and pave a way for the solution to find him.

***

Aaron could hear a sound, like a bell chiming—but couldn't understand what it was. It sounded again. Slowly the fog of his meditative state cleared and he realised it was his door annunciator. 'Enter,' he called.

'Sorry to disturb you Sir. This just came in on the encrypted channel.' Lieutenant Commander Albrecht stood at the door with a message pad in her hand. Aaron let her in and moved to his console, activating the message and noting the time: 14:32. He had been in a meditative state for most of the day, and still a solution evaded him.

'Commander, have you replied to this?' Aaron called from his console.

'No. I couldn't decode it so I recorded it and brought it straight here,' Kate replied.

'What time did it arrive?'

'About seven minutes ago.'

'It doesn't make any sense. It says that the Coalition Space Corps wants us to divert to Medros 6 and await further instruction. It's an old encryption but still valid; but there's no originator or authentication.' Aaron paused. 'Is Simon still on duty?' *Dumb question*, he thought, *these two are always on duty together*. He pressed the communicator on his console.

'Navigator, can you come to my cabin please,' he paused, 'and wake Commander Mannix, she needs to be read in on this.' Two minutes later, the door chimed again and Simon Holm entered, with Petra close behind him. Aaron directed her to the console where she read the communique.

'Simon, what's at Medros Six?' Aaron asked.

Simon thought for a moment. 'Nothing, it's basically a rock...no life...a barely breathable atmosphere and not much else. It's in the middle of nowhere, totally off any main flight paths.'

'Who's in the chair now?' Aaron asked.

'Holland Sir,' Kate replied.

'Good. Call David and meet us in the ready room in ten minutes,' Aaron commanded and Simon and Kate headed back to the door. 'Number One, a moment please,' Simon and Kate left and Aaron turned to Petra. 'Can you collect our guest and bring him to the ready room in about fifteen minutes? It's time everyone found out what we're doing.'

As she walked past towards the door, their hands brushed, a momentary and almost imperceptible contact, but Aaron felt that now-familiar electric shock; the hairs on his arm began to stand and he had that strange fluttering in his stomach again. Their eyes met for the briefest of moments, but to Aaron, it seemed that their gaze locked for an hour.

Petra refocused. 'I'll go and wake your guest.'

'Y...yes,' Aaron stammered, his throat felt bone dry. 'Be careful...he may be a good friend but he has a reputation...if you know what I mean.'

'Yes Sir, I understand. I think I can handle myself, don't you?' Without waiting for an answer, she opened the door and was gone. Aaron just stood in the same spot, his mind reeling, his heart racing.

Simon, Kate and David were waiting for their Captain when he entered the ready room ten minutes later.

'I know I've been a bit vague lately, but you'll all see why soon.' Aaron moved to his desk and brought up the message they had received from Coalition Space Corps. 'Anyone have any thoughts on this?'

Dave Carter spoke up and shook his head. 'Only that it makes no bloody sense at all! Medros six is so far out of the way; why send us there?' As he finished, the door opened and Petra entered, followed by Admiral Dokad.

'I want to introduce my guest,' Aaron said, 'and the reason for this trip. Admiral Dokad, this is my senior staff.' A hush came over the room as Aaron made the introductions—the Admiral dismissing any formalities. When introductions were complete, Aaron turned back to his staff.

'Please sit, this will take a bit to explain. I was asked by Prime Grainger to deliver the Admiral safely to Earth. He also intimated that we could run into some complications and we should be careful; I think we know what he meant now. My problem is that I hate not knowing what is going on around me and I will not put my crew in harm's way unless we are all aware of the risks. The developments we have seen make it imperative you all know what the score is. Admiral, can you please enlighten my staff?'

Admiral Dokad stood as Aaron sat beside Petra. 'Firstly, I must apologise for any danger I have placed you in and thank each of you for helping me. Believe me, your actions may be the most significant ever.' He paused to gauge their reaction before continuing.

'I believe you all are aware of the structure of our society. What no-one is aware of is that it is currently in crisis. Our

Emperor is gravely ill and will soon die. This would normally be a period of transition with his named successor taking over. Unfortunately his successor, his eldest son, is a weakling, with no military experience and more importantly, no backing from the Todak council. There is a great deal of posturing and intrigue going on.

'To stop this, Da'Lak, the heir apparent, formally abdicated his position and will name another to take the throne on the death of his father. There has been an undercurrent of dissatisfaction and several Todak's have removed themselves from the council and a program of de-stabilisation has begun. The apparent assassination attempt on me was part of this.' He paused, catching breath.

'But this, in itself, is nothing new for us. We have a rich history of coups, uprisings and power games. In isolation, all this is just business as usual in Krell politics. But there is another element that I believe is more far reaching.

'The rebelling Todaks have joined forces, something that is very unusual. But what's even more interesting...they have elected their own leader. And this leader has formed alliances with dissidents on some of the Coalition colonies. This human element seems to be led by one person...but the identity still eludes me.

'As you all know, the peace treaty that has allowed both of our societies to thrive has led us to dramatically reduce our military forces. It seems that our mutual opponents, however, have been doing the exact opposite and arming themselves at an accelerated rate.

'The reason I must meet with President Malik is to identify who the human component of this action is, and stop it before it becomes too difficult.' He stopped and studied his audience, noting the grave faces.

Aaron looked quizzically at the Admiral. 'I still don't

understand the significance of the transmission we received or where Ga'Dok fits.'

'Ga'Dok is the leader of a minor family siding with the dissidents,' Dokad answered, 'but he has risen much too fast to be discounted. The fact that he commands a battle group attests to that,' he stated with conviction. 'Why anyone would request you to wait at Medros Six is mystifying, but it is part of Ga'Dok's family holdings. Actually, it is the reason his family met with hard times. His father's father invested heavily in a mining operation on that rock. It was a spectacular failure, one almost of legend. They were trying to mine a new source of energy, a mineral that humans had played with unsuccessfully; Trisidium.'

The very mention of this caused the hairs on the back of Aaron's neck to stand. He interrupted Dokad.

'My great, great, grandfather had some stories about that mineral! It's extremely rare, as it is only found in a few places in the whole galaxy. In its unrefined state it's inert and not very impressive. At one time the human race tried to harness its potential. One of the most brilliant human minds, Eugene Sarclan, discovered that it could be processed into an energy source to power existing nuclear reactors, with a huge increase in output and efficiency.

'At the time Earth was dying and energy was in very short supply, Trisidic Reactors...as they became known...could have been the answer we had been looking for. We discovered one problem though...nothing could shield us from the radiation and thousands died. Sarclan also developed a genetic patch...basically a mutation of the human genome that enabled us to cope with limited exposure.'

'Unfortunately, or fortunately, depending on your point of view, the coalition government decided to ban any use or development of Trisidium. All reactors were demolished and any refined ore remaining was sent into our sun. There was some political and civil unrest as the company that developed the technology went into liquidation. With his company now defunct, Sarclan began a campaign of political sniping, fanning unrest and rebellion.

'The security forces gave his group a name…the Sarclan Sedition. Eugene Sarclan was a genius, but also a sociopathic egomaniac. Eventually he was subdued and, with the last of his followers, he left Earth never to be heard of again.' Aaron focussed on Dokad. 'I never knew your people also played with this mineral.'

The Admiral looked back at Aaron. 'Unfortunately we did. It has a much worse effect on the Krell physiology than yours. Millions died before it was banned. We thought we would never hear of this mineral again. We were wrong! It appears that our Emperor has been exposed to Trisidic radiation. That is what's killing him and, I fear others in the Imperial family may also have been exposed.'

The gravity of the situation was now evident. It was David Carter who spoke next. 'Then this message must be a trap, or a ruse to locate us. If we answer, our subspace transmission may be tracked.'

'Simon, what is our displacement status?' Aaron asked.

'Currently twelve, and steady.'

Aaron started pacing again. 'What would happen if we increased the displacement?'

'Shit skipper, I really don't know.' Travelling in hyperspace was a very delicate operation and any changes while in the worm hole were not something to be considered lightly. 'It'd throw our reinsertion way out…I've never done it before.' Simon sounded worried.

'If we increase the displacement, we change our entire flight profile, not to mention the fact that we really don't know what other things we would alter. We've calculated our reinsertion to the millisecond…any change in the displacement will change our reinsertion timing. Effectively, we may arrive earlier, but Earth will not be in the same place. Nothing will! I'll need to work this out very carefully, but it's not something I'd recommend.'

Aaron could see it was a huge dilemma for Simon. 'Ok, let's assume it is not a viable course of action. I'm just thinking out loud and I want all of you to do the same. I agree…if we comply with this request, we'll end up in a world of hurt. Also, I believe that if we respond, it will allow our position to be pin-pointed. How about a delayed transmission,' Aaron suggested. 'What if we drop a drone and it sends a response timed to give the impression the transmission is from Condor? That should give us enough time to clear the area.'

'Could be done,' Dave Carter added. 'We drop a drone in its' own displacement field, leave a timed message, and be long gone when it transmits.'

'Seems we have been well and truly dropped in the proverbial,' Simon added wryly. 'While we are reasonably safe here in the worm hole, we are still three and a half hours from any Coalition assistance. We might as well be on the far side of the galaxy.'

Aaron spoke again. 'We still have one ace…we could jump.' He paused, waiting for any comments. 'Simon, I need you to work out where we can reinsert and initiate a jump immediately…just a precaution. I think Dave's proposal will work, but just in case…' his voice trailed off, Simon got the message.

'Number Two, you and Lieutenant Holland set up the drone, set the delay timing for fifteen minutes; any longer would look suspicious. Also, send a message to Earth and

Argos informing them of the situation; heavily encrypted of course. David, spin up the weapons again and wake everyone up; we need to be ready. Number One, I need you to take the con.' Aaron turned to Dokad. 'Admiral, would you care to join our bridge team?'

As Aaron and the Admiral entered the bridge, Simon motioned to his skipper. 'The only jump point that coincides with a possible reinsertion will be in'—he looked back at the clock—'twenty two minutes.'

Aaron patted his navigator on the back. 'Good work. We'll know if the drone worked or not by then; proceed as if we are going to initiate. How long would the jump take?'

'Three minutes and twenty six seconds.'

'Drone's ready, Captain,' Petra called from the con.

'Release,' Aaron replied. The Communication drone was ejected from the rear torpedo bay. It was caught, momentarily, in Condor's displacement wake, but soon began to fade into the distance.

'Number Two, what's the sequence?'

Kate looked up from her console. 'Fifteen minutes: a dual burst transmission to Earth and Argos; ten seconds later a standard sub space transmission to reply to the original message; thirty seconds later the displacement field will collapse and the drone will commence its self-destruct sequence...timed for another thirty seconds.'

Thirty seconds would give the drone enough time to reinsert into normal space before self-destruct. The last thing anybody wanted was an explosion inside hyperspace. With the drone at a virtual standstill and Condor still travelling at a displacement of 12, there should be more than enough distance between them when it exploded. All eyes were on the timer on the view screen.

Kate Albrecht's voice broke the silence. 'Transmission should be now.'

Suddenly the sensor alarms sounded. Ensign Croker watched in horror as every sensor the ship had suddenly went crazy.

'What the?' he cried. 'The self-destruct must have cycled early, but that explosion was far too big!'

Aaron leapt to his side. 'That is a lot more than a drone self-destructing. Kate, did the transmissions go out?'

'Can't confirm, but that explosion was twenty seconds after the second transmission was due to go,' she replied. 'Looks like someone didn't like our answer.'

Croker looked very worried. He motioned for Phillip Harper to join him. Aaron moved out of the way.

'What's the problem, Ensign?' he asked.

'Sir that was a huge explosion *inside* hyperspace...we can expect a sub-space shock wave, but with our sensors out, I can't see it,' Harper replied. Both he and Croker were frantically working on the sensor console.

Minutes flew by; with tension on the bridge building. No-one spoke, the only sounds came from Croker and Harper as they desperately raced against time to restore the ship's eyes. Finally, Harper spoke. 'That should do it.' As if by his command, the sensors came back online.

Croker's fingers raced across the panel, searching for any indication of the shock wave. 'Got it...it's out to about fifty million kilometres and growing, it's expanding at a DF of fifteen.' He paused, watching the read outs. 'Initial reading was fifteen now fourteen point five...and still growing!'

Aaron's face was a mask of concern. A shock wave in their worm hole would smash the ship like an egg shell.

'Navigator, will it catch us?'

Simon was now beside Croker with a Nav Pad, frantically working on the readings. Minutes passed before the image projected on the sensor screen showed the growing shock wave as a red ring.

'Put it on the Bubble,' Simon shouted. 'Make the explosion epicentre the reference point!'

The Bubble glowed and settled to show epicentre of the explosion as a brilliant red spot, and the shock wave as a growing red ball expanding from it. Condor was outside this field but was slowly being overtaken. Croker, Harper and Simon were a study of concentration, making more and more calculations until finally Croker looked up, relief etched across his face.

'Captain, we'll be okay. It's slowing down; should start to dissipate in about five minutes...already its expansion is down to DF nine.'

Just as it had started the energy wave disappeared and there was a collective sigh of relief. Again disaster had been avoided—for Condor at least. An explosion in space generates a ball of energy that dissipates slowly over time. A planetary explosion does the same but the atmosphere, terrain and other factors can limit its reach; in space there are no such limiting features. And in hyperspace the effect could be even more catastrophic, as previous accidents had proved.

'Do we know of any other ships in the area?' Petra asked. The thought of other travellers being caught was horrific. 'We should send out a few probes to make sure.'

Aaron nodded. 'Good idea...make it happen, and record all data on the shock wave propagation.' He looked back toward Dokad. 'What sort of idiot would deliberately use a weapon in sub space?' he asked in disbelief.'

The Admiral shook his head and leaned against the

comms console as Petra commenced to launch four new probes; hopefully they would find nothing, but they had to be certain.

Aaron spoke briskly. 'Send one directly into the epicentre; I want to know just what that was. If it was our drone, then we are the fools and need to make sure it can't happen again. If not, it means that whoever did that has the ability to fire a weapon at a target in hyperspace.' That thought made him shiver.

Croker was scratching his head as he worked his console.

'Is there a problem, Ensign?' Aaron asked.

'Sir, if that was an explosion *inside* a worm hole my calculations show the shock wave should have grown to at least five hundred million kilometres in diameter.'

'So?'

'Sir, this one dissipated almost completely at just over one hundred million...like it just bled away. No, that's not right; more like it just dumped instantly somewhere else.' Croaker was obviously concerned.

'Well if it did, at least it didn't get us.'

Simon joined the conversation. 'That's not the point... you're wondering where it went, aren't you?'

'Yes, it had to go somewhere; that much energy just can't dissipate without trace.'

Aaron now saw what Croker was getting at. 'OK, you two start working on finding out what happened. After all, we have no idea what that much energy would do in sub-space. No one has been this stupid since the Krell wars, and then the result was catastrophic!' Aaron was referring to an incident hundreds of years previously, an incident that caused many deaths and consumed an asteroid belt.

Gradually the bridge returned to normal, but Dave Carter

kept the ship at battle readiness for another hour, just in case.

Finally, at 09:45 hours on Friday, February 7, 2921, Condor reinserted into normal space between Earth and Mars; immediately she was hailed by an Earth Coalition patrol ship and asked if any assistance was required. Then four more patrol ships joined her and provided an escort to the same dock that currently housed Valiant. Their track took them past the launch site for Rhapsody and the circus that was evolving around that event, scheduled to occur later that day.

Aaron contacted the patrol leader. 'What's that all about?'

The patrol ship's captain, Commander Donaldson replied. *That's Rhapsody of the Stars, Damien Albrecht's latest sin palace. Well, at least for those who want to mortgage their lives to pay for it! She'll be launched later today.*

'Thanks, Commander.' Aaron turned to Kate, 'Albrecht; any relation?'

Kate shook her head. 'Don't ask, Sir,' she said, 'don't ask.'

***

It took another hour to secure Condor to the dock and complete the administrative formalities. Crew leave had already been authorised, with accommodation at their chosen destinations arranged. Everyone was very keen to get down planet-side. For some, it was their first visit to the home of the human race; for others, simply a return after a long absence. Emotions were mixed, but a visit to this special planet always caused an effect. Aaron activated a ship-wide comm.

'This is the Captain. I want to thank each of you for everything you did during this trip. Accommodation has been arranged where you requested and will be billed to the company. We will be here, on Earth, for at least the next week so make the most of it. Enjoy and be safe...that's all.' He closed the channel and turned to his bridge crew. 'That goes for all of you too see you all later.' Everyone was smiling and didn't need a second invitation. They were all eager to have some shore time.

'All I have to do is collect Prince and head home.' Aaron felt strange saying that in reference to the family compound, but it *was* home. 'By the way, you don't seem to have any accommodation?' he said to Petra as he powered his console down.

'No. I thought that, since I had just joined, I'd stay aboard with the security detail...look after things,' she replied.

'Aaron, really,' Dokad asked pointedly. 'Are you *really* going to leave this lovely creature locked up in this ship for a week? Why not take her with us...at least it might help diffuse the family situation. Besides, I would like to get to know you a bit better my dear.'

Aaron felt his pulse rise sharply. The thought of taking Petra along intrigued him, but Dokad's attention to her caused him an uneasy sensation he couldn't explain. 'Sounds good to me...what do you say, Number One?' his throat was suddenly dry again.

'Thank you, Sir. I've always wanted to come to Earth.'

'Good, get your things and we'll meet at the shuttle bay in ten minutes.'

As they entered the pod, George's voice entered Aaron's mind. *You have an incoming communication from Argos...it will be channelled to your cabin console.*

Petra left the pod on the second accommodation deck where her cabin was, and Aaron and Dokad proceeded to the next floor and their cabins. They parted company; Aaron entered his cabin and went straight to his console. He opened the communication; it was a couple of hours old even using sub-space communication systems—it still took time to cover the distance between Argos and Condor, especially with Condor being inside a worm hole when it was sent. He read the text, shook his head and read it again to confirm the contents.

The final line was most telling—*be very careful where you place your trust*—the warning kept roaming round in his head as he packed.

He stopped as if coming to a sudden decision. He contacted Petra via the secure command link. 'Number One, change of plans' he tried to sound upbeat. 'I've decided to take the yacht...much more comfortable. Can you get her ready?'

She agreed and said she would have *Junior*—as she called the yacht—ready in about ten minutes. Aaron busied himself with changing the departure schedule and contacting the dock commander to obtain the necessary permissions. He was so engrossed with his actions he almost forgot the cat. Aaron picked up his ready bag and left the room, with Prince by his side, the cat securely fastened to his lead.

Admiral Dokad was waiting and exited his room as soon as Aaron pressed the annunciator. He glanced at Aaron. 'Expecting more trouble?'

Aaron had decided that the warning from his Prime needed to be heeded. He had strapped a disruptor to his hip and had another in his bag for Petra. 'After this trip, who knows?' he shook his head. 'I've also decided to take the yacht. It's much more comfortable than a shuttle.' They entered the pod and Aaron selected the hangar deck.

True to her word, Petra had *Junior* prepped and ready. The hangar roof slid open as the two men entered the bridge deck. Petra was at the pilot station. Aaron handed her the comm pad he was carrying and bent down to remove the cat's lead. Prince immediately leapt onto Petra's lap and curled up. This brought a hearty chuckle from Dokad and he looked at Aaron.

'Seems your cat has adopted someone new,' he gave Aaron a knowing smile. Aaron just nodded, his mind still working on Grainger's message.

Petra entered the authorisation codes from the comm pad and started the take-off cycle. Aaron sat at the co-pilot's console and followed her movements. Even after only one flight in the yacht she seemed completely at home, flawlessly taking the vessel out of the hangar in the limited space of the dock. As soon as they cleared Condor, Petra powered the deflector array and turned the yacht towards the hangar's space door portal. The force field flashed white as it matched harmonics with the deflector and they were back in space.

Petra turned to Aaron. 'Since this is my first time to Earth I've programmed a flight path that will give us a good overall view of the planet...I hope that's OK?' She could sense that he was wrestling with something. He didn't answer, just nodded.

Their flight path would be a polar orbit starting with the North Pole and then heading towards the south. It wasn't a direct path, but one that gave them the best possible orbital tour of the planet. Petra skilfully orientated the ship so they could all get the best view; it was one that Aaron remembered from many years ago.

The vast majority of the northern hemisphere was covered in ice and snow and had been for centuries. Continental Europe, Russia, China, and most of the Asian region, was still one huge frozen waste. For most of the old USA and Canada, it was the same, a chillingly amazing sight, both beautiful and terrifying at the same time.

'This is what happens when stupidity and greed govern,'

Aaron said with a sad note to his voice.

They continued over the Equator and the south of the Americas came to view. Here the scenery was different. Lush greenery was everywhere with settlements of human habitation blended into natural surrounds. They continued south over Antarctica, now not a completely frozen waste but an area with a number of thriving communities. *Still*, Aaron thought, *there's a lot more snow and ice here than I remember...maybe the balance is swinging back again?*

Petra aligned the ship for re-entry and began the sequence. Aaron sat back to allow her the freedom to command the ship.

Dokad spoke. 'Aaron, I must ask something. When we were in that final confrontation, you mentioned something about your ship jumping.' Aaron stiffened in his chair. Dokad continued. 'There was a report from one of the dissident groups that Freebooters had some new drive technology, something from the Eldorans that could revolutionise space travel. Do you have that technology?'

Aaron turned to face his old friend, unsure of how to proceed. He looked deep into Dokad's eyes, searching for any clue that may help him formulate his answer. Then he remembered that in all the years and dealings he had with this man, there had never been any deception between them. He spoke freely.

'Yes. It was installed by Eldoran engineers so we could evaluate it. So far, it is proving to be somewhat of an advantage, but there are limitations that may make it unusable, long term.'

Dokad nodded. 'That is the missing piece.' He smiled back at Aaron. 'The communication Ga'Dok received from his superiors suggested that he should capture your ship, if possible. I assumed it meant me, but the ship itself may have been the target.'

Aaron interrupted. 'It wouldn't do them any good; part of our trial agreement with the Eldorans is to keep it secure. To that end, they have installed a self-destruct system. If anyone...us included...tries to interfere with the drive system, it will destroy itself and my ship with it. They will remove this only when we have ascertained that there are no operational problems. We are not trying to hide it, just evaluate it...same as we have done with all other technologies from them.' He paused, thinking for a moment. 'So, Ga'Dok was supposed to lure us to Medros six, capture the ship and steal the drive?'

'That would be my conclusion; and when he saw he was failing he opted to destroy it instead,' Dokad answered.

'By risking a sub space disaster,' Aaron was incredulous. 'That's insane!'

'I never said Krell politics were sane,' Dokad retorted. 'As with human history, we have had our share of megalomaniacs in charge...that seems to be the one constant similarity between our races.' He sat back, suddenly looking very old and tired. 'That is why we must stop this madness.' He sat quietly for a few minutes. 'Aaron, what are your friends the Eldorans like? They're a bit of an enigma.'

'Admiral, you are *so* correct,' Aaron agreed. 'They seem almost god like, they come and go and we never know when or where they will pop up next. They change their appearance almost at will, yet they still use technology... albeit very advanced technology.'

'Do you know where their home planet is?'

'No one has ever been to their home planet. We have tried to discuss it with them. Their answer is that they are from another realm, whatever that is. Yes, they really are an enigma.'

The ship was just entering the atmosphere and Petra had a huge smile on her face as she reconfigured the yacht for atmospheric operations. The wings extended and she disengaged the artificial gravity.

'Twenty minutes till we land,' she announced as they broke through into a cloudless sky, the beauty of a verdant Australian landscape spread out below them.

10

They approached the compound from the south, giving them a good view of the lake and the complex—at their height of one hundred metres it was very impressive.

Petra looked over to Aaron. 'Is that where you grew up?'

'Yes, but most of it is used by the company; the family only takes up half of the upper ground floor. The rest is either office space or accommodation for staff.'

The comms interrupted any further banter. *Abracorp base to unidentified aircraft, please identify yourself.*

Petra replied. 'This is Freebooter shuttle FTS Condor Junior, requesting landing permission.'

The response was immediate. *Permission granted. Please proceed north of the compound and use pad four to land. Once you have landed, please taxi to hangar one.*

Petra confirmed the instructions and initiated the landing cycle. As their airspeed dropped, the antigrav took over, the wings retracted and Petra guided the ship to the designated landing pad—she didn't actually touch down—keeping the landing gear just a few centimetres off the ground and entered the hangar. There was a ground crewman to guide her into the assigned park. She followed his instructions and gently grounded the ship.

Aaron looked out his view port. There standing behind the doors were his brother and sister-in-law. He looked over to Petra and the Admiral. 'Can you give me a couple of minutes?' He smiled—a nervous smile but one edged with hope.

'Of course, take your time...just signal us when you're

ready.'

Petra lowered the port side access ramp and Aaron slowly exited the ship. It felt like he was walking in slow motion, long forgotten emotions and memories starting to flood his mind. The doors in front of him opened and his brother emerged. They stood, facing each other for what seemed like an eternity until Jeff finally broke the silence.

'Welcome home Brother.' He extended his hand and Aaron gripped it tightly.

'Thanks, Jeff...it's been too long,' Aaron choked the words and both brothers grabbed each other and embraced. 'Far too bloody long' he repeated. They broke apart as Sonia came out the doors and joined them. She threw her arms around them both, ecstatic that she had finally been able to get them on the same planet and hopefully bring them back together. Aaron waved for the others to join him and Petra was quickly at his side, the Admiral taking a little longer.

'Jeff, Sonia, I'd like to introduce my First Officer, Petra Mannix.' Jeff shook her hand and Sonia gave her a gentle kiss on the cheek. 'And an old friend,' Aaron moved aside to allow Jeff to see the Admiral. 'Admiral Dokad, I believe you and my brother are well acquainted?'

Dokad bowed his head. 'We most certainly are. How are you Jeffery?'

'Well Sir...and yourself?' Jeff enquired.

'Still alive...thanks to your brother and Commander Mannix.' Dokad said with a chuckle

'Well, I can assure your safety here,' Jeff replied. 'Come along. We have rooms ready for you. I'll have your luggage brought up.'

Petra excused herself. 'We forgot Prince,' she said, as she walked back into the ship.

The men moved through the doors while Sonia waited for

Petra. A few minutes later she came back down the ramp, the cat beside her. Sonia smiled and bent down to pat the small animal.

'I've heard about this cat; he is a beauty,' Sonia said, as Prince lapped up the attention. Then she stood up and looked directly into Petra's eyes.

'So! What are the arrangements?'

'Pardon?' Petra was caught off guard by the question.

'Petra, may I call you Petra?' Sonia started. 'It has taken me more than twenty years to get those two on the same planet, let alone in the same house, so I need this to go smoothly. It's obvious that you and Aaron are more than Captain and First Officer; how do you want to handle it?'

Petra let out a sigh. 'He is the Captain and I'm the First Officer, nothing more.'

'Oh! I'm sorry, I just thought...' Sonia's voice trailed off.

She took Petra's arm and they walked through the doors, Prince trotting happily between them. There was no sign of the men so Petra and Sonia went to the house; a butler met them at the door.

'Phillip, please bring us some tea to the garden room,' Sonia asked.

'Yes, ma'am,' he replied as he turned and walked away.

They walked into the garden room. It was huge, with fifteen-metre high clear walls—all made of glass— something of a rarity. In total, the room covered an area of two hundred square metres and was filled with hundreds of exotic plants.

'This is beautiful!' Petra gasped, having never seen some of these plants and flowers. She reached out and touched an orchid. 'They're so delicate,' she said softly.

The butler returned bearing a tray that held the tea pot

and cups. He placed it on a table beside the orchids. Sonia sat and poured two cups. 'Milk?' she asked.

'Yes, thank you,' Petra replied. They sat and sipped their tea before Petra spoke again. 'Your butler seems very efficient.'

'He's not really a butler he's actually a robot, or as Jeffery puts it, an artificial. We have several of them. They do most of the work around the farm...not many humans want to do that anymore.

'We did have a real butler, but he left for one of the colonies. So Jeffery decided that we could use one of the robots. He had one designed as a butler, which worked out very well; I believe they are now one of the robotics division's biggest income earners...it seems that clients will pay a handsome premium for a specialist butler.'

'Really; I thought the home of the Human race would have most things done by robots or artificials?' Petra observed.

'Back in our history we did. Many jobs and daily tasks were given over to machines and robots. Even getting from one place to another was left to the control of artificials. Then things started to go wrong; people had nothing to do and Earth went through a time of anarchy.

'It was around the time of the Exodus and those who remained here decided to limit just how much automation was acceptable. There's an old saying: *idle hands make the devil's work.* Thankfully, for once, humans have learned from that mistake.

'We did have one section of our society that embraced a totally dependent lifestyle. They called themselves Mechanista. They emigrated to their own planet and have done very well, or so we believe. Nobody ever sees much of them anymore.

'Now, has Aaron talked about this reunion? Has he

mentioned what happened?' Sonia was desperate for information.

'No, nothing...I only joined the ship a few days ago; everybody on Argos is aware of the feud, but I don't think anyone knows what caused it. If anyone knows anything it would be our Prime; he and Aaron are very close,' Petra replied, trying to keep her distance from any family issues.

The door opened and the butler announced that the baggage from Junior had been brought to the house. Sonia took charge. 'Phillip, put Captain Abraham and Commander Mannix in the two spare rooms at the end of the hall and the Admiral in the main guest room.' He left and she turned to Petra. 'Your room is in the family section, but at the opposite end of the hall. If that's not suitable, we have a number of spare suites above.'

'Thank you, I'm sure it'll be fine.'

'Well, I suppose we should find the others to have a drink before dinner.' Sonia led Petra out of the garden room and down the hall to Jeff's office. Inside, Jeff, Aaron and Dokad had been joined by Sol and JT. They all had a large glass of scotch in their hands.

'Knew where they'd be...Jeffery keeps his best scotch in here.' The men were glued to a vid screen as the two women walked in and Petra glanced over to see what they were watching.

The image of a huge star ship filled the screen. In the foreground and dwarfed by the enormity of it, a group of formally attired people stood on a dais behind a clear panel, giving the illusion that they were standing in space, in front of the ship. Behind them, there appeared to be hundreds of spectators, all safely inside the dock facility.

'The President's wife is about to christen that monstrosity,' Jeff announced.

Petra couldn't believe the size of it. 'What is it?' she asked.

Jeff answered her. 'That, young lady, is *Rhapsody of the Stars*, the most expensive den of iniquity in the known universe.' He looked across at Petra and the confused expression on her face.

'Sorry, you wouldn't know. Rhapsody is the largest space cruise liner ever built, and Abracorp built it. She can carry seventy five thousand paying guests to places considered unreachable by cruise ships, until now.'

As Jeff spoke, a woman on the dais waved a champagne bottle as if to smash it on something. The image zoomed to the front of the huge ship. A grapple arm mimicked the woman's movements and a real bottle of Champagne was smashed on the front of the ship, accompanied by much cheering and handshaking as the huge vessel slowly moved back from the viewing window. Everything was choreographed perfectly, the bottle smashing, the ship moving to simulate being launched, with much cheering and more champagne bottles being opened.

Jeff turned to his eldest son. 'Well, now that monster's gone we can get down to some real work.' They both smiled and raised their glasses in a mock toast.

Sonia stood with her hands on her hips. 'That's all well and good, Jeffery, but you have two ladies here and you haven't offered either of us a drink. I have never known you to have such bad manners where a new female in the house is concerned!' Jeff stood and offered his apologies, went to the cabinet and returned with two glasses of his best single malt.

Jeff stood before Petra, studying her intently. 'Mannix,' he said finally, 'any relation to Colin Mannix?'

Petra was saddened by his words. 'Yes, he was my father,' she replied quietly.

Jeff was taken aback. 'Was, what happened?'

'He was killed three months ago on Varga. There was a rebel attack on the capital. He went in with the rescue teams to assess the damage and to help survivors. He was killed when a building collapsed on him.' She choked these final words out.

'I'm terribly sorry,' Jeff reached out to console her. 'I knew him for many years, both as a client and a friend, but I never knew he had a family.'

Petra looked into Jeff's eyes, hers brimming with tears. 'Not many people did. My mother was Vargan and she kept mostly to herself. I spent a lot of time away at school and then at the academy.

'When my mother died Dad sort of closed off from the world; it seemed he only lived to work, and for me. He never missed any special event in my life; silly things like birthdays, big events like graduation … he was always there.' She stopped, cleared her throat and took a long swig of her drink.

'Anyway, enough of that...why are you so upset by this ship? After all, you said you built it.'

'Yes we did but...that ship is designed as a pure pleasure palace...if you get what I mean. All sorts of pastimes: gambling, brothels...anything you can imagine. Ships like this make a mockery out of our thin veil of civilization! I can only hope that bloody pile burns up in some interstellar disaster.' Jeff's outburst surprised everyone as he was not usually prone to such passionate displays. He shrugged and went to the cabinet to pour another drink.

The butler appeared at the door. 'Dinner is ready. I have laid it out on the porch.' They all stood and followed Philip to the table.

Dinner was a quiet affair consisting of three courses,

allowing plenty of time for Jeff and Aaron to get reacquainted. At first they appeared to be sparring, cautiously feeling out the other's defences, but as dinner progressed the atmosphere lightened and they began to talk more openly. Sonia couldn't have been happier—the event she had worked hard on for over twenty years was now unfolding in front of her.

The table had just been cleared and the coffee pot brought in when Jason and Amanda—Jeff and Aaron's parents—arrived. They had left their home on Caprica five days previously and at Amanda's insistence, had cut almost a full day off their normal flight time. After scanning the room she spoke. 'I felt there was something incredible going to happen, and I was right!'

'Yes I agree. Seeing you all here together calls for a celebration,' Jason beamed as he left the room, only to return a few minutes later with two very old and dusty bottles. 'I've been hoping that one day I'd have a reason to open these.'

'Where did you get those?' Jeff looked at the two old bottles.

'Son, I was head of this family for many years. I suppose I still am, and I built part of this house. I still have a few hiding places that you haven't found.' Jason grinned as he opened the first bottle. It was a magnificent Para Port, fitting for the occasion.

Aaron's memory of his father was of a very formal person, with only very rare displays of emotion or affection—but tonight was different. At one point he walked up to his son, gripped his hand and spoke quietly.

'Glad you finally came home, your mother has missed you terribly,' his voice broke slightly and he grabbed his son in a tight embrace. 'Damn it, I missed you too.' Jason broke free and looked at both of his sons, his eyes misting with emotion as he spoke. 'What the bloody hell did you two idiots fight about in the first place?'

Aaron tried to speak but was cut off by his mother. 'Leave them alone, Jason.' She held her arms to Aaron. 'Come and give your mother a hug.' Amanda Abraham was not a tall woman, at just under one hundred and sixty centimetres with dark curly hair that was greying delicately. Her face was round, with eyes that were full of kindness, and her full figure moved with grace as she enveloped her long-lost son in a hug—the kind of hug that only a mother can give.

Aaron thought back to the many times, as a boy, when his mother's hugs had solved his problems. 'I hope you two boys have sorted things out, I don't want to lose you again.' She kissed her son on the cheek and broke away. 'Now, will you please introduce me?' She hadn't changed. A gregarious woman, she was always eager to greet anyone new.

'Mother, this is Commander Petra Mannix, my First Officer,' Aaron stated.

Amanda took a long look at Petra as she shook her hand and said to Aaron, 'Of course she is.' A knowing smile formed on her face as she held Petra's hand. 'Welcome to the Abraham family, my dear.' She led Petra to a lounge on the porch. 'Now tell me all about yourself.'

As they sat, Jason turned to Aaron. 'I have been trying to follow your exploits but without any contact, it's been difficult. Fill me in on what you have been up to for the last thirty odd years.'

It was then that the full impact of his life dawned on Aaron. He had spent almost a third of his life to date, away from his family—and it *had* been far too long. The men settled into another port as Aaron began to bring his father up to date. Sonia smiled as she surveyed the scene; this was a much better result than she had hoped for.

It was almost midnight when the night came to an end and everyone headed to their rooms. Aaron and Petra walked together down the hall. As they reached their doors, Aaron turned and spoke. 'I hope my family hasn't been too much of a shock; my mother can be a bit intense.'

'Nonsense, she's delightful. We had a good chat, sort of helped me get to know my captain a bit better,' Petra grinned cheekily.

'Oh no, not the childhood stories,' Aaron groaned, but Petra just gave him one of her innocent but suggestive smiles before she said goodnight. Before Aaron could say anything else, she was gone.

Next morning the house woke to the smell of fire smoke, the real kind fuelled by wood. Memories came flooding back—he and his brother working with their father digging holes and building fire pits. As soon as he saw Jeff he asked, 'Are you still using the pits we dug all those years ago?'

It was Jason who answered. 'I told you two then, if we build them right, they'll be there forever.'

This was a momentous occasion, being the first time the whole family had gathered together for breakfast in more than thirty years; the two younger siblings—Salina and David—joining them. While everyone was getting settled, Jeff beckoned Aaron to the side window, seemingly to point out some feature of the country beyond. Instead, he spoke quietly so no one else would hear.

'Make breakfast quick. President Malik and his staff will arrive in about twenty minutes and they want to get straight to business...he specifically asked that you attend the meeting.'

'Why? I have no interest in Coalition politics.' His inclusion puzzled Aaron.

'Don't know...but evidently your Prime requested it.' Jeff answered.

At that moment Dokad entered the room and was greeted warmly by Jason. 'Admiral, please accept my apologies for neglecting you last night.'

'No need. It was a very important family occasion and I was privileged to be here.' He sat and accepted the plate of food that Phillip placed before him. A traditional Krell morning meal, it consisted of a spiced porridge, made from a maize-like grain, topped with two raw eggs. Accompanying this was a long black sausage, the ingredients of which no one at the table really wanted to know.

'This is wonderful,' Dokad exclaimed. 'How did you get this? I didn't know Earth had any Krell foodstuffs?'

Sonia beamed. 'Phillip here is an absolute magician in the kitchen. I asked him to see if he could make something from your culture. It may be a little different as I don't think he could find everything he needed, but he is very good at improvising.'

The Admiral took a bite of the sausage. 'Fantastic! If he had to change something, it has made it better. This is the best Jarol I have ever had! Thank you.' He smiled and continued to eat with gusto.

They had all finished their meal and were enjoying some fine coffee when Ajay—Jeff's PA—came to the door. Jeff stood and motioned to Aaron and JT to join him. Aaron tapped the Admiral on the shoulder and they all excused themselves from the table.

As they left, Sonia looked over to Petra and Salina. 'Salina, could you please show Petra around? I have so much to do for tonight.'

Salina agreed and winked at Solomon, the only male left in the room. 'Looks like you have us both to yourself.' She gave him a wicked grin just as her elder brother came back in.

'Sol, come on. You're included in this.' JT smiled at his sister, who returned him a withering glare as the two men left for Jeff's office. Once the door was closed, Jeff touched a concealed button on his desk and a section of the bookcase opened.

'One of the Second's tricks...takes us straight to the Folly,' Jeff said as he led them into a well-maintained ancient elevator. He closed the doors, selected the floor he wanted, and they started to descend.

'Sorry for all this skulduggery, but it was requested by Malik,' he said as the elevator started to descend. It stopped at Floor *SB5*. The doors opened to reveal the interior of a room, very similar to the office above.

Passing through a door on the far side they entered a larger room set up for meetings. In the centre was a large circular table that could seat at least twenty. There were a number of people already at the table, including the three admirals who had, just yesterday, witnessed the final test of Valliant's weaponry; the President of the Coalition, Salim Malik and General Klastok, commander in chief of the Coalition ground forces. Malik stood and walked over to Admiral Dokad.

'My friend, I am so glad you made it safely here.' He turned to Aaron. 'My thanks Captain; I hear you had an interesting voyage.'

Aaron took the President's hand and shook it. 'Yes Sir... that's one way of describing it.'

Jeff spoke as the others took their seats. 'I suppose you're all wondering why we're meeting here. When my ancestor built this place it was a most desperate time for Earth. With all that was going on, he strove to build the most protected bunker he could. This room is totally sealed. It has its own air supply, purification system, intrusion countermeasures... in fact; it was designed to protect any meeting in here from any sort of prying eyes and ears. I trust it meets with your approval?'

Malik spoke softly, 'A perfect place for our discussions, thank you for agreeing to this. It appears we share some problems with the Krell. Admiral Dokad, can you please deliver the information you have?'

For the next thirty minutes Dokad had everyone's undivided attention as he related the information and events that had led to this meeting. His closing words hung in the air.

'From what I have learnt, and just told you, there is now a subversive partnership forming between dissidents in both of our cultures. Our indications are that the human side is led by one person...who, we do not yet know...but he is someone with access to great resources both in equipment and personnel.'

There was silence for a couple of minutes as the reality of what had just been said sank in. Finally it was Malik who spoke.

'Thank you, Admiral, for risking so much to bring us this information. I can verify some of it personally. There have been a number of rebel incursions on various colonies in the past six months. Until now we just ignored them as local politics, but it is evident that the situation may be much more serious.

'It is not widely known as yet, but there has been a coup on my home world; the government has been toppled and fundamentalists have seized control. The coalition base has been destroyed, but worse than that, the rebels have captured the Coultrane.'

This revelation stunned everyone. ECS Coultrane was one

of the largest battle ships in the Coalition fleet—she was brand new and one of only three of her class in existence.

Admiral Wilson shook her head. 'How was that even possible? Firstly, she was in orbit, and, secondly, there's no way anyone could board her without authorisation!'

Just then the door at the far end of the room closed. No one had seen this new person enter, and now he spoke. 'Quite simply...it was orchestrated from inside the ship.'

The speaker was a short man—almost completely bald. His eyes were dark and without any expression and his mouth was framed by thin, cruel lips that seemed set in a permanent sneer.

'Director Crompton...as usual, a timely entrance,' the President said, a hint of sarcasm edged his voice.

Anthony Crompton, head of the Coalition Intelligence Directorate, was not fazed by this at all. He was used to the response he drew in most meetings; his was probably the most hated job in the whole Coalition administration.

Previous chiefs of operation had made huge mistakes; personalities bordering on megalomaniacal had been in his position and had abused the power of the position for their own personal agendas. Heads of State had been assassinated, governments de-stabilized and private citizens ruined in the guise of protecting the status quo.

Finally enough was enough and a coup, of sorts, saw a new breed of operator emerge. Crompton was one of these types—highly intelligent, analytical, insightful and result oriented. He had been chosen to overhaul the old organisation and to his credit, in the forty years since he took over, there had been no return to the old cavalier attitudes. However, old wounds ran deep and he had to continually defend his organisation.

Crompton looked at everyone in turn and his gaze settled

on Aaron. 'Captain Abraham...do you have any information about the explosion?'

'Not as yet. We sent a probe back to the epicentre but no results have come through...it was programmed not to transmit anything until later today, just in case.'

Crompton placed the large valise he was carrying on the table and opened it. He withdrew two large bound books—a strange thing to all, as nothing was recorded on paper. He kept them closed and sat down.

'Our intelligence gathering is ongoing in this matter. Admiral Dokad has corroborated what we have found out, but there is still a piece missing. The destabilization on Ummah is not an isolated event. At this precise moment, there are twenty-four other colonies that are going to fall in much the same way...probably some have already.' He paused to gauge the group's reaction; the stunned looks told him all he wanted to know.

'Mr President, we in the intelligence community have been warning of this for several years, but our warnings have been largely ignored.'

Malik looked as if he was going to speak, but Crompton held up a hand. 'Please Mr President, allow me to finish. The two books I have here are the complete and redacted reports into one of our greatest mysteries.' He reached into his bag again and produced yet another slimmer volume. 'This contains all the information we have been able to piece together into another ancient happening that ties completely with the first reports.'

Crompton stood and took a small data drive out of the bag and plugged it into the computer interface in front of him. 'Rather than read a couple of thousand boring pages, I have brought the salient pieces together.' A screen descended from the ceiling and came to life in front of the group.

'Please bear with me, some of this will seem farfetched, but all will gel later. Just over two hundred years ago the largest colony ship...*Baleraphon*...left Earth; her journey was programmed to take two hundred years to reach the chosen destination. Approximately twenty years later, we lost all contact with the expedition.'

Admiral Wilson broke in. 'Crompton, this is history. We all know this story...what's your point?'

'Admiral,' Crompton replied, 'to get to the point, *some* history is needed.' Wilson shook her head but sat back and indicated for him to continue.

'As we all know, there were one million seven hundred and fifty thousand colonists in stasis for the journey. There were also ten thousand crew members working on a ten year rotational basis so they would all still have the opportunity to start a new life at their destination.'

Wilson made to interrupt again, but a sign from Malik shut her down.

Crompton continued. 'There are a number of things that have never been released about this whole episode. There were also three million viable human embryos, also in a state of stasis. The *entire* crew were members of the Sedition, and the venture was funded by the Sarclan group, via a number of bogus shell companies—something that we have only just uncovered. Add to this the events leading up to Sarclan's expulsion from Earth and the course he and his followers took when they left, and the only conclusion is that Baleraphon didn't disappear and wasn't destroyed, but was actually diverted to a new destination by the Sarclan Sedition.'

'Are you completely fucking mad?' Wilson could not control the outburst. 'That's not possible...it's unthinkable!'

Crompton stood and glared at the Admiral. It was no

secret that there was no love lost between the two—various incidents with bad intel had given Space Corps reason to distrust the intelligence community.

'Or, Mr Director, is this another attempt for the Directorate to start up an active division?' She was referring to the old 'black ops' operations that had caused so much trouble in the past.

'Admiral,' Crompton sounded strangely humble, so much so that everyone, even Wilson, gave him the floor. 'Believe me, I wish there was some other conclusion. Given the time, the resources and Sarclan's expertise, this is the last scenario I want. But it is the only one that fits. If we are correct, he could have a standing force of over seven million...that's our estimate of his potential military capability.'

'But that's just supposition...what are the facts?' Malik asked.

'Sir, I have summarised everything we have been working on and,' he turned to Aaron, 'Captain Abraham, I'll wager you a bottle of thirty-year-old single malt that your probe reports Trisidic radiation from that blast. Watch and see what we could be up against.'

The group watched the presentation Crompton had prepared and twenty minutes later, a deathly silence filled the room as they assimilated the information they had just seen.

Admiral Morris was the first to break the silence. 'So your assumption is that Sarclan stole the Baleraphon, found some safe haven and started a colony. In all these years we've never heard or seen any evidence of this, and now you're intimating that he has somehow infiltrated the governments of twenty five Coalition colonies. That he is the master mind behind all these rebellions. To what end?'

Crompton considered Morris's words before answering. 'I

can think of only one thing, revenge. He's out for revenge on those who he believes destroyed his life here and, if our assumptions are correct, he has the manpower to do it.'

Morris countered 'How could this have happened? Sarclan would have needed so much support to pull this off...everything from records being falsified to sensor logs being erased. How is it possible?'

Crompton spoke quietly. 'We don't know; but a total of twenty five colonies will fall to so called rebels, which will in fact be a take-over by Sarclan. The Krell uprising at the same time is just too much of a coincidence for anyone to believe.

'If this is all correct...and I expect corroboration to start to come in soon, he could soon have over twenty million in a military force. The Empire and the Coalition can't field anything to match him. As for how it happened...we let it. The Baleraphon mission was the most ambitious ever...no other mission had entailed so much...a two-hundred year journey!

'The longest ever done previously had been seventy-five years, and that was a one off. We threw every piece of technology at that mission, the latest in replication systems, cloning systems, weapons. The latest and best of everything we had was on that ship, plus it was the only ship to ever be powered by Trisidium.'

JT stood and spoke. 'Then that's the key to finding where he went...Trisidium; they must have had a source for refining! As I recall from the official story, Baleraphon was equipped with a processing plant. In fact, it was the reason the original destination was chosen ... there appeared to be a source of the ore there. If all this is true, and Sarclan did divert Baleraphon, he must have known of an ore body they could exploit! After all, the ship only had a limited amount which wouldn't supply a full colony for long.'

Admiral Dokad interrupted. 'We already know of one very rich ore body...Medros six. It was supposed to be deserted, but it is so far out of the way no-one ever goes there...or so we thought.'

'We didn't even know of its existence then,' Morris interjected.

'Neither did we,' Dokad replied. 'In fact, we didn't discover Trisidium till many years later according to the timeline here.' He pointed to the image on the screen. The discussion continued along similar lines for quite a while until Malik spoke up.

'Quiet please.' He waited till the conversations ceased. 'It's quite obvious we don't have all the facts and we could keep this conjecture going forever and get nowhere. I suggest we adjourn till next Tuesday, as we had originally planned. By then, we will know if we are, in fact, in the grip of another Sarclan Sedition, or not. If more colonies fall to rebel forces, then we must assume the worst and plan accordingly. Until we know more, there is nothing we can do.'

The nodding of heads around the table indicated all agreed.

'Admirals Wilson and Morris, I would like you to start working with Crompton on our logistic requirements and, more importantly, our current resources. Admiral Grogan, can you have a list of all Space Corps assets we have available and their disposition? General, we will need a full review of our ground forces for our meeting.' All agreed.

'Then I suggest we leave this till next Tuesday at ten hundred hours,' he said finally.

Crompton, Wilson, Klastok and Morris headed for the hangar and their shuttles. Grogan held back, indicating he would join them later and pulled Jeff aside.

'Jeff, these new Mantas might be very urgent now. Can

you and Silas have a production timetable by Tuesday?'

'No problem, Admiral. Silas is working on that as we speak…our end has already been done so we will have a full program ready for you Tuesday. How soon can you supply the ships?' Jeff asked.

'Give me the word and I'll have the first batch to you in two days,' Grogan replied.

'As soon as funding is approved, we can start.' Jeff looked the Admiral in the eye as he spoke, understanding the urgency of the situation.

'Good. I have funding I can use for five, at the cost we have been discussing, so I'll arrange for them to be transferred tonight. They should be on site Monday evening, latest.' Grogan extended his hand to seal the deal. Contracts would be signed in due course but the relationship between the two men was based on trust—far more binding than any contract.

As Jeff and Admiral Grogan bid each other farewell, President Malik spoke to Aaron. 'I know that this situation goes against all that Freebooters believe in but I don't see any way of you avoiding this. The Coalition and the Empire make up a sizeable part of your trade business…not just you but all Freebooters. If we fall, what happens then?'

Aaron studied Malik's face, seeing only honesty. 'You may be right, Mr President,' he said reluctantly. 'But until our Prime decides a course of action, I can't do anything. I have been involved as a private citizen so far; any general Freebooter involvement must be decided by the Prime and, in all probability, the Council of Seniors.'

'I understand,' Malik conceded. 'Thankfully, Grainger will be here for the meeting Tuesday.' He turned to Jeff and changed the subject. 'I have always been fascinated by this construction and the stories about it. It always seemed to be a bit of a myth.' He gazed down the passage way. 'So much to see...' He said as his voice trailed off.

'Yes, sir' Jeff answered. 'It's been a bit of a family joke for many years you know...the Second's Folly and all that... most of the family thought him a bit mad. Strange thing is though; as things now stand, this might be the best piece of real estate on Earth, if all that we have just learnt is true, well...it won't be a folly anymore.' They walked back into the room and entered the elevator to the surface. It was already 6.00 pm and Sonia was going to be impossible if they were late for her party.

11

*W*hile the meeting was taking place, action at the house was furious.

Sonia was in her element, directing the settings for the night's celebrations like a conductor in front of an orchestra. Phillip was designated *pit master* and was overseeing the BBQs; the staff kitchens below were in full production and there were guests to greet in the afternoon.

Petra was grateful that she and Salina had been overlooked and they had slipped quietly away so that Salina could show her around. They commandeered a small shuttle and did a quick tour of the property. Sal had little interest in the operation—she just wanted the chance to escape to one of her research stations. As the half hour aerial tour ended she turned to Petra. 'Want to see something fascinating?'

Petra had no idea what she was up to but agreed and Salina turned the small craft towards the coast. 'So, what's the deal with you and my uncle?' Salina Abraham wasn't known for beating around the bush—she was always direct and sometimes a little too blunt.

"Nothing, he offered me this job on Tuesday,' Petra replied, hesitantly. 'I took it and our first trip was here.'

'Really, that's all, nothing more?'

"No, we only met earlier this week … why the questions?'

Salina looked intensely at Petra. 'I'm pretty good at reading people and there's more to the two of you than meets the eye.'

Petra was desperately trying to sound disinterested. 'He offered me this job and I accepted, that's all there is.'

'Ok, for now. Sorry if I was prying.' Salina finished the conversation and started her landing cycle. They had arrived at their destination.

The research station they landed on was twenty kilometres off the coast, east of Sydney. It was here that Petra saw the real Salina Abraham. Gone was the slightly dour and prickly demeanour; here she was truly alive and very animated.

They spent the next few hours touring the facility, Salina talking enthusiastically all the time. Petra began to understand her passion and to understand just how much damage humans had done to the planet, her appreciation of the work Sal was doing growing each passing minute. The last part of the tour was the best—they took one of the mini subs to tour an artificial reef that had been constructed for fish habitat while all the time Salina kept up her commentary. They were both so engrossed that time flew by till, finally, Salina checked her watch.

'Shit!' She exclaimed and turned the sub back toward the station. '3.00 pm, we better get back! We really don't want to be late for tonight—Mother would not be happy!'

They arrived back at the house at 4.30. Already several shuttles were on the apron, and more were on approach. Being family, Salina claimed priority and parked in the family hangar. The two raced for the pod and arrived at the service entrance.

'This is a quiet way to enter the house, if you get my drift,' Salina said quietly. 'We used this as kids to sneak in and out...always worked for us back then.' Their entrance went unnoticed, and they split up, Salina going back to her house to dress. Petra walked quietly down the hall towards her room and was almost there when she heard a voice behind her.

'Petra, glad I caught you. Did Aaron fill you in on the dress for this evening?' It was Aaron's mother, Amanda. She was holding Prince in her arms, the cat purring contently as she stroked his head. 'Lovely animal...Aaron was always fond of cats.' She approached Petra and gave her an enquiring look.

'No. I was just going to wear my uniform.'

'Typical bloody men! Sorry, but he should have remembered tonight is formal...all Sonia's events are. Come with me...we'll sort this out.' She led the way towards a door at the far end of the hall.

The room was empty except for three very comfortable chairs. One wall was mirrored with the moveable sides. 'One of the benefits of being an Abraham...there's always a great selection of clothes.' She smiled and indicated for Petra to turn. Amanda summed the younger woman up and moved toward a small panel on the far wall. She pressed the pad and the wall opened to reveal hundreds of dresses. 'Oh! I am sorry. Does your culture have any clothing requirements?'

Petra laughed. 'No, Argos is very casual but we do dress up occasionally,' and the two women began to pour through the vast selection before them.

It took just over an hour before Amanda was satisfied with the choice. She looked at Petra's image in the mirror. 'That'll knock his socks off,' she commented.

'Who's socks?' Petra questioned.

Amanda tilted her head to one side and gave Petra a knowing grin. 'It's as plain as day how Aaron feels about you and, if I'm any judge, how you feel about him.' She held up her hand, to stifle any comment Petra might make. 'Don't protest, I *am* his mother and I have a feeling that there's more to you two than either of you understand.'

'But we only just met a few days ago,' Petra frowned, feeling somewhat uneasy. The woman before her was his mother and, from her own upbringing she knew that sometimes mothers had a sixth sense where issues concerning their children were concerned.

'Does that really matter? I knew Jason was the one for me the day I met him...it did take another six years to snag him...and I still love him as much today. Now, tell me you don't feel the same about my son and you can go back to wearing your uniform,' Amanda smiled.

'I'll keep the dress,' Petra said quietly, 'and you're correct, there is something...something I can't explain.'

'So, how did the two of you meet? And don't give me any of that *he offered me a job* rubbish.' Amanda's eyes showed that she wouldn't be fooled by any subterfuge.

'We met at a restaurant, on Monday night last week, Earth time. We had both been stood up and we sort of started talking and ended up having dinner together.' Petra finished there, hoping she had said enough.

'And that's all?"

Petra looked into Amanda's eyes and instantly knew there was no way she would be fooled. 'Pretty much...we had dinner, talked till midnight and then I left. The next day, we met at the Prime's residence.' She looked at Amanda, her eyes pleading. 'So that's the story to date but there is something...a feeling I can't explain. Please don't say anything to Aaron.'

'What! And miss all the fun of watching you make him squirm? You must be joking! My lips are sealed. Now off you go, the festivities start in under an hour but wait for me...you need to make an entrance.' Amanda opened the door, winked conspiratorially and let Petra out into the hall.

The party was as expected. Sonia had invited a number of potential partners for her children. JT was prepared and managed to avoid most of them but one had struck a chord and he was actually starting to enjoy her company. David, on the other hand, was not so lucky and had eventually resorted to sneaking back to his own house to escape his mothers' machinations. Salina fared best. Early in the evening she had attached herself to Sol and there she stayed, sending a clear message to her mother's chosen potentials.

Aaron was concerned—it was now after eight and he hadn't seen Petra since he returned. Salina had told him they had arrived back a bit late and she was going back to her room to dress—but that was a couple of hours ago.

He started back into the house but stopped when he looked up to the top of the stairs; there between his mother and father was Petra. Since they had met, such a short time ago, he had only seen her dressed in uniforms, or normal casual clothes. But here before him now was a different person. Everyone was formally dressed; men in either formal suits or dress uniforms and the women in evening gowns—but Petra had outdone all.

The dress she wore seemed to shimmer as she moved. The neckline plunged almost to her navel but was joined by a translucent fabric. Her shoulders were bare but she had a silk shawl draped seductively over her arms.

The buzz of conversation seemed to quieten as they descended the stairs, with all eyes centred on Petra. Amanda Abraham was renowned for making an entrance wherever she went, but tonight she surrendered that job to Petra. She whispered to Petra as they approached Aaron.

'That's how to make an entrance, my dear.' She turned to her husband as they reached Aaron. 'Jason, the orchestra has started. I'd like to dance and Aaron,' she moved closer to her son and whispered, 'close your mouth or you'll swallow a fly.'

Aaron was stumped for words but finally spoke. 'You look amazing.' His throat was dry and his voice little more than a croak.

'I think you need a drink…then we can dance.' Petra had clearly taken control as they moved through the crowd to the bar area. Aaron selected two glasses of champagne and raised his to Petra.

'To the most stunningly beautiful woman here,' he drained his glass and offered his arm. 'Care to dance?'

Petra smiled and took his arm. 'Thank you,' she whispered.

They danced as if they were alone, lost in each other, until Aaron felt a tap on his shoulder—it was his father.

'Care to trade?' Jason said as he took Petra's hand. 'You can't expect to hog her all night.' They swapped partners and Amanda looked at her son as they glided around the floor.

'She's incredible, Aaron. Don't let her get away.'

Aaron smiled as he replied. 'I don't know what you're talking about…she's just one of my crew.'

His mother rolled her eyes. 'If that's all, then you're the dumbest man I've ever met,' she chided.

The orchestra finished and dinner was announced. Everyone moved to the tables set up on the lawn and took their allocated places. The food was excellent—beef, lamb, pork and poultry perfectly roasted over the ancient fire pits under Phillip's expert guidance, roasted vegetables accompanied the meal. It seemed to Aaron, that the meat tasted better here on Earth than back on Argos, even though some of the breeds were the same.

President Malik was in his element, circulating, massaging egos and working the crowd. It was at 11:00 pm that he called for attention and made his presentation to Salina. She was awarded a presidential medal for her service to the environment and her work in the area of marine ecology.

At the same time, he announced that she had successfully completed her Doctoral studies and had been awarded her PhD in Marine Biology.

Her acceptance was short and polite, even though she was furious at all the fuss. She did what she did because of her passion for the ocean and the desire to see it fully recover from the ravages of previous human stupidity—not to be publicly celebrated! None of these emotions were evident as she concluded by thanking the President for taking time to present her medal in person.

Aaron was returning to the assembly, with fresh drinks for Petra, Jeff, Sonia and himself when the comm link activated and the sound of George's voice entered his head.

It appears that Crompton was correct...the probe found significant Trisidic radiation at the explosion site. By the way, I have been playing with Mr Harpers' sensor program. I believe it has incredible potential and I suggest you secure the rights to it.

Aaron considered this and replied. *Good. Contact Henry and have him start on the contract—I'll discuss the details with Harper and send them to him later. Send the probes' data and your analysis to the Yacht's computer. Also transmit a general alert to all our ships...suggest something about piracy and warn them all to be extra careful. We'll fill in the gaps when we know what we are dealing with.*

Consider it done, wait...you have just received an encoded message from Argos. What do you want done with it?

Relay it to the Yacht, he thought, then severed the connection.

Aaron re-joined the others. He handed them their drinks and took Petra's arm. 'I have a communication from Grainger; I think I should have a look at it. Will you be OK for half an hour?'

'More than all right, I'm really enjoying this...you have a great family by the way,' she smiled, her eyes flashing with happiness. Aaron nodded and walked back toward the house.

Petra watched him leave, wondering what the problem was and thinking on what had transpired in the last couple of days. Amanda approached and touched her arm, 'penny for your thoughts?'

Petra smiled as she replied. 'Just thinking; he's been estranged for over thirty years and yet it feels like he's always been here. There's no disconnect, no defence, nothing I was expecting.' She sounded perplexed.

Amanda took her arm and guided Petra to a quiet spot. 'There has never been a single day he wasn't in our thoughts, and I'll guarantee he's felt the same. Sonia told me about the reunion, in the hangar; it was just as I expected and it's something you need to understand, if you're to become one of us.' Amanda quickly silenced Petra's protest with a wave, 'stop, and please understand this. Being an Abraham and part of this family is hard, sometimes. We tend to do things our own way; yes they fought and, in the heat of anger, Aaron stormed out. But he's made his life a success, elsewhere but, and this is the key; he's always been an Abraham and he can't ever change that.

'When they met in that hangar, the thirty years vanished, they were just two brothers who had had a fight and realised it was time to get over it. I expected nothing less, when they finally met.'

'But other families, even on Varga, have continued feuds for generations?' Petra commented.

'Yes, but they weren't Abrahams, were they? Now come on, we have a party to enjoy.' Amanda turned and led her back to the crowd.

***

It only took a couple of minutes for Aaron to reach the hangar and set up in the Yacht. *I must give this damn boat a name* he thought vaguely as he took a cup of coffee from the dispenser. He sat at the console in his cabin and opened the communication. It took a few minutes to decrypt it and he read it slowly and re-read it, twice. He shook his head wondering where all this would leave Argos and the Freebooter way of life.

Grainger confirmed that he was heading to Earth for the meeting on Tuesday—something Aaron knew he would never do unless the circumstances were dire. As a private citizen, Aaron had the freedom to work with any party he chose and in any capacity, so the events leading up to today were of no real consequence for Freebooters as a whole.

But as a foreign entity, the Prime attending what could only be described as a war council was a different matter— his cover story of a tri-lateral trade meeting between The Coalition, The Empire and Argos was thin.

Aaron sat back in his chair to consider the facts and the implications—he still had significant concerns and doubts. Although the facts did seem to fit, like the pieces of a jigsaw, he was unconvinced that everything was on the table. His thoughts were interrupted by the sound of footsteps coming up the ramp. He opened the cabin door and Petra entered.

'Are you OK?' she asked. 'You've been gone so long I thought you might be unwell.'

Aaron looked at the time on the console screen, 03.25. He had been sitting here for more than three hours! 'Sorry, I just lost track of the time,' he apologised sheepishly.

'Want to talk it through?' Petra asked, her face a mask of concern.

'There's a lot to discuss, don't you want to get some

sleep?'

'By the look of you, there will be no sleep until you get it off your chest. Use me as a sounding board, that's what a first officer is for after all—maybe we can work out whatever is bothering you?' She brushed a wisp of hair away from his eyes, even with all his doubts and concerns, Petra in that dress was difficult to ignore.

'OK,' Aaron relented, 'but you may regret this.' He started to recap events to date. An hour later he had brought Petra up to speed with everything that had happened. Finally he slowed down. 'My main worry is the way it all fits so perfectly, everything is too...' he was reaching for the right word.

'Smooth?' Petra suggested.

'Yeah! Everything just fits too smoothly, like each piece of information was designed to meld with the previous one and the next one, no gaps, it's too complete...' His voice trailed off as he went back into his thoughts.

'Well, what are you going to do about it?'

Aaron said nothing, busying himself at the console for the next few minutes. Finally he looked back at Petra. 'There, I've sent Grainger a message asking to meet first thing when he arrives, before the others can get to him.' He sat back waiting for an answer.

'How long will the reply take?'

Aaron gave a shy smile. 'About four hours. Maybe we should get some sleep.' Aaron stood, 'the cabin across the hall...you can use that if you wish.' His words said one thing but he desperately wanted another. 'And there's a dispenser there...you can get another uniform.'

It was 05.00 and too late to go back to the house...Petra's heart was racing. Everything Aaron was saying said, *'walk across the passageway to the other room'*, yet everything from his actions and demeanour said exactly the opposite. Her voice was soft and shaky as she replied. 'If that's what you want...'

Aaron's response surprised them both. 'No, it's not what I bloody well want!'

He took the two steps across the space separating them, scooped her up in his arms and kissed her, passionately... she responded, crushing herself into him. Aaron fumbled with the door, desperate to open it...finally it released and they almost fell through. Still locked in the kiss, they stumbled through the lounge area toward the bedroom. As they entered, Petra pushed Aaron onto the bed.

'Just stay there and watch.' Her voice was calm and breathless as she reached behind and began slowly unfastening her dress. She then reached up and slid the delicate gown off her shoulders. It dropped to the floor revealing her almost entirely. All she now wore was a tiny thong, stockings and high heeled shoes.

Aaron reached for her. 'I thought you looked taller,' he said huskily. He reached up, cupped her firm breasts and gently tweaked her nipples.

'Easy, now it's my turn.' Petra smiled as she undid his shirt front. She ran her tongue over his bare neck and down to his chest, giving his left nipple a gentle nip. Aaron groaned as she slipped his trousers off, exposing him. Aaron reached down and removed the flimsy thong that separated him from his prize.

Gently, at first he began to tease, his fingers barely touching her. Petra's moans told him he was doing what she wanted. She took a firm grip on his manhood and began to stroke him. Her kiss was demanding, almost as if she wanted to devour him; it was too much for them both. Aaron pushed her to the bed, lifted her legs and entered her in one swift thrust.

There was no finesse; they were both too desperate, the tension of the past few days driving their passion beyond comprehension. Their hips thrust in unison, building in tempo, their cries and grunts of pleasure filling the room. Finally, their lust temporarily sated and their bodies exhausted, they fell asleep.

Aaron stirred, glancing at the clock—09:25—four and a half hours since they went to bed. He gently rolled over and there beside him was Petra, still sleeping. She was on her left side, facing him. The sheet was mostly off her and he marvelled at the beauty beside him. Her red hair was tousled and covering half her face—he gently moved it aside to see her better. His gaze flowed down her body, across her firm breasts, memories of earlier this morning flooding back. Down further, over her firm round belly till his view was blocked by the sheet, gently draped across her hips.

'Do you approve?'

His voyeuristic pastime was dashed. 'Yes, I could never tire of this.' His eyes returned to her face, those green eyes challenging him. Words left him, his mind went blank and he stuttered something incomprehensible.

'Aaron, stop!' Petra placed her hand on his mouth and she slithered closer to him. Their lips met.

'Petra...I've got to say this while I can. The night we met, I felt something I have never felt before, and it scared me. Now I understand why I've been so dumb lately. I think I'm falling in love with you.' Aaron stopped, not knowing what he should say next.

'Only think? I *know* how I feel, Aaron Abraham!' As the words hit his ears, Petra sprang on top of him, pinning him to the bed. She bent lower, her breasts brushing his chest, tantalising him. 'I knew the moment you sat down...I didn't understand it, but I knew my life had suddenly changed.'

She crushed against him as they kissed again, this time Aaron rolled her onto her back, their lips still locked. He broke free and started kissing her neck, down her throat, across each breasts, teasing her nipples and lower—down over her belly, past her navel till he reached the velvety folds of her pleasure zone.

'Yes, yes.' Petra moaned, the sensations driving her crazy, her back arched and her thighs clamped his head where she wanted it. Aaron's tongue was teasing, tantalising—almost cruel in the way he worked. Long strokes; quick flicks over the nub of her clitoris; every time he changed an intense shockwave of pleasure slammed through her body. She was pulling his hair but not letting his tongue leave the spot.

Suddenly, she released her thigh lock, pulled him up by his hair until he was positioned above her; her legs wrapped around him and she guided him into her, thrusting her hips upward to greet him.

'I want you in me now!' Petra demanded.

Finally, an hour later, with both of their needs satisfied, they lay snuggled in a loving embrace. Petra propped up on her right elbow. 'Well, Captain, what do we do now?'

Aaron looked at her intently. 'I don't know about you, but I think I need a shower before we go to brunch.' The clock read 10:30 as Aaron headed to the console while Petra started the shower. The reply from Grainger confirmed the meeting for Monday at 15:30, just after his expected arrival. Aaron was relieved and shut the screen down and headed for the bathroom. He found Petra standing under the shower, water streaming off her body. He quickly joined her, wrapped his arms around her, kissing the back of her neck, his hands quickly finding her breasts. 'What are you going to tell my mother, now that you've had your wicked way with me?' he joked.

'Wicked way? Believe me, when I've had my wicked way with you, you won't be this energetic.'

'Ha! Sounds like a challenge...I just hope I'm up to it! In the mean-time, we need to get up to the house; brunch will be served in about ten minutes...and you can do the explaining!' Aaron quickly washed, they dried together under the air blower and had started to dress when a call from the house came through; evidently their absence had been noted. With a feeble excuse of some urgent trade problem they quickly finished dressing and raced back to the pod. A few minutes later, they walked onto the rear terrace where everyone was sitting for brunch.

'Everything OK?' Jeff asked as they sat.

'Yes, just a small issue to sort out...you know how it is,' Aaron replied to his brother.

'I certainly do,' Jeff smiled and gave his brother a wink, while he busied himself bringing the coffee pot to the table.

Amanda and Jason were seated opposite Aaron and Petra. Amanda leant forward and asked Petra, 'Did you enjoy last night, my dear? You seem to be in very good spirits this morning,' a knowing smile crossing her face.

'Yes, thank you. I had a wonderful time.'

'I'm so glad. Sometimes these things can be such a drag.'

Aaron stood and moved away from the table, an itch behind his left ear signalling that there was a comm from the ship. The voice of George, the ship's brain echoed in his head.

You have been summoned to a meeting by the Eldorans. Simple and matter of fact, but George's message was anything but clear.

'What do you mean, summoned?' Aaron questioned aloud.

They have demanded a meeting, urgently. To get there you will need to leave now! George responded.

'Did they give any clues as to what they wanted?' Aaron was intrigued. The Eldorans had never demanded before; requested, asked politely yes, but never demanded. He also knew that George would not exaggerate—if he said demand that is what was communicated.

No, just demanded and stressed extreme urgency.

'Can we use the yacht?' Aaron enquired.

Yes, and I can transfer to my post there if required, George suggested.

'No, just program the coordinates and file an exit request... we'll go from here.' He paused for a moment and walked out of earshot of the others. 'Another thing, transfer all the data from the trip here, I want to have another look at what happened.' Aaron stopped speaking and the rest of the conversation continued subliminally. He walked back to the others and motioned Jeff to join him.

'I've to go to a meeting...urgent thing...but before I go, can we have a couple of minutes?' he asked his brother.

'Sure...let's go to the study.'

Aaron beckoned Petra to him. 'Can you prep the Yacht for immediate take off? She nodded and turned to leave the room, saying farewell to all at the table.

Aaron joined his brother as they headed to his office. Once in there, he closed the door and began. 'Jeff, I have some concerns with what has happened; it all seems to fit too well. What's your take on it all?'

Jeff considered his answer. 'I must admit I have some

concerns as well…especially with Crompton being involved… but it all seems logical.'

'Yes, too logical,' Aaron mused. 'Let me tell you what my concerns are.' Over the next ten minutes he gave Jeff an abridged version. He finished with, 'and now I have been summoned to a meeting with the Eldorans. They *never* summon, so that only increases my apprehension.'

Jeff shook his head. 'I can see what you're getting at…from the Freebooter perspective…but consider the Coalition. If the rebel conspiracy which Crompton suspects happens, we could be facing a reduction in members, at best. At worst, it could be the end of the Coalition, which would be disastrous for most of the colonies. Remember, most rely on the Coalition for support, trade and protection. If it fails, then they will be easy targets for any opportunistic force that emerges from the rubble.'

Aaron thought on this and finally spoke. 'I think we need more information. Can you look into things while I'm gone? We can then discuss it when I return.'

'All right, I'll do some digging. When will you be back?'

'Should be around 3:00 pm tomorrow…the Eldorans have chosen a meeting place very close…something they've also never done before. It all just keeps getting more intriguing.' Aaron stood and held out his hand which Jeff took and shook firmly. 'Some home coming.'

Jeff laughed. 'As I remember, you always were a magnet for drama.' Aaron left the room and went to the pod.

The Yacht was prepped and ready when Aaron arrived. The flight plan had been approved and Petra was already sitting in the pilot's chair, a wicker hamper sitting beside her. She gave a quirky grin. 'Your mother insisted.'

'Good! Let's get under way,' Aaron said as he sat in the second chair, picked up the hamper and examined the contents. 'Sure can't beat home cooked food.'

Petra closed the access ramp, energised the antigrav and the vessel lifted a few centimetres off the hangar floor. She turned the ship to face the hangar door and transmitted the code to open—the door slid down into the ground and she slowly moved out onto the apron. Together they worked quickly through the final pre-flight check list. Then she asked, 'Destination coordinates please?' Her flight plan only covered to the outer marker, no further.

'Should already be in the auto pilot,' Aaron replied. Petra checked and brought up the destination in the Bubble.

'Strange, there's nothing there, just empty space,' her voice edged with concern. 'Not the sort of place I would expect, given what is going on.'

'No, that's exactly where they'd want us to go,' Aaron replied.

'Who?' Petra queried, interrupting his next sentence.

'The Eldorans; let's get going, we don't have much time.' Clearly he had assumed the Captain's role again.

At his command, Petra initiated the atmospheric drive and the craft leapt into the Sky. In five minutes they had transitioned into space and the main drive took over. Twenty minutes later, they reached the outer marker and Petra handed control over to the auto pilot; immediately it altered course and initiated the displacement drive. Now all they needed to do was sit back and wait. The journey timer indicated they would be at the meeting location in two hours and seventeen minutes.

Petra turned her chair towards Aaron. 'Ok, we are now on our way, what's going on?'

'I really don't know,' he replied. 'The Eldorans contacted Condor and demanded we meet them. They have never demanded anything before, so it must be important.'

Petra thought on this before she spoke. 'You don't think it has anything to do with the sub space explosion do you?'

'No, it couldn't have. Why do you ask?'

'Look, I know your opinion of Professor Fraslok, but hear me out. While I was at the academy I had the opportunity to attend some of his tutorials. One was on displacement theory and sub space; not how we use it, but our concept of it. He theorised that sub space and normal space are separate and that our idea...that we somehow displace normal space when we enter a worm hole...is incorrect. His idea is that our worm hole is actually in the separate place we call sub space and not part of normal space.'

She paused, gathered her thoughts, and took a deep breath. 'He also theorised that sub space actually is the separator between different dimensions. So if that explosion was potentially damaging in our dimension, it follows that it could have the same effect on any other dimensions that intersect with sub space at that point.'

Aaron couldn't help himself. 'Total crap, Loonie Lennie is nuts.'

'Is he?' Petra was beginning to get angry at Aaron's arrogant stance regarding the professor. 'He was correct with the heat signature traceability...you thought that was impossible...and he has been right about a number of other things. Why couldn't he be right in this?'

'Because it would throw our entire universal theory out the window...the theory upon which all our existence is based...theory we used to develop space travel in the first place!'

'Would it? We don't know that for sure. As you said, it's still a theory, and that theory was based on limited knowledge centuries ago. But what *if* the professor is right?

Maybe we should ask your friends when we see them...they should know.'

Aaron studied her with new understanding. She was very intelligent, and this was one of her areas of expertise. Her incisiveness and ability to question existing ideas was both refreshing and challenging. Their discussion continued until it was interrupted by the sound of the reinsertion alarm.

Taking their seats as the auto pilot shut down the displacement drive and Junior transitioned back into normal space.

Aaron's thoughts raced. *If Petra is correct, we have just passed outside of our Universe.* The thought was too big for him to comprehend but, at the same time, part of him felt that she was right. The ship kept moving, slowly, towards nothing—they could see nothing on their present course. Seven and a half minutes later they came to a full stop.

'I don't understand...where are they?' Petra's voice was tinged with confusion and concern. A full sensor and visual scans gave no indications of anything being near them.

Suddenly, Aaron noticed a slight change in the view screen. 'They're here,' he muttered softly.

'Where?'

'Right there,' Aaron pointed to a section of the view screen that was out of focus. Slowly the section that was out of focus changed; disappearing completely to be replaced by a huge ovoid shape. 'There they are...that's their ship.' The shape slowly coalesced into a solid white form—no openings, no view ports—just a solid shape.

Then everything went black.

12

*I*t felt like only a few seconds later that Aaron woke, and found he was naked and lying on a firm but pliant surface.

The lighting was subdued with a blue tint to it, and it was quiet. He detected movement to his right and as he lifted himself up off the surface, he saw an approaching figure.

'Good to see you again A-Bra-Ham,' a familiar deep, sonorous voice said.

Aaron realised who the figure was. 'It has been too long, Jok-Tar.'

Jok-Tar moved past him, and stood by another table, occupied by a still-unconscious Petra.

'We took the liberty of completing a full scan of you both,' he said absently. Aaron wasn't concerned; he knew this was standard practice for anyone who was granted access to an Eldoran ship. 'Your companion is a fine specimen of a human female. She is in excellent health and should bear you strong offspring.' He made himself busy with a console that just appeared beside him. 'She will need some enhancements though.'

His words sounded final, but Aaron sought to clarify his intentions. 'Why?' he queried.

Aaron studied Jok-Tar intently. He was tall and well-muscled. His face was a study in elegance, with deep blue eyes, a broad regal nose and full lips. His hair was jet black and hung to his shoulders. His nakedness was only because his guests were naked, as Eldorans always appeared to take a form complimentary to their guests. Aaron suspected that this was not the true state of Eldoran physical form; his experiences with them had given him the idea that it was a less corporeal existence.

Petra started to stir before Jok-Tar could answer. She opened her eyes slowly, and visually scanned the form standing beside her bed, as if appraising what she saw, before speaking.

'If I am dead, I have certainly gone to heaven,' she smiled appreciatively towards Jok-Tar.

'I...thank you,' he replied hesitantly.

'It is I who should thank you! I'm Petra Mannix.' His presence was obviously pleasing Petra.

Aaron smiled—he had never seen an Eldoran embarrassed before. Jok-Tar turned toward Aaron, his empathic reaction to Petra's interest becoming obvious.

'I will leave you and your mate, A-Bra-Ham,' he said as he took two steps and disappeared.

Petra rose and moved towards Aaron before she stumbled. Quickly he reached out to steady her. 'Take your time... you've come a very long way in a very short time,' he said with a smile.

'What's so funny?' she asked.

'Jok-Tar's reaction to you...he was getting an erection... what were you thinking?' he chuckled.

'That is not at all amusing. I usually get that reaction from men, especially if I'm naked...present company included.' She smiled a teasing sparkle in her eyes.

Aaron smiled back and said nothing.

'Clothing please,' he commanded. Their clothes appeared on their beds and, as they dressed, Aaron began to explain.

'Eldorans are somewhat more than Empaths, they are telepathic...and they try to compliment those who they appear before. I believe the physical form they assume is what they believe will put their guest most at ease. They are fastidious about health and wellbeing, that's why they gave us a physical examination when they brought us to their ship. This isn't the first time I have been on one but, usually our meetings are conducted in a neutral setting.

'For the examination we needed to be naked, our clothing was certainly inspected just as thoroughly. Jok-Tar appeared naked because we were. The first time I met him he appeared as an incredibly beautiful woman, so he must have read your thoughts this time.'

'Well, if that's the case, let me go back to sleep...I really need to finish that dream!' Petra teased. Jok-Tar reappeared at that precise moment, this time fully clothed.

'A-Bra-Ham, we have much to discuss.' He turned to Petra. 'Man-Nix, we need to give you some enhancements, if you are to come with us.' He paused and looked at Petra, 'Do I have your permission?' Petra looked at Aaron with questioning eyes.

'Don't worry,' Aaron reassured her. 'If you don't want to do this, you don't have to; but I have had several enhancements that have not harmed me in any way.'

'Man-Nix, we would never do you any harm,' said Jok-Tar. 'These enhancements will allow you to accompany A-Bra-Ham as he travels with us.' His tone was matter of fact and reassuring.

Petra looked at both of them. 'Ok then, what do I have to do?' she asked.

Another Eldoran appeared and glided over to Petra. This one was in the guise of a woman—an older, motherly form. Her hair was slightly grey and she had kind, caring blue eyes. Her nose was long and her mouth generous.

'Come with me, Man-Nix.' She held her hand out and Petra took it; they both vanished. The room reconfigured from sterile examination to one with a comfortable lounge. A table bearing a selection of foods and coffee appeared beside Aaron.

'I trust this is acceptable?' Jok-Tar enquired. 'Man-Nix will be back shortly so we can delay our conversation till then if you wish.' Aaron nodded his agreement and reached for one of the rock cakes, his favourite sweet. It amazed him how a race that he had never seen eat or drink human food, could get these things so right. Aaron had just finished his cake when Petra reappeared. She walked across the room and sat beside him.

'The enhancements have been carried out? I trust you did not experience any discomfort?' Jok-Tar enquired from Petra.

'Nothing…it seemed that I just went from that other room to here…I didn't experience anything in between,' she replied. 'What was actually done?'

'Most of the enhancements we give you are to help you access more of your capabilities; to give more active control of your brain. There is an old theory that humans only use a small part of their brain and while it is a gross exaggeration, there is still some truth in it. We have developed ways to allow us more conscious control of our brain…it helps with many things you will see and experience as we visit other realms. None of what we offer will ever harm you. Now, please have some refreshments,' Jok-Tar gestured toward the table.

Petra loaded a small plate as Jok-Tar continued. 'I apologise for the manner in which we requested this meeting, but time is of the essence. Your recent experience has had great and far reaching effects. There was a significant amount of damage to other realms. Many life forces were extinguished…violently…and that is something we haven't experienced for many, many cycles.

'There are others who live in the inner realms that have been affected adversely and wish to retaliate...that is why you are here. We must convince them not to take action; convince them that you can handle your own affairs. But understand this...none will tolerate any more attacks in sub space...the very survival of the universe may be at stake.'

Aaron had never heard this degree of conviction in the Eldoran's voice before—things were getting very serious. Petra looked puzzled.

Jok-Tar smiled at her. 'I think I need to explain.'

'Yes please. I lost you at *please, have some refreshments*,' she replied.

Jok-Tar gave a subdued chuckle. 'I remember when we started to explain our existence to A-Bra-Ham,' he looked to Aaron. 'Remember?' Aaron nodded as Jok-Tar continued, 'your traditional understanding of the structure of the universe is somewhat flawed; the concept is of a linear universe...to simplify your stellar theory.

'In reality, it is a multi-layered structure with many layers or realms, each realm interwoven with all the others. There are areas where they converge and become almost one. These areas are the most sensitive to any disruptions and where you were attacked in sub space is one such place.

'Between each layer is void...this you call sub space. Sub space is the...' he was searching for an analogy that would help his explanation. A moment later he continued, 'Yes; the mortar that holds the realms apart...and together at the same time, just like a brick building of your past.'

Petra nodded her understanding as Jok-Tar continued. 'And as with a brick building, damage the mortar and you damage the whole structure. That is what happened when that weapon was detonated in sub space.'

Petra chimed in and told Jok-Tar of Professor Fraslok's theory.

'A very astute fellow,' he observed. 'Sub space is indeed separate to normal space and it is the separator between the realms or, as he calls them, the dimensions. Unfortunately, we are now faced with a huge problem. Sub space has been breached from your realm. This caused horrific damage in some of the other realms,' Jok-Tar said.

'A meeting has been called in the tenth realm...the realm that suffered most. This meeting is under the Protocol of Intercession, meaning that all delegates are free and protected. Also, if any wrongdoing is discovered, the culprits are not harmed or detained. This is the only way we could get all to sit and discuss this matter, and also preserve your safety.' He paused while his guests finished their refreshments.

'There are, as far as we know, twelve realms, with yours being the twelfth. Eldora is in the fifth and all between there and the eleventh are inhabited. The realms are like different universes, with many galaxies each.

'The most important thing is sub space...it separates each and supports each...but it is a fluid situation. There are many places where the realms converge; in those places it touches several realms simultaneously, and these areas are extremely vulnerable. When the breach occurred, we detected a substantial energy release at that point.

'Some argue it was a deliberate act; that the placement and timing allowed the energy to propagate into other realms causing varying degrees of damage. Some are calling it an act of war.

'There is an organisation that unites the inner realms, sort of like your Council of Seniors on Argos, or the Coalition Council. When the disaster happened, an urgent meeting was called and we were tasked with bringing representatives of the twelfth realm to a central location to answer to the delegates. This is most serious...we have never been called on to do this before.' Aaron was about to speak but Jok-Tar waved him to silence.

'My friend, there are some who want to invade your realm to pacify it. Believe me, they have the ability. The only problem is we are the only ones who can successfully navigate the path through the eleventh realm. For any invasion to succeed; Eldora would be required to assist and, if the council decides on this course of action, we are treaty bound to do so.

'So far my sire, Eldrac-Tar, has been able to keep the peace but we cannot have another incident. You have been brought here to answer to the delegates and to negotiate a solution.'

'You're joking! I'm just a trader. I'm not a general...or a politician...why me?' Aaron was now on his feet and pacing.

'No, you are none of those,' Jok-Tar agreed. 'But you have proven to be an honest and truthful friend to us and I could not think of a better representative of your race, A-Bra-Ham. Time is short, we must have you on Reglaos in twenty of your hours and you have so much to learn.

'We can give you the information, now that both of you have the necessary enhancements. Would you consent to a session in an education chamber? It will make the process much easier and more complete. I must impress, this is a critical stage for your race, indeed for all races in your realm, for either we succeed now or you will face certain domination.'

Petra and Aaron agreed and the old Eldoran woman returned. 'Follow me, please,' she said, leading them toward the far wall of the room. Once there it just seemed to disappear and they were now in a different chamber. There were two beds and the woman indicated they take one each.

Once they were comfortable, she commenced working with a small device. The lights dimmed and the ceiling started to shimmer, changing colours, faster and faster, until it all merged into one blur. Just as quickly, the lights returned to normal and Aaron and Petra sat up. The old woman returned and asked how they felt.

'I feel fine...I think,' Petra replied. She looked around the room as if she was seeing it for the first time. 'This seems the same, but I see...more. Yes...I can see more.'

'Excellent!' the old woman said. 'Your training has been successful. You have been taught many things: cultural background on the main races you will be meeting; instructions on protocol; but most importantly, how to properly use the enhancements we have given you.'

'How long were we here?' Aaron asked.

The old female smiled. 'Sixteen of your hours...there is a bathroom for your use to your left. Jok-Tar is waiting for you...please join him when you are ready.' She didn't move, just pointed toward the far wall, then turned and left through the opposite wall. The bathroom was welcome and after relieving themselves, they both walked toward the wall the old Eldoran had indicated. As they reached it, the wall became transparent and they walked through and into another room. There, sitting at a round table was Jok-Tar, three other Eldorans and a smaller, insect-like creature.

'Excellent, you seem to have mastered the enhancements well!' Jok-Tar congratulated them. 'Allow me to introduce you.'

One by one, Jok-Tar led Aaron and Petra to each new person. 'A-Bra-Ham and Man-Nix be pleased to meet Eldrac-

Tar, my sire and head of the Tar clan; Zal-Tar, my sibling; Mondrac, one of Eldora's elders; and Tocmal of Reglaos.'

This last creature was small and stood on two very sturdy legs. It had four arms, each ending in a three fingered hand-like attachment; compound eyes were set to each side of its slightly domed head which was attached to his body by a thick, short neck. When he spoke they heard a series of clicks and whistles with their ears but, thanks to the enhancements, these sounds were translated and they could understand every word he said.

'I am pleased to be in your presence though I would prefer if it was under better terms.' Tocmal reached out one of those arms and Aaron took it as a gesture of greeting.

'I too, am pleased to meet you and agree that the timing could be better.' This seemed to be the correct response and everyone took their seats.

"What we are gathered to discuss is the breach that happened from your realm. We know that your vessel was in the vicinity and that it released an object in hyperspace. Fifteen minutes later, your time, there was an explosive release of energy that ruptured the very fabric of sub space causing immense damage to some other realms? We need understanding of why you did this.' Tocmal's words were translated but they gave no indication of any aggression.

All eyes were now on Aaron. 'You are correct in that we were in the vicinity; also correct that we released a probe. But we did not initiate the explosion.' He continued with his explanation, detailing the events that led up to that moment and why he had acted as he did. 'It was our contention that if we transmitted a message from our ship, it would have been targeted. That is why we used a communication probe. Unfortunately, we cannot identify who launched the weapon...we have suspicions but no evidence.'

Mondrac spoke up. 'A-Bra-Ham, who do you suspect is responsible?'

'To be honest,' Aaron answered, 'all I have is suspicion. I have absolutely no evidence so I am reluctant to apportion blame when I can't substantiate it.' He was aware that he was, in essence, on trial; not just for the breach, but for his character.

Mondrac looked deeply into Aarons' eyes as if scouring his soul. Finally he spoke again. 'Good answer. We should all remember it is too easy to cast aspersions in the heat of the moment, only to find we were incorrect later. I thank A-Bra-Ham for his honesty.'

'All the data from the incident is in the memory bank on my ship; I had it sent there when we reached Earth. I would appreciate you viewing it, maybe we missed something. In any case, a fresh analysis may be beneficial,' Aaron suggested. Understanding the urgency, Petra went with Zal- Tar to retrieve the data.

'A-Bra-Ham, when we reach my home planet, you will see first-hand the damage we have suffered. Tragically, there were many casualties, so be prepared for a less that friendly welcome,' Tocmal stated sadly. 'We are usually a very welcoming species but, under the circumstances, it may not be so.'

Zal-Tar and Petra returned with a data pad. They transferred the information to a device beside Jok-Tar. The wall to their left began to display images and data, everyone watched intently. It was Tocmal who noticed a small aberration. 'You believe it was one of these five ships that fired the weapon?'

'That's correct,' Petra answered.

'I do not believe so. If you examine the track they took when leaving, and impose the track of the weapon, then we must assume that they could not have delivered it; they were going in another direction.'

Aaron watched the simulation again and again till he was sure of what he saw. 'You're right; the difference in trajectory is too much! There must have been another ship...another cloaked ship.'

'So we have another mystery; one you will need to solve when you return,' Jok-Tar said. 'We are now entering Reglaos territory and will assume orbit shortly. I would suggest you return to your ship and dress in more formal uniforms. From now on, appearances will be a key point.'

Fifteen minutes later, Aaron and Petra returned, now dressed in their best Freebooter dress uniforms—navy blue trousers and jackets buttoned to the neck. On their shoulders their rank insignia sparkled, gleaming black boots and white peaked caps with the name "Condor" emblazoned across the visor completed the uniform.

They were just in time to watch the Eldoran ship settle into a parking orbit above Reglaos. The sight was astounding. The planet was slightly larger than Earth, the standard most humans used, but it was astonishingly similar. It had a large area of ocean covering a little over half the planet. The land masses were very green and, except for obvious settlements, looked unspoilt.

Petra was enthralled as Tocmal walked over to Aaron. 'Man-Nix seems fascinated with our planet, and I can see why. It really is a beautiful sight, but I would ask something of you, A-Bra-Ham.'

'Of course, ask away.'

'We could use my shuttle to get down to the planet, but I was wondering if we could use your ship?' The request came as a complete surprise, and Tocmal sensed this. 'After meeting you, and analysing the data you have, I would rather you arrive on our planet by your own means, as a free being. Arriving in the company as we had planned may send the wrong message. Maybe I could accompany you, with your permission.'

'I see your point. I'd be honoured if you would join us,' Aaron replied.

'Good, I'll have the sensor data transmitted to our defence force so they know what is coming. I really don't want some young flight officer trying to impress by shooting down an alien ship.' He gave what passed for a chuckle and moved away to send his communication.

A wise decision human, Mondrac's voice entered Aaron's head. *Now you will arrive as a guest and equal, not as a suspect...yes, a wise decision.*

Tocmal returned. 'It is all settled. I have an arrival trajectory that will allow us to tour some of the worst hit areas. While I know you are not responsible, I believe you need to see this so you can convey the seriousness to your peoples. Shall we go?'

Aaron agreed and the three left for the hangar. It amazed Aaron how the enhancements he and Petra had were now part of them. When they were moving about the ship alone they could, it seemed, simply visualise where they needed to be and almost magically, they were there. Now, with Tocmal, who didn't have the same ability, they followed the path in their mind to the hangar, through doors and passageways.

They arrived at the hangar and Tocmal stood back, admiring the ship. 'This is indeed a fine vessel; what is its designation?'

For a moment, Aaron didn't understand, but finally it dawned, 'Oh, you mean what do we call it? Well, the truth is I haven't actually named it yet. It's my private shuttle and is part of a larger vessel we call Condor.'

Petra interrupted. 'I call it Condor Junior. It looks the same only much smaller. The designation I have used is FTS Condor Junior, the FTS stands for Freebooter Trade Ship.'

'An excellent designation...if you approve we shall use that for this trip.' He looked to Aaron for approval. Aaron nodded. They walked round the ship, Tocmal enthralled by the construction. He ran his hands over the skin and turned to Aaron.

'The surface coating, what is it?'

'A composite we manufacture called Acrilan; very tough and easy to work with.'

'I would like to show you a substance we use...I think it may be beneficial to coat your ships. Who knows, this may be the beginning of trade between our realms.'

Aaron hadn't thought about trade but the little creature was right. After all, he was a trader and should always be looking for opportunities. As they walked up the entry gangway, Petra went to the pilot seat but Aaron's mind was focussed on Tocmal's comment.

'How many does it need to operate?'

Petra answered. 'In reality, one can operate her. She can accommodate ten, in comfort, but can be flown by one person.'

'I noticed you assigned the ship a gender. Is it alive then?'

Aaron laughed. 'No. It's just very old human custom to give ships female gender. I don't know why...the reason's been lost in time.'

While Tocmal and Aaron were talking, Petra had initialised the ships systems. The reactor and main generator were now on line and the gravitron drive was at idle. 'We're ready Tocmal. Do you have a flight plan?'

'Yes, I had Jok-Tar transmit it to the ship...it should be in your data bank.' Petra interrogated the data bank, found the file and set the program into the nav system. She increased power to the antigrav and the ship floated off the deck, turned through 180 degrees and moved toward the wall. As they approached, a portal opened and Junior slipped out of the Eldoran cruiser.

Jok-Tar's voice sounded in Aaron's head. *Enjoy the tour; it is indeed a beautiful planet. We will join you on the surface.*

The flight path took them on a polar orbit. Both poles had large ice fields and the rest of the planet was almost familiar with continents, islands and oceans, some looking almost impenetrable, others open and green. In fact everywhere they looked green was a dominant colour.

They descended through the atmosphere, Tocmal impressed with the craft's manoeuvrability. The clouds parted and they were greeted with the vision of a very lush, almost primordial forest.

Unidentified space craft please transmit your flight approval. The voice boomed around the bridge.

'May I respond?' Tocmal asked. Aaron nodded.

'This is Admiral Tocmal on board Freebooter Trade Ship Condor Junior,' he began. 'Who am I speaking with?'

Admiral, this is captain Sodrel, commanding a flight of three interceptors. Sir, we were sent to investigate reports of unidentified craft. Now we know who it is, may we accompany you?

'That would be most welcome. Captain, form your flight up in front and flanking us. Make it a good show...we don't want to give a bad impression. We are proceeding to Zeril to inspect the damage.'

The three sleek arrow shaped ships formed up as Tocmal requested, with the lead ship forward and slightly above them, the other two flanking Junior.

Suddenly Junior lurched, the nose dipping to an alarming angle. Sirens screamed; a huge vibration slammed the ship, followed by an unmistakable boom of an explosion, then another.

Petra fought hard to bring the ship under control. 'Who's firing on us?'

Tocmal grabbed the comms. 'Captain, what is going on?' As he spoke, the starboard interceptor exploded.

Ground fire...we are taking ground fire.

'Then leave us...attack whoever is firing!' Tocmal ordered.

Aaron was working the engineering station, trying to see what damage they had sustained. Junior lurched as another explosion reverberated through the hull.

'Main power is out. Atmospheric drive is down,' he cried as he frantically tried to get the power system back on line. Junior was falling fast, their altitude now only 3,000 metres and decreasing rapidly.

'Antigrav is functional but no power. If I can re-route the battery...' his voice trailed off. Seconds flew by, altitude fell away. 'I can give you seven seconds of antigrav, but that's all I can do.'

Petra was a study of concentration. 'I think you two should strap yourselves in, this is going to be messy. What can she take?'

Aaron leapt into the second seat and initiated the safety straps. 'Structurally six G's, but I don't want to hit that hard. What's on your mind?'

'No time. Just sit back and watch your life go by.' She had managed to slow the ship slightly but at this speed they would still hit at 15 G's, way too high to survive. 1500 metres flew by–1000 metres; the ship was more stable now and under partial control, but still spinning slowly. Petra waited till they were at 250 metres before she hit the antigrav. The system energised and the ship started to respond. 'This is where it gets messy.'

With only seven seconds of power, she had no choice but to initialise the antigrav at full power. The result was like jumping off a ten story building. The sudden deceleration hit them with 12G force. The only thing that saved them was the inertial dampening system, but it couldn't sustain the energy. It failed as they passed through the 70 metre mark, the full force of their deceleration now trying to crush them in their seats.

'Forty metres ... 9G still,' Petra lowered the landing struts, hoping they could absorb some of the impact. The ship hit the ground at 7G's. The magnetic clamping system in the landing struts took a large part of the force, transferring the landing energy back to the battery, giving them a few milliseconds of power to the antigrav. That's what saved them: a few thousandths of a second additional power.

Their seats had absorbed part of the energy and, considering they had just crashed on an alien planet, they had all survived. 'Everyone ok?' Aaron asked.

Tocmal and Petra both replied that they were.

Aaron removed his straps and moved to the sensor console; nothing was working. 'Fuck,' he swore. 'We're stuck now. No power, no sensors; we're sitting ducks.' He left the console, went to the rear of the bridge and opened a section of the wall revealing a weapons store.

'I think we should be prepared. I don't think whoever shot us down is just going to leave.' He unclipped and handed a long disruptor to Petra and Tocmal as well as a blaster side arm.

Tocmal looked at the weapons as Petra gave him a quick

instruction on their operation. He smiled and turned back to Aaron. 'Do you have any more? I seem to have two appendages that have nothing to do.'

Aaron laughed and handed him two more blasters. 'Now, shall we prepare to greet the fiends who shot at us?' Tocmal left the bridge, striding purposefully towards the airlock, Petra just behind him.

Aaron shrugged and followed. 'I don't have anything better to do.'

Petra and Tocmal stopped. 'Yes you do,' Petra said. 'You know this ship better than anyone. You need to figure out how to get power back. Tocmal and I can be the welcoming party.'

Aaron was about to speak when Tocmal interrupted. 'She is correct A-Bra-Ham. We have no power, no communications and an unknown number of unfriendly creatures out there. You must do what you can to restore some power.'

Aaron knew Tocmal was right, but it still irked him. He opened another section of the wall and pulled out three small portable comm units. 'Ok, I don't like it, but I'll see what I can do. These will give you comms out there; limited range...probably no more than a couple of thousand metres...so stay close.'

They took the units; Tocmal was having some difficulty as the ear pieces were designed for humans not Reglaons. It took a few minutes but they finally jerry-rigged a way for him to use one.

Aaron strapped on his blaster and they walked to the airlock. The ship was listing heavily to port, indicating the port landing strut had either collapsed or sunk into the ground. Petra and Tocmal opened the airlock and jumped the two metres to the ground. Pieces of the strut were strewn under the port wing confirming it had collapsed.

Petra moved quickly to the rear of the ship as Tocmal headed forward.

'Captain, I'm at the rear of the ship. There's a large hole where the atmospheric drive should be...it's totally gone. The Gravitron drive seems intact but the power couplings and conduits are a mess...we need a dock to fix this. I don't think Junior is going anywhere right now.' As she finished, the two remaining Reglaon interceptors descended to inspect the damage.

Tocmal moved out from the relative cover of the ship and began waving to them. 'A-Bra-Ham, I think you should make communications your main objective...I think they are trying to tell us something.'

'Ok you two...back inside.' Aaron called as he dropped an emergency ladder out of the airlock. He left it for the others to climb aboard and went further aft, opened another storage area and pulled out a couple of items. He took these to the bridge and began pulling access panels apart.

As Tocmal and Petra entered the bridge they found him attaching two cables to the internals of the comm console. He stood, checked his work and flicked a switch on each of the units he had brought in. The comm console lit up and Aaron punched the air with a huge smile on his face. 'A couple of emergency power units; they should give us comms...for a while at least.' He motioned Tocmal to contact his ships.

'Captain Sodrel, this is Admiral Tocmal...can you hear me?' They waited for a few seconds then Tocmal repeated his call. 'Captain Sodrel...can you hear me?' Again they waited but this time Sodrel replied.

Admiral, we hear you. What is your situation?

'Captain, we have survived but the ship is badly damaged... we may need assistance to leave,' Tocmal replied.

Admiral, I suggest you leave as soon as possible. There are about twenty individuals approaching your position from the south...they do not look friendly. I estimate you have 15 minutes before they arrive.

'Then, Captain, I suggest you do something to delay them. Destroy them if you must!' Tocmal was clearly angry.

But Sir, do you know where you are?

Tocmal began talking quickly, too quickly for Aaron and Petra to accurately translate. The discussion went back and forth but finally Tocmal turned back to his companions. 'We have a huge problem. It appears we have crashed nearly three thousand metres into Lasdrik, a forest that has huge religious significance for Reglaos. I won't go into details now but we usually don't even fly over it...it is ancient and part of our culture. Sodrel only followed us after he received an official pardon from the Palace. Unfortunately, he cannot assist us as no Reglaon would *ever* do anything to cause damage to this place. Only the religiously devout come here on pilgrimage, or the conservators to make sure it is well. That tells us something.'

'What, that we're screwed?' Aaron quipped.

'No, that we are not facing twenty Reglaons, which is a good thing.' Tocmal's tone left no doubt that facing twenty natives was far worse than any other option.

Admiral, I have royal permission to bring in a recovery team...they can be here within the hour.

'One more thing Captain...has the Eldoran delegation been informed of what has happened?' Tocmal asked.

I do not know Sir, but I will find out and inform them if it has not been done. Sorry I cannot do more, Sir.

'It is of no consequence. We will just wait here to welcome our guests. I will see you later at headquarters.' Tocmal cut the comms. Aaron left the bridge and returned with another four power units. He started to disassemble the sensor console and bypass the power supply. 'A-Bra-Ham, please...we cannot use sensors in this place. We can risk no damage.'

Aaron looked up from what he was doing. 'Not even passive sensors...just environmental readings?'

'That will be acceptable...but what will environmental readings give us?'

Aaron smiled as he powered the console. 'An edge...just an edge.' The console screen slowly came to life. Aaron adjusted the sensors to improve the resolution and there on the screen they saw an infrared display, the damage to the systems making his task even harder. Finally, he managed to compensate for the damage and was able to reach out far enough to locate the impending visitors, now about five minutes away. They were making heavy going through the forest, using blasters to clear a path. 'Definitely not locals,' he speculated.

'No...vandals!' Tocmal's voice had a cold edge—he wasn't happy with what he saw. 'We need to set a perimeter and stop them!' He stood, taking a long look at the screen. 'I'll go and scout out where we can stand...it is better I do this alone...I can move faster. I shall return in a few of your minutes.' He left the bridge and went back to the airlock. Aaron and Petra watched the small creature leave. He had only moved a few feet away from the ship when he stood upright, moved his back and released a pair of very fine wings. He leapt into the air and flew quickly to one of the trees at the edge of the crash site.

'Well, that little guy is full of surprises.' Aaron exclaimed, chuckling. He noticed the approaching force had slowed considerably indicating they had run into a very dense piece of forest. Tocmal quickly returned and began telling his companions his plan. As he finished, Aaron opened the weapon store again and retrieved spare power supplies for each of their weapons. 'This should give us plenty of fire power,' he said as he handed out the packs.

'Please remember, this forest is sacred,' Tocmal pleaded as they left the ship.

Tocmal flew to his high vantage point. Petra used the port wingtip for cover and Aaron moved to the rear of the ship, taking cover behind a large rock outcrop. Thankfully, Petra had managed to crash the ship in the only clear section of the forest for many thousands of metres and the ship was at the furthest edge from the direction their adversaries were coming. Between the ship and the forest was a clear 100 metres without any vegetation, giving them a good field of fire.

The Reglaon sun was low in the sky, setting behind the ship. Aaron smiled as he thought *good, the sun will be in their eyes*.

A-Bra-Ham, how does the rock feel? Tocmal's voice clicking in the comm unit.

The question amused Aaron, but he reached up and felt the rock. 'Hot...bloody hot actually.' He was amazed at the temperature he felt emanating from its surface.

Excellent, this will hide you from any heat seekers. Man-Nix, is the wing feeling warm to you?'

Petra reached up. The sensation was strange until she realised what she was touching. 'Admiral, somehow the absorption field is still active...I can feel it just off the wing.' She smiled, understanding this would offer her a degree of protection as well as cover.

Good, we are all in position. Wait for my call before firing. Tocmal was whispering into his comm unit. *The enemy is close...they are at the edge of the clearing...be prepared.*

Aaron adjusted the sights on his weapon. The light was now very low and he could just make out the edge of the clearing. The low vision system kicked in and he could now see the field of battle clearly. At the same time, Petra selected to switch her sights to infrared; each one of the encroaching raiders was now visible. 'Captain,' she whispered, 'infrared.' The simple statement caused Aaron to switch also.

A dull thud, more like a muffled drum startled Petra. The wing above her head flared to brilliant white as an energy bolt slammed into the absorption field. She didn't flinch as she waited for Tocmal's call.

A loud explosion to the rear of the ship, this time pieces of the hull flew in all directions; still no return fire.

'Wait...they are starting to move,' Tocmal whispered.

Five shapes started cautiously towards the ship. They moved in about five metres and hit the ground. Three deafening explosions hit the ship, two on the wing and upper body, one at the rear. More parts of the hull exploded. Petra huddled lower as pieces of the hull flew around her. Five more shapes began to edge their way towards their companions; this time they moved past and hit the ground; now ten metres into the clearing.

'They're getting close Tocmal,' Petra whispered.

Just a few more seconds, ready...Petra and Aaron steadied their breathing as they took aim, Petra taking the front five and Aaron targeting the rest.

NOW!! Tocmal's voice screamed in their ears.

Petra and Aaron opened fire, their disruptors sending high energy blasts towards the enemy.

The intruders returned fire, hitting the absorption field and the large rock. The field did its job, absorbed the energy and fed it into the battery banks. Aaron's rock had no such luxury; it was being carved up. Blast after blast slammed into it, chunks flying in every direction.

But still Aaron kept up his withering fire, ducking and weaving behind the boulder, dodging energy blasts and flying debris.

Their weapons were set on maximum; enough energy in each blast to vaporise a body; every time one of the attackers was hit square on, they erupted in a fireball. Some of the assailants weren't so lucky. One, hit in the arm, just sat stunned, unable to comprehend why his arm now ended at the elbow.

Realising their vulnerability, the attackers retreated—they turned and began to run, crouched as low as they could.

A blood-curdling howl came from the forest. Petra swivelled her weapon towards the site of the sound; what she saw sent a cold shiver down her spine.

Tocmal—his hands spitting fire—was descending from his treetop perch. He fired continuously, each hand seemingly independent of the body it was attached to.

Petra moved out from behind her cover and began firing at the retreating enemy.

Aaron followed her lead. Dropping his large disruptor he drew his two blasters, firing toward the enemy. Of the ten who originally began to creep toward the ship, only two were still standing—both of these now dropped their weapons, fell to their knees and tucked their arms behind their heads.

'Petra...stop!' Aaron called. 'Cover these two.' He then proceeded through the carnage—kicking weapons away from bodies and nudging them to see if any were still alive. Only the one missing an arm and another with a nasty abdominal wound survived. 'Bring those two over here,' he ordered.

Petra complied and stood guard, watching the four as Aaron went to see how Tocmal was faring. He didn't get far before Tocmal emerged from the forest. He looked up to Aaron, his large compound eyes glowing red.

'A-Bra-Ham you are wounded.' Tocmal cried. Blood trickled down Aaron's face from a nasty gash somewhere on his scalp.

'It looks much worse than it is, didn't duck quick enough, one of those chunks of rock must have sliced it.' Aaron wiped the blood away and started to move toward the forest edge.

'No need to check, my friend...none survived.' He moved past Aaron, as Petra went back to the ship. Tocmal removed the head coverings of the four wounded.

What this revealed shocked and astounded Aaron. The body of their attackers was human but the head was almost canine. A long snout formed the top half of the mouth with two eyes set deep into the head, facing forward. The ears were also dog like, standing out from the side on the head.

'*Galdoran scum*!' Tocmal spat. 'You fools never learn. Many times you have tried to fight us and every time you have been defeated. Do you not have any brains in those ugly heads?'

Aaron moved to his friend's side. 'Tocmal, maybe you should holster some of your weapons?' Tocmal looked down to his arms—each was pointing a blaster at one of the captives. 'They may be able to give us some information... if they live.'

Tocmal looked up and shook his head. 'We Reglaons tend to be a little aggressive when provoked,' he admitted. As he holstered three of his weapons, the sound of the recovery vessel moving overhead filled the clearing. 'I would suggest that the two of you will need new uniforms,' Tocmal chuckled as he moved away. It was true; their impressive blue uniforms were now only grubby, torn rags.

'So much for making a good impression,' Petra laughed as she returned with a med kit for Aaron's wound.

13

*A*aron and Petra quickly went back into Junior to retrieve their clothes and personal effects.

The recovery effort impressed them. The Reglaon engineers only took half an hour to secure the ship and transfer it to the recovery vessel, their skill and efficiency impressing Aaron as he stood at the edge of the clearing, watching everything that was taking place.

'Do not fear, A-Bra-Ham. Our engineers will take extremely good care of your ship. She will be returned to you fully functional and in pristine condition...or they will answer to me!' Tocmal said with authority. As he spoke, the large recovery vessel started to climb away from the clearing. Another smaller craft entered the area, transitioned to vertical operation and settled gently to the ground. It was much larger than a shuttle and, as the airlock opened, they saw why. Fifty heavily armed Reglaon troops came down the access ramp and dispersed to the edge of the clearing. When they were satisfied with their dispersal, another figure emerged from the ship and came towards them, it was Jok-Tar.

'I am pleased you are alive my friends. It appears you have triumphed.' He embraced both Aaron and Petra, something Eldorans rarely did. 'Now, if you will excuse me, I wish to converse with these creatures.' He bowed slightly and walked to the Galdoran leader. Jok-Tar reached his target and kneeled down in front of him. Aaron watched as he saw the emotions change from defiance, to one of abject terror. Clearly Jok-Tar was someone this creature feared. Jok-Tar kept staring—the Galdoran becoming ever more fearful each second. Suddenly, it let out a howl that was filled with pain and terror and then it collapsed to the ground in the foetal position, where it lay whimpering.

Tocmal placed a hand on the arm of both Petra and Aaron. 'Eldorans are the most loyal and honourable friends but are equally the most ferocious enemies. We are lucky to be the former.' Aaron watched his friend gently place a hand on the top of the Galdorans' head. Instantly, the whimpering stopped and he began to regain his composure. A few minutes later, Jok-Tar rose and re-joined the group.

'That is something I never enjoy,' his voice was heavy and sad, 'but sometimes necessary. They have a ship, not far from here and only a token two sentries...such is their arrogance. We will need him to come with us, he will be compliant, but we need to proceed with haste...whoever is behind this will be waiting for answers.'

Tocmal agreed and directed the operation. He, Jok-Tar, Aaron and Petra, accompanied by five additional Reglaon soldiers, struck out from the clearing—the Galdoran captive meekly following any direction he was given. They followed the path of destruction the invaders had cut through the forest, making their progress quick and quiet. The mood of the Reglaons deepened with every damaged tree or bush they passed.

Twenty minutes later, they saw their destination. Hidden in a shallow depression was a ship. Tocmal emitted a series of whistle and clicks, unintelligible to Aaron and Petra. *Better you don't know what he said* Jok-Tar's voice sounded in their heads. Two of the soldiers moved silently away to either side of the ship, returning a few minutes later to confer with Tocmal.

'My friends report there are two sentries outside and one other Galdoran on board the ship. Jok-Tar will have his new pet call the sentries out...then we will take the ship.' Tocmal moved back to the soldiers who melted into the forest, nothing marking their passage. Jok-Tar placed his hand on the top of the Galdorans' head again, and it began to speak into a communication device on its arm.

'This is Commander Xylem...we are returning. I have wounded and need assistance.'

Yes commander, the reply broke the silence and the two sentries moved away from their posts and approached the path. They only took a few steps when two Reglaon soldiers were on them. Silently they subdued the Galdorans as a third soldier moved up the ship's gangway. There was a brilliant flash inside, Tocmal stood.

'We are clear now...follow me.'

The ship was larger than Aaron had first thought—larger than necessary for an incursion such as this. Jok-Tar and the Galdoran officer went forward to the bridge to report to the Galdorans' leader. Tocmal and three soldiers started to search the ship. Aaron was fascinated. He saw at once both remarkable similarities to human engineering, but also huge differences. They arrived on the bridge as the Galdoran finished his report and cut communications.

'We have told the superior that the mission was a success and that all of you were killed. We also mentioned that there was a larger Reglaon presence than anticipated and we need to remain concealed till that is recalled.' Jok-Tar seemed very pleased with himself. 'And I believe I know who is behind this operation. This will prove very interesting in the coming days.'

Aaron's communicator buzzed. *A-Bra-Ham, I think you need to see what we found. One of the soldiers will meet you at the airlock...have Jok-Tar bring his pet, we may need him.* Jok-Tar shrugged, motioned to the Galdoran who followed Aaron as he led the way back to the entry. They met the soldier and he led them back to a hold area. Here were six stasis pods, the same pods used back in the twelfth realm. The hairs on the back of Aaron's neck stood and a cold shiver ran down his spine. He moved to the first pod, brushing away the condensation on the clear Acrilan surface, totally unprepared for what he saw inside.

'What the......' his voice trailed to silence as he cleared more of the condensation. He moved quickly to the other pods, the same sight greeted him. Dead faces—dead human faces, twelfth realm humans. 'This isn't possible,' he said under his breath.

Tocmal was now at his side. 'They are all dead...we can find no life signs. Do you know who they are?'

'Yes, well and no. They are human, obviously, and from their clothing, they are from our realm, but what are they doing on a Galdoran ship...and on Reglaos in the tenth realm? It makes no sense.'

'You appear to recognise them...do you know them?' Tocmal's voice was firm; he wanted an answer.

'Not personally. From their clothing I know where they come from, or are supposed to. See the insignia...the skull with the letter "T"? That's the emblem of a rather pathetic group of human misfits, people we call pirates...' Aaron's voice trailed off, clearly baffled by this discovery. 'Jok-Tar, ask your friend about these.'

Jok-Tar turned to the Galdoran and soon had answers. 'I can't do much more...he will not survive it.'

Tocmal shot a withering stare at Jok-Tar. 'Do you think I care? Look at what these degenerates have done! Ask him?'

Again Jok-Tar stared into the Galdoran's eyes. It started to whimper again, then slowly it spoke to Jok-Tar, quietly, too quietly for the others to hear. Finally it let out another howl of agony and Jok-Tar broke the connection. He stood, disbelief written on his face.

'Such deception! These bodies were to be scattered over the battlefield, leaving the impression this was an incursion from the twelfth realm. The goal was to make the council believe this realm had been invaded and the twelfth's rebellion was now a direct threat here and, by implication, to all the other realms. What they did not plan for was A-Bra-Ham's ship. They were expecting your shuttle, Tocmal...and they knew your destination. You were the prize here. Humans killing the commander of Reglaos defence forces...what a message that would send!' This was the first time Aaron had seen anything like emotion from Jok-Tar. 'An elaborate, despicable plan. I am sorry my friends, I didn't believe any of the inner realms were capable of such deception.'

'Yes, I see...but how did they get these bodies?' Tocmal clicked.

Jok-Tar hesitated. 'They brought them from the twelfth realm,' he said quietly. 'It seems they have found a way to navigate through the eleventh.'

Outside, the three soldiers who had eliminated the guards were standing over the bodies of the Galdorans they had killed, each holding a long bladed knife in one of their hands. Everyone watched and, as one, the three raised their knives and sliced cleanly through their own necks, collapsing over the bodies of their victims.

Petra gasped. 'Why, Tocmal?' Her hushed voice was full of emotion.

Tocmal replied solemnly. 'To take a life in the sacred forest is unforgiveable, to the devout. They had no other choice but to take their own lives. Personally, I do not hold with these ancient superstitions, but I respect those who do.' He turned to Jok-Tar. 'Three good Reglaon soldiers sacrificed because of these things.' In his rage, his eyes were starting to change colour, becoming redder and redder each second. 'I don't care how much damage you do to this thing!' he pointed to the Galdoran. 'We must find out all we can. Jok-Tar...look outside...look what these monsters have done!

Tocmal moved away from the open hold access ramp and bowed his head as his rage subsided. 'A-Bra-Ham, please tell me what you know of these humans.'

Aaron looked at each of the pods. 'Not much. As I said before, they're pirates. They live at the edge of our galaxy, a place we call the Badlands. It's a region of space we try to avoid because of the navigation hazards...gravity wells and cosmic storms...it really is a hell hole!

'Many years ago, a Coalition officer, Darius Tragarian, led a mutiny on one of their ships. He, and others from two different worlds, stole a huge and extremely valuable cargo and disappeared into the Badlands. Since then, their numbers have grown. They are a real nuisance to any vessel in that area, but they usually don't get involved with politics. They're just criminals, living by raiding small, weak colonies and preying on freighters. They call themselves Tragarian Raiders.'

'I can see the brilliance of the plan, but I don't believe that Galdor could devise this without assistance.' Tocmal mused. 'If a group of pirates...one that doesn't have great resources...can infiltrate our realm, navigate the eleventh and kill the senior military commander on Reglaos, what message would that send to the other realms? No, this whole event...the meeting, the ambush...it has all been orchestrated and masterfully executed.' He paused and walked around each of the caskets. 'Jok-Tar, what do you think the outcome would be?'

Jok-Tar thought a while before answering. 'The council would immediately sanction action be taken against the Twelfth Realm...even approve an invasion to protect the other realms. You are correct, Galdor doesn't have the guile for this...they are just the instruments of war, puppets if you will...someone else must be the puppet master.' He paused and looked at each one of the bodies. 'Their move must come soon, probably at the council meeting tomorrow. Tocmal, how would you feel about being dead?'

Tocmal stepped back from Jok-Tar. 'What do you mean?'

'We have already told the Galdoran leader that the mission was a success. What if we have that confirmed by the palace, or a leak from one of us? Let the pieces fall, and then swoop down when the perpetrators reveal themselves.'

Tocmal thought on this. 'It might just work. A-Bra-Ham's ship has been taken to a very secure facility and only a few of our senior command know the truth...the others we can contain for a few days. Yes...this might just work.'

***

The meeting of representatives from the Inner Realms was set up in the royal audience chamber, the Reglaon Mother Queen's throne standing higher at the head of the table. Delegates began entering the chamber mid-morning, the meeting due to begin at the tenth period which—considering Reglaos had a 38 earth hour day—was quite an early start. The chamber itself was designed to impress, with high vaulted ceilings, ornately carved cornices and wood everywhere, giving it an impressive, but homely ambience.

Mondrac and Eldrac-Tar led the Eldoran delegation, with other Eldorans in the audience gallery as observers. Gradually, the seats at the table were filled with the representatives, protocol dictating there must be two from each world in attendance. In all, there would be three hundred seats filled, meaning that proceedings would be long and tedious.

Mondrac had attended many such meetings, but dreaded them all the same, with the usual pompous, long-winded speeches extolling the virtue of each delegate's home world. The political manoeuvring with alliances forming and dissipating made more for a tragic comedy than anything else. He was resigned to the fact that all they would see here was posturing—any real decisions would be made quietly behind closed doors, later.

The table was now full, except for four delegates and the Reglaon ruler. Just before the designated time, four creatures strode into the room—two Galdorans and two from Nileros. Zarof, leader of the Galdoran delegation, stood tall, his canine head held high. He strode confidently to his allotted seat and waited till the Nilerans joined him. Nilerans were humanoid and the head of the Nileran delegation was a strikingly beautiful woman. Nefaris was shorter than the Galdoran who stood back to allow her to take her seat. Her hair was black and lustrous, falling gracefully down her back. The scarlet robe she wore, encrusted with sparkling jewels was discarded as she sat down. The garment underneath was a stunning, full length gown in brilliant white. It hugged the contours of her body and every eye in the room was focussed on her.

One must give Nefaris credit; she certainly knows how to gain attention. Mondrac commented telepathically.

Eldrac-Tar nodded in agreement, i*t was a great entrance. They left no doubt as to where their allegiances lie. Sometimes that is a mistake so early in the day.*

As the tenth period was announced, the main door to the throne room opened and in walked the Mother Queen, ruler of Reglaos. She took her place at the head of the table as an attendant adjusted the comm unit for her. All eyes were now on her as three new, hooded observers quietly entered the rear of the room, unnoticed.

The Mother Queen began her speech. 'Representatives of the Inner Realms, I bid you welcome. It is under grave portents that we gather and I would rather we could meet in better times, but that is not to be. As most of you know, Reglaos has been ravaged in the incident we are all here to discuss. Several million of our people have had their lives terminated prematurely; this weighs heavily on the heart of Reglaos.' She paused, gauging the mood of the room. 'But, we are determined to find the true culprits and bring them to justice. All I charge each of you with is to seek the truth and not waver, no matter where it takes us. Again, I thank all of you for joining us and welcome you.' She was not known for long speeches and, thankfully, today was no different. 'I now open this meeting and call for the first delegate to speak.'

For the next few hours a number of delegates rose to pass their condolences and offer support to Reglaos. Mondrac was studying Zarof, the leader of the Galdoran delegation. *He is about to explode...just watch him brother.*

Eldrac-Tar shifted his gaze to the Galdoran, testing his half-brother's theory. *You are correct; the only thing keeping him in check is Nefaris. Watch as she occasionally touches his arm, very lightly...he calms immediately.*

The Mother Queen called on the Eldoran delegation to speak. Eldrac stood. 'Mother Queen, as all have said we, of Eldora, are appalled at what has transpired and we stand ready to assist Reglaos in whatever way we can. But, I counsel all here not to jump to hasty conclusions...we must seek the truth and act accordingly.'

This was too much for Zarof; he leapt to his feet and growled.

'Eldorans are weak! They would have you believe that their pets, the humans in the twelfth realm, are innocent. But we have evidence, evidence that proves conclusively that they were the perpetrators of this crime, and they have found ways of penetrating the eleventh realm. They have come to Reglaos and attacked one of your senior people... Admiral Tocmal...who they killed. Their petty war has now spilled to our realms...look!' He paused as he had images placed on the huge view screen at the far end of the table. 'Here is your proof! They shot down the Admiral's shuttle, killing him and the Human prisoners he was bringing here. They have desecrated your sacred forest and violated your customs. They must be punished!''

Here it comes, Mondrac thought.

'People of Reglaos, people of the inner realms, we must respond, we must protect our future and our homes from this aggressor. Galdor stands ready to invade and pacify these lawless criminals. All we need is assistance from Eldora to complete the task.' He stopped and glared at Eldrac-Tar.

Eldrac-Tar stood and looked at the images being shown on the screen, images showing the bodies of Aaron, Petra and most importantly, of Tocmal. The bodies were lying beside what looked to be the Admiral's personal shuttle, itself exhibiting damage consistent with having been shot down. It then panned across the bodies of the Tragarian Raiders, the perceived perpetrators of the atrocity. The images panned back again, clearly showing the faces of Aaron and Petra and the head of Tocmal. Finally Eldrac-Tar spoke, his voice heavy. 'Most disturbing images Zarof, how did you come by them?'

Zarof leapt to his feet, his voice rising in volume as he sensed victory. 'From one of your own people; it seems that, even in your own clan, there are some who do not believe you act in the best interests of the inner realms. Some who think that your obsession with Humans has gone too far, some who believe you have betrayed all we stand for.' He stopped as Nefaris reached for his arm.

'And may I ask who your informant is?'

Not even Nefaris could contain Zarof now. 'Your own offspring, Jok-Tar, he is a true friend to all in the inner realms...not a betrayer like you,' he said, spitting those last words.

Eldrac-Tar looked to the head of the table. 'Mother Queen, it appears I am being accused of treachery. Do I have your permission to defend myself?'

'There can be no defence from this, Eldoran! Your own offspring has condemned you!' Zarof screamed.

'Galdoran, you will be silent!' the Mother Queen spoke firmly. 'Or you will be removed. Eldrac-Tar, long have you been a friend of Reglaos but the evidence is damning. If you have a defence, you may proceed, but be careful.'

Zarof sat, a victorious leer spreading across his face.

'Thank you Mother Queen,' he continued pointing to the view screen. 'I agree these images are damning...I do not deny that. But I do not accept they are the truth.'

Zarof again leapt to his feet. 'Are you blind, can you not see?'

'SILENCE!' The Mother Queen shouted into the communicator. 'One more outburst and you will be removed, Zarof of Galdor!' Zarof growled but sat, seething.

'Again, my thanks,' Eldrac-Tar bowed to the head of the table. 'This image seems to show the lifeless bodies of two humans and, sadly Admiral Tocmal...everybody can see that. But is it truth? Admiral Tocmal...are you in this room?' Nefaris now had a firm grip on Zarof's arm, holding him back.

A small figure at the back of the room stood, threw back the hood on his robe and walked toward the table. 'I am indeed, Eldrac-Tar of Eldora.'

'A-Bra-Ham and Man-Nix of the Twelfth Realm...are you in this room?' Two more figures stood, removed their hoods and approached the table. The likeness to the images of the dead bodies on the screen was unmistakable.

'What is this deception? These are imposters!' Zarof was on his feet again. This time his outburst earned him a quick response from one of the royal guards and he was stunned into silence.

Eldrac-Tar faced the head of the table. 'Mother Queen, I apologise for the theatre I have just orchestrated but those images had to be discounted. To explain, I ask for your indulgence a while longer. There was indeed an attack in the sacred forest of Lasdrik but it wasn't perpetrated by any in those images,' He turned to Tocmal. 'Admiral, if you would continue.'

'Of course, Mother Queen if I may,' the regent nodded and Tocmal began. 'Yesterday we arrived in orbit. Instead of taking my own shuttle I decided it would be better if we came in the human's vessel. We followed the flight plan I had registered for my shuttle previously, to give our guests a better understanding of how Reglaos suffered. As we approached the forest, we were fired upon. The ship was badly damaged and one of our interceptors destroyed.

'Unfortunately the explosion altered our course and we crashed in a clearing in the Sacred Forest. So far, the truth and this imaginative,' he gestured to the images on the view screen, 'version are the same.' Tocmal stopped to allow the images to be studied. 'Could we please have Zarof wakened? He needs to hear this.' Tocmal waited as one of the guards, with his weapon at the ready, revived the Galdoran.

With Zarof awake, Tocmal continued, 'Now, this is where things change. According to what you see on the screen, we were attacked, and killed, by human outlaws. The truth is quite different! Here is a recording taken from the weapons we used, in our defence.' He changed the data feed and a new scene began. It showed the Galdoran attack and their defeat. The room was silent; even Zarof said nothing.

'We obtained the location of the ship they used and followed the track they had cut through the forest. Here, we found the bodies of the human raiders, already dead and in stasis. We had the force commander communicate with his superior, informing him that the plan had succeeded, but they needed more time as the Reglaon defence force was scanning the area.' There was a murmur of condemnation coursing around the room; Tocmal sensed he had the room's undivided attention.

'We staged those images Zarof had; we also took the time to bring the bodies of the dead and the survivors back.' The main doors opened and the four survivors were led in together with sixteen stasis pods. 'We were forced to leave three Galdoran bodies and three of our own at the scene. Three of our soldiers killed the Galdorans and felt honour-bound to terminate their own lives, as is the ancient religious tradition.' Tocmal's voice was filled with sadness as he indicated to Eldrac-Tar to continue.

'Mother Queen, while the criminals here are obviously Galdoran, we do not believe they acted alone. Information we have indicates that Galdor and their ally have found a way to breach the Eleventh Realm...that is how they transported the bodies here. At this stage, we do not have the identity of the other conspirators, but we have our suspicions.' He paused looking long and hard at Nefaris.

'We also have conclusive evidence that the subspace

breach was not entirely the fault of the Twelfth Realm. We will need further investigation, but we believe that the major part of the energy released was generated here, in the Tenth Realm...meaning there was an attack from within.' His assertion brought a gasp of horror from some of the delegates.

'We will, of course, make this data available to all here but we ask the council's approval to continue our investigation.' There was a murmur of approval from the table. 'I ask A-Bra-Ham, representative of the Twelfth Realm, to speak, if you are agreeable Regent of Reglaos.' Again, the Mother Queen nodded her approval.

Aaron stood and looked round the room at the many different species, humanoid and non-humanoid, gathered together for a common purpose.

'Delegates I am humbled to address you. All the peoples of the Twelfth Realm are very young when we compare ourselves to you, young and brash...full of curiosity and thirsty to learn. Not long ago, my people, Humans, thought that our world was flat and that there was nothing in space. Now, we travel to the stars in our realm. We have discovered that there are many different species in our own realm, and now we are privileged to be here with you.

'We are not perfect, we do make mistakes. But, I assure you of this...if the problem is in our realm, we will fix it. We can't do that alone. As we have just seen, others in the inner realms have played a part in this tragic incident. All I ask is that we work together to ensure this never happens again! Mother Queen...delegates...I thank you for allowing me to speak.' Aaron finished and resumed his seat.

The Mother Queen stood, studying the two Galdoran delegates. 'Delegates of Galdor, how do you explain this treachery?' she demanded.

Zarof stood, brushing aside the guard's weapon. 'Galdor explains nothing!' he said defiantly. 'If these events happened, as the Eldorans' *pet* says, then these are rebels and will be dealt with by Galdor. But I do not believe a word the Human says. Galdor is free and we will roam wherever and whenever we choose.'

'Zarof of Galdor, you are gravely mistaken. These rebels, as you call them, have committed crimes on Reglaos, crimes that will be investigated and punished on Reglaos, not Galdor,' the Mother Queen fired back.

Zarof said something unable to be translated, kicked his chair out of the way and started walking toward the door but was stopped by royal guards. Nefaris stood and confronted the Mother Queen. 'Mother Queen, you cannot detain any delegate...the Protocol of Intercession forbids it. Remove your guards...we are leaving.' She left the table and joined Zarof.

The Reglaon Regent left her chair and walked to Nefaris. 'Yes, the rules guarantee your safety and you are free to leave, but hear this...if any Galdoran or Nileran vessel enters this realm without our permission, we will call it an act of war and both of you know only too well what that means!' Though shorter than them, she still had an intimidating presence.

'Careful insect...do not make threats you cannot support!' Zarof spat.

'Galdoran, I make no threats. I simply state fact. Now leave!'

As the door closed behind Zarof and Nefaris the Mother Queen returned to the table, resumed her seat and addressed the meeting. 'My friends thank you for coming so far. It is unfortunate that things have transpired as they have...a most disagreeable business. Let us continue.'

The meeting carried on for a few more hours, with resolutions and counter resolutions being put forward on a number of items. One overriding concern was the possibility of Galdor being able to traverse the Eleventh Realm, something everyone looked to Eldora to solve.

***

Petra and Aaron were installed in an apartment in the Eldoran Embassy and were more than grateful for finally being able to rest. It had been nearly sixty hours since either of them had had slept. One common thread that Aaron had found with most humanoid species was the need for cleanliness. The Eldorans were no different.

The apartment came complete with a large bath that could probably hold four, or more. Neither of them had enough energy to even fill the thing, so they settled for a quick shower and retired. Then they slept peacefully until the sound of someone knocking on their door woke them. Aaron rose, donned a robe and opened the door. One of the embassy attaches was there with an invitation for them to join the Ambassador and the delegation for breakfast in half an hour. She also indicated that a selection of fresh clothing had been placed in their room. Before she left, she gave Aaron directions to the dining area.

Aaron returned to the sleeping quarters. 'How do you feel?' he asked Petra as he opened one of the cupboards to check the clothes that had been supplied.

She groaned, sat up and looked at him. 'Like I just fought twenty Galdorans...what about you?

'Not much better, but...duty calls. We have been invited to take breakfast with the Ambassador so you better get your arse into gear...we only have about twenty minutes. Here, check the wardrobe, they left us some clothes.' Aaron was already on his way to the shower.

From the wardrobe, Aaron chose a pair of grey trousers, blue shirt and a pair of fine leather loafers. Petra took a bit longer. She tried on a couple of outfits before deciding on practicality—denim jeans, white tee shirt and joggers. Now ready, they left the room, arriving on the terrace just as Jok-Tar and his sibling were sitting down.

'Welcome Man-Nix, A-Bra-Ham. I trust you rested well?'

'Very well, thank you,' Petra answered. They were joined by Eldrac-Tar, Mondrac and the Ambassador Goldoc-Mul. To Aaron's surprise, breakfast was more human than he thought possible; bacon, eggs and toast, with a variety of spreads and a hot drink, similar to tea. The conversation was mainly about recent events and how to respond, with Eldrac-Tar putting forward a number of alternatives which he suggested he and Aaron discuss later.

'A-Bra-Ham, you seem a little pre-occupied. May I ask what is concerning you?'

"Yeah, I'm in a bit of a quandary. Ever since we met your race, we have considered you to be somewhat different. We looked at you in awe, almost reverence. You seemed so far more advanced as to be almost god like. Yet here we are, enjoying a very human meal together.'

Jok-Tar was looking furtively toward Aaron. Finally he spoke. 'My sire, I think we need to discuss this with A-Bra-Ham and Man-Nix.' Eldrac-Tar nodded and indicated for Jok-Tar to continue. 'A-Bra-Ham, I believe we have a misunderstanding between us. Your initial assumption was that we are not really humanoid. The general consensus of your people is that we existed in a non-corporeal form, however, as you now can see, we are most definitely flesh and bone just as you are. A-Bra-Ham, please accept our apologies for allowing this misconception to progress...we should have stopped it immediately.

'Throughout human history, there have been interferences by some far less altruistic beings, two of whom you met at the meeting. Galdor and Nileros have interacted with your race a number of times, and always purely for their own benefit. Now, it seems, they wish to repeat their past but more directly. You must take this threat as real and significant! If these two races have found a way to traverse the Eleventh Realm, then you, and your realm may be in mortal danger.' He stopped and looked to his sire.

'As my offspring has said, we regret not clearing this issue before but, the threat from invasion seemed to be real. Your realm must take this seriously or else face total subjugation.' Eldrac-Tar's voice conveyed the gravity of the situation.

Aaron smiled as he replied. 'I agree, while our perception of Eldorans was confused, what we now face is almost unbelievable, and that will be our greatest challenge... getting others to believe, before it is too late.'

'That will be your task when you return, for now we have other matters to address,' Mondrac began. 'Today, Tocmal will take you to your ship so you can see their progress. This afternoon, the Mother Queen has requested your presence. Evidently, she wants to become better acquainted with you. While this is happening, I will have a discussion with our prisoners. There are many things I need to understand before we can move forward.'

The discussion continued for another half hour, with Eldrac-Tar telling them a message had been sent to Grainger explaining why they wouldn't be back in time to meet with him. They also asked that he postpone any action till Aaron and Petra returned with more information.

Petra only half listened to the conversation—most of her attention was focused on the patio and garden. The structure reminded her of images she had seen from ancient Earth civilisations; heavy marble columns, very high ceilings and terrazzo floors. The garden was very similar to the one at Orange, formally laid out with many plantings that seemed familiar.

'You are interested in our garden?' Goldoc-Mul asked.

'Yes, it feels very familiar, Mister Ambassador.'

'That is because it was designed from images of many gardens on Earth. We Eldorans may have reached the pinnacle of our development, but we lost so much on the way. We have no art, no music and most certainly no gardens like this. Our contact with Freebooters has inspired us, something we are eternally grateful for. You will see this for yourself, when you eventually come to Eldora.' Goldoc-Mul sat back, allowing his guest the freedom to enjoy the scene. An aide entered and informed them that Admiral Tocmal had arrived. Petra and Aaron stood, thanked the ambassador for his hospitality and left with the aide.

14

*T*he damage to Junior was extensive. Aaron's heart sank as he surveyed his ship. 'I doubt if she'll ever fly again,' he said sadly.

'Nonsense...we'll have her ready to take you home in four days!'

'Come on Tocmal, that's not possible. Just look at how much work is required.' The rear section had already been cut away, the atmospheric drive completely destroyed, all the power couplings and conduits to the Gravitron drive were either badly damaged or destroyed. Add to this the structural issues that would now appear and Aaron couldn't see any option but to scrap her.

'A-Bra-Ham, I do not lie. If I say she will be ready in four days...that is what *will* transpire.' He sounded hurt by Aarons' lack of faith.

'If you say so, then I must accept it,' Aaron agreed despondently.

'Good, that is settled! Now, what to do for the next few days? I can't let you stay at the embassy all the time...that would be improper.' Tocmal thought for a while. 'I have a domicile away from the cities. After the reception this afternoon, we shall go there, if you agree. You will find it a most relaxing experience.' Once this was settled, they continued with their inspection.

The Reglaon engineers had managed to reverse-engineer the Acrilan composite used for the exterior of Junior. Whole sections were now in production and would be fitted just as soon as agreement on the atmospheric drive was reached.

The chief engineer, a female named Hallak, had examined the details of the old unit and suggested she could fit a Reglaon unit in its place. Aaron agreed and the final specifications were confirmed.

The Gravitron drive was another area of interest as with all its couplings gone it was just so much wasted space. Hallak assured them that the standard Reglaon drive would be more efficient than the original. Finally, Tocmal led them to another lab; here he had two sections of Acrilan from the ship.

He handed Aaron a blaster and asked him to fire at the sheet of composite. Reluctantly Aaron obeyed. The result was as expected with the Acrilan exploding. Next, Tocmal asked him to fire on the second sheet, again Aaron complied. This time, nothing happened, the blast seemed to somehow dissipate. Unable to believe his eyes, Aaron fired a second blast, this time at full power, and the result was still the same.

'A-Bra-Ham, this is coated with the resin I told you about.' Tocmal explained. 'We use it on all our space ships...that's what makes them so hard to destroy. Unfortunately for the pilot the other day, we do not do the same for atmospheric craft. With your permission, we will apply a coating of this to your ship.'

With the results he had just seen, Aaron agreed enthusiastically. They left Hallak to get on with the job of rebuilding Junior. 'As we have some time till we must be at the palace, I would like to show you something.' Tocmal announced as he entered his shuttle.

They left the orbiting repair dock and headed back to the planet. Tocmal took a different route, still heading toward the city he wanted to show them—Zeril. It had suffered most and had almost been completely destroyed. The remains of the city gave the impression that it had been large and open. Some of the buildings that had survived were elegant and thoughtfully designed to complement, not dominate, the surrounding, something humans still had problems achieving. Throughout the rubble there were Reglaons, digging desperately, trying to find lost family members, a sight that Aaron and Petra would never forget.

Tocmal's voice was heavy with sadness as he spoke. 'Over 7 million of my people perished here, and for what? We still have no idea of the purpose of all this destruction and death. If we were at war I could understand it, but we are not. A-Bra-Ham, do you have any idea as to the purpose for this?' He cast his arms wide to encompass all they saw before them.

Aaron shook his head. 'Sadly my friend, I don't. I can think of no reason for this or what purpose it might serve. I also can't see how the blast in our realm could possibly cause all this...it just wasn't strong enough.'

'It was not. We know that this destruction was caused by energy released in this realm, not yours. Like you, we have our suspicions and no evidence...but it is clear that both explosions were connected, but how is still a mystery.' Tocmal said as he turned the shuttle away from the devastated city.

Fifteen minutes later, they approached a mountainside. As they got closer, the side opened and they flew into a tunnel which led to a massive cave, revealing thousands of large space ships. Tocmal guided the small craft into a vacant dock space. The three disembarked and Tocmal led them to a viewing platform.

'This is a secret few have ever seen. Our defence forces are vast. We have many thousand fighting vessels and the crews to man them. Many have been deployed and soon many more will follow. We believe we know who the aggressor is and we will not be caught waiting for them to attack again.' As they continued the tour, Aaron and Petra were staggered by the scale of the operation. Finally, Tocmal guided them back to the shuttle and they left for the palace.

The reception was in two parts. Firstly Aaron, Petra and Tocmal were invited to a private audience with the Mother Queen. Without the usual attendants that always accompanied the Regent, the meeting was relaxed and informal. After two hours many issues had been discussed; the most important being the establishing of permanent ties between the two realms. It was also agreed that when they returned, Tocmal should accompany them. His standing on Reglaos, his grasp of recent events and inner realm politics would be invaluable in establishing the relationships needed. The second part was the official reception. The huge hall where the council had met was now being utilised as an informal reception hall.

As with any function back in the Twelfth Realm, this was an opportunity for political posturing and grandstanding. Aaron and Petra were the centre of attention; most delegates vied for their people and planet to be in a favourable position when the eventuality of inter-realm trade was realised. Luckily, this was Aaron's forte and he played it as a master. The opportunities were everywhere and Aaron was in a position now to be able to take advantage of the many opportunities opening up. His years of negotiating trade deals were evident and impressed those who spoke with him. Although he could see the possibilities for his own companies, he also saw immense potential for all in his realm. The Mother Queen gave him the title of Twelfth Realm Ambassador and, although this was completely unofficial, all other delegates approached him as such.

After four hours of meeting and greeting, both Aaron and

Petra were exhausted and thankful when Tocmal took them aside.

'I think it is time to make a tactical retreat,' he chuckled as he led his companions through the melee. They had reached the side of the room, close to the exit, when the Regent called everyone's attention. Graciously she thanked everyone for their attendance and wished them all well; the reception was over. Tocmal almost dragged Aaron and Petra out the door and straight into his shuttle. 'If we had not made it here now, you would probably not get out for many hours.' Tocmal chuckled again as the shuttle rose into the air.

The flight to his country residence took them over some of the most beautiful scenery Petra had ever seen. 'Tocmal, your planet looks like it is uninhabited. The forests appear to be virgin territory. How many live on Reglaos?'

Tocmal chuckled. 'Many billions, in your terms...you need to understand our history. Initially we evolved from a swarm creature. Our ancestors lived in caves and built large communal domiciles...you would call them hives. The legend of the sacred forest tells us that that was the place where our forebears were granted the power of reason...that's why it is so revered. While most Reglaons have a degree of faith, only a few are devout, but our social structure has not changed greatly...we still have our Regent.

'Eons ago she would have been the only breeding female. Each colony or hive had a queen. Thankfully we have evolved past that, but the social and political structure is still reminiscent of then. We have many underground cities...it is a favoured lifestyle in our society...as well as a number of above ground cities, as you have seen. Very few know our true numbers or strength, and we prefer it that way. The only issue we have ever had is with Galdor. Even though they are in a different realm, they still covet what we have. They have tried to subdue us a number of times and have been defeated each time. Some creatures never learn, no matter how painful the lessons become.'

As he finished he began to descend, finally landing on a pad in the centre of a clearing. He completed his power-down sequence, opened the main airlock and led them out. They followed a trail that seemed well worn, up a small hill and stopped above an idyllic stream.

'This is so beautiful,' Petra gasped.

'Yes, it is beautiful, but I advise two things: don't go into the stream; and always carry a blaster...this forest has some very large and hungry predators. Humans would bring a welcome change to their diet.' Tocmal turned and led them back to the shuttle pad.

At the front of the pad was a door, so cleverly concealed that it was almost invisible. He opened the door and allowed his companions to enter. Sounds were coming from further in the domicile. 'Excellent...that will be my mate. She has taken time to be with us.' He carefully closed the door behind them explaining, 'We don't want any unwelcome guests.'

Tocmal led them through the structure. It was much taller than either had expected and Aaron asked why.

'Simple...we are flying creatures and the height of the roof allows us to stretch our wings when the mood takes us.' He looked at Aaron, as if sharing some secret. Aaron's stunned expression caused Tocmal to stop. He beckoned Aaron down to his level and whispered, 'It is essential...Reglaons mate on the wing.'

They finally reached what Aaron took for a sitting area; here they met Tocmal's mate, Saddari. Reglaons can't sit, their physical structure made this impossible. Instead they utilised an elevated couch making their final rest position close to 60^0 to the horizontal with their upper body supported by the device. Thankfully, Tocmal had some human-like chairs that proved to be very comfortable. With the introductions completed, they settled into to the business of relaxing, something they all desperately needed after the recent events.

Saddari offered them some wine. Eldrac-Tar had, according to her, made the suggestion. It was a soft red and quite enjoyable as the conversation drifted around. She was an artist with many commissioned works hanging in cultural spaces in a number of Reglaon cities. There were even some scattered in the domicile. To Aaron and Petra they were stunning, landscapes and images of natural beauty of the planet.

Saddari had also taken time to learn about human food and while it was very different to theirs, she had brought in the necessary ingredients to make a human meal. She and Petra decided to work together on this as Aaron and Tocmal seemed comfortable in their discussions. A call from the palace informed them that unfortunately Aaron and Petra would have only the next day free; such was the eagerness of delegates to meet with them.

The next morning Tocmal suggested they take a walk in the forest, also insisting that they carry weapons. His warning was taken seriously, some sounds they heard were reminiscent of large predators on Argos.

'One thing I do notice,' Petra spoke as they stood on a hill behind the domicile site, 'is the almost total lack of intrusion. Reglaons seem to take extraordinary measures to preserve the natural sanctity of the planet.'

Saddari answered. 'We do. We have seen many other worlds where this hasn't been done and, as a species, we take the preservation of our planet very seriously.'

'Then Humans could learn much from you. When you eventually come to the Twelfth Realm, we will show you what damage we have done, and just how much we could benefit from your philosophy,' Aaron replied.

The time went far too quickly and it felt like only a few hours later that Tocmal and Saddari were accompanying them back to the city. The next three days were a blur, with endless meetings from daylight till deep into the evening.

The opportunities for trade completely staggered Aaron. While no commitments were formed, agreements to discuss mutual opportunities were made for their next visit.

Finally, word came that the repairs to Junior had been completed. Everyone assembled at the Eldoran embassy to finalise plans to leave. It was decided that Mondrac should accompany them as well as Tocmal—his expertise in inner-realm politics could prove invaluable.

The discussions with the prisoners had yielded much intelligence and Tocmal quickly returned to the defence ministry to brief his subordinates, the others remaining at the Embassy awaiting his return.

'A-Bra-Ham, what do you know of portals?' Mondrac asked.

'No idea...it means nothing to me. Why?'

'The prisoners told us that the energy released in this realm was a failure of their portal. They believe that a surge of energy, from the *other side,* caused a catastrophic overload resulting in the damage here. Do you know what they mean?'

Petra broke in. 'Aaron, remember the old Exodus Gateways? Some called them portals.'

He nodded and turned to Mondrac. 'In the early days,

Humans developed huge structures that generated worm holes. They used these Exodus Gates, as they were called, to send colonists to distant worlds. Most have now been dismantled, though I think there are half a dozen still in existence. They're mainly used for large non-time-critical freight operations.'

'That fits with what the prisoners said. Possibly Tocmal's people will solve the mystery...he is sending a ship to investigate. Now to your ship...it is complete and the Reglaons have improved a number of systems. We have installed the navigation data to allow you to transit the Eleventh Realm. Use it wisely my friend, only Eldorans have had this until now,' Mondrac's tone warned Aaron he was serious.

When Tocmal returned, Aaron, Petra and Mondrac joined him on his shuttle. They made the short journey back to the repair dock to find Junior completely renovated, with nothing to indicate she had sustained any damage. The only noticeable difference was the colour change. Gone was the polished silver hue—Junior was now a mid-blue colour, a by-product of the molecular fusing between Acrilan and the Reglaon resin.

As he walked around his ship, Aaron was amazed at the skill displayed by the Reglaon engineers. He was joined by Hallak who gave him a complete rundown on the repairs. Several systems had been upgraded. Because the drive system was now completely different, a short test flight was essential. The results were far better than Aaron had ever expected. Before, Junior had only a maximum displacement factor of 15; now that had been increased to 28. The weapons systems had also been tuned and augmented; Aaron was impressed by the amount of work they had carried out in such a short period of time.

On their return to the dock Aaron and Petra thanked the engineering team for their amazing workmanship; then made themselves comfortable while they waited for Tocmal to arrange the necessary clearances for departure. As usual with bureaucratic formalities, the process took much longer than Tocmal had anticipated. His mood was foul when he finally returned with the clearance. He was clicking and buzzing so furiously that no one even needed to translate.

Shortly after the 17th period they finally cleared the dock and headed for the outer mark of the Reglaon exosphere, a full two hours later than planned. As soon as the mark was reached, Petra programmed the displacement drive and they slipped quietly into their worm hole. Six hours later they reached the optimum location and prepared to jump to the Eleventh Realm.

Aaron was operating the sensor console when he noticed something wasn't right. 'Wait, don't do anything yet! Tocmal, can you have a look at this?' Tocmal joined him and together they poured over the readings.

'It makes no sense...the Mother Queen told them what would happen. To so blatantly ignore her is unacceptable. Mondrac, please verify A-Bra-Ham's readings.'

Aaron switched the sensor to the Bubble, something Tocmal hadn't seen previously. The Bubble formed and the sensor readings converted into a holographic image.

Mondrac shook his head and a great sadness seemed to descend upon him. 'I confirm your readings...those are indeed Galdoran vessels.'

'Petra, raise shields and power up the weap-'

'Wait, A-Bra-Ham!' cried Tocmal. 'They have not seen us yet. If we suddenly increase the energy output, they will! As good as this vessel is I do not desire to tackle four to prove it! I suggest a slow build up, that way they will not be alerted to our presence.'

Aaron nodded and the process of slowly bringing the weapons and shields on line began.

'Also, there is something else you need to know.' Tocmal moved away from the sensor console and over to comms. 'We discovered something incredible when we gave your ship our resin cover. When it bonded with the Acrilan base a strange phenomenon occurred. We found that the molecular bond actually diffused any sensors and, more importantly, reflected and refracted light. The result is that at this level the ship is invisible to our sensors and yours, as well as being very hard to detect visually onscreen.

'If those Galdoran scum perform sensor sweeps, they will see nothing. Slowly building our power will help keep us undetected. I think we should move closer and have a look at what they are hiding...see what that thing is.' He pointed to a large, indistinct object in the Bubble, approximately 500,000 kilometres away.

The four ships were positioned to form a defensive line around it. While he was speaking, Tocmal was working at the comms console. Once he completed his task, he looked up. 'There, I have sent a short message to Reglaos, giving them the coordinates and disposition of our friends. It will take several hours before any assistance arrives, so we should be careful.'

Junior continued its advance, slowly increasing power to the weapons systems. Their goal was to discover what these four ships were protecting as they crept nearer, trusting their new capabilities would cover their sneaky approach. Their track was taking them closer to one of the sentry ships, passing within 20,000 kilometres of it. Their momentum had reached 50,000 KPH and Tocmal indicated that this should be enough. Petra reduced power to the drive and

Junior now coasted towards their goal with Aaron keeping a discrete distance, weapons locked on the Galdoran vessel.

'I'm getting some weird readings from that structure... massive radiation leakage from something.' They crept closer still, the Galdoran sentry now falling behind.

'A-Bra-Ham, what is the range of your visual scanner?' Mondrac asked.

'Good point, we should be able to get a reasonable look at this thing now.'

The view screen changed, beginning to focus on the point in space that the sensors indicated. The image was still slightly fuzzy as Aaron worked to enhance it. Then it appeared clearly on the screen.

'What the..?'

They were all staring at the large image before them.

It was a huge ring hanging in space. Part of it seemed to have been torn, or blown off, by some cataclysmic event, leaving less than half of it intact, but that was enough for him to identify it.

Suddenly an alarm started to scream; Aaron worked furiously at the sensor console.

'Petra...all stop!'

She immediately complied and the ship decelerated to a standstill.

Aaron kept working at the console. 'Bullshit,' he exclaimed, 'this can't be right!'

'What can't be right?' Petra asked.

'The radiation...it's Trisidic.' He looked to Tocmal and Mondrac. 'Does anyone here use Trisidium as a power source?'

They both shook their heads and Mondrac replied. 'No-one, A-Bra-Ham. We know all too well the dangers of that mineral. It is banned throughout the inner realms.'

'We need to get out of here, the radiation level is increasing. Whatever happened here was massive, Petra, reverse course...now!'

Petra started to comply when Tocmal pointed to the Bubble. The main sensor feed was still directed to it and showed that two of the four sentry ships had left their posts and were heading toward Junior's position. 'Mondrac, can we jump here?' she asked.

'No, the optimum point is where that structure is... we need to go to the alternative.' He consulted the nav system and sent the coordinates to Petra. 'Unfortunately, that is where we must go.'

'Crap,' Petra swore under her breath. 'That means we need to pass the sentry ships again!'

'I do not believe they have detected us as yet...study their course,' Tocmal said as he watched the Bubble. 'A-Bra-Ham, can you enhance this sector?' Aaron switched the scale of the Bubble. Now it displayed a much smaller range, giving them very good tracking of the sentry ships' course.

'Track them...but we can't leave.' Aaron began prepping a drone. 'We need to get a closer look at that thing.'

'Aaron, fire that probe and they'll know where we are,' Tocmal warned.

'I know, but we have to,' he replied as he launched the drone. 'Petra...manual control...show us some of the fancy flying Kate saw. Mondrac, please man the sensor console and record all the data from the probe.' Aaron was now in the command chair. 'Petra, just keep flying...I'll take a shot when I can. They'll still be firing blind...the only time they'll get a bead on us is when we fire.'

'The other two have changed course,' Tocmal added.

'Ok, time to even the odds. Petra new course, two-one-zero by one-one-seven…now!'

Petra threw the ship onto the new heading.

'Increase power two thirds.'

Again Petra complied. Junior responded instantly, her speed increasing rapidly.

'New course, two-two-five by zero-nine-zero.'

Again the small craft responded and as it assumed its new heading, Aaron fired two torpedos at the nearest sentry ship. Without waiting to see the result, Aaron called. 'New course one-four-zero by one-one-four, power back to one third.' Petra swung Junior to the new heading, reducing power at the same time.

Aaron fired another two torpedos at the second ship. Junior suddenly shuddered violently. 'Looks like they found us…no damage, the absorption screen took the blow.' Aaron called. 'Petra, give me control, I need you on the engineering station.' She switched all ship control from the pilot chair to command, leaping to the engineering console a she did so.

Much better Aaron thought as he started to fly Junior. There were now only three ships searching for them, the only indication of the first sentry ship was a dissipating ball of energy. 'Well, we got one, Mondrac. How's the data coming?'

'I am recording everything, but the drone is experiencing difficulties.'

"I thought it might…too much radiation. Tell me when it fails completely, and we'll bug out.' As he spoke, Aaron threw Junior into a very tight climbing turn to the left, dropping power to almost zero.

Two enemy torpedos flew over Junior, barely missing her; Aaron despatched these with the lateral blasters. That gave the Galdorans another clue to their location.

Two ships fired as one and Junior was slammed off course,

spinning out of control.

Aaron fought the controls, desperate to regain command of his ship, alarms screamed and the main view screen blacked out. Petra's hands flew over the engineering console, interrogating alarms and re-initialising systems. Slowly Junior started to respond.

'Nasty bastards, let's see if you like this!' He threw the ship into a new heading, firing all four forward torpedos. The new course quickly brought his rear tubes to bear and again opened fire.

The Galdoran sentry ships tried desperately to dodge the torpedos, but this gave Aaron the chance he wanted. His forward disruptor bank was fully charged and he fired it as the first sentry zigged away from the torpedos. But the Galdoran turned the wrong way—the blast from the disruptor slammed into it tearing a huge portion of the hull away.

'Two down...now things are a bit more even!' Aaron yelled.

'A-Bra-Ham, the drone has ceased operation,' Mondrac's voice, boomed over the bridge.

'Ok, let's get out of here! Petra, what's our status?'

"All systems green. Disruptors and blasters at full capacity but we only have six torpedos left.' As she spoke, the Bubble flashed again, indicating that the third Galdoran ship had become another victim of the torpedos.

'Only one left,' Aaron mused as he searched for the last vessel. He found it, racing away at maximum acceleration. 'Number one, take the con and set course for our next insertion point.'

Petra left the engineering console and resumed control of the ship. She changed course, brought Junior to the new heading and increased power to maximum cruise. Aaron was now at Mondrac's side, pouring over the data the drone had sent back. He fed the data into the computer and started a modelling program.

'This'll take a while, but it should give us a good idea of what that was.' He turned to Tocmal, 'My friend, what you have done to my ship it's amazing. They had no true indication of where we were and the disruptors...they were at least twice as effective. What did your engineers do?'

'Their job A-Bra-Ham, just their job.'

'Well, they did a fantastic job. Thank you,' Aaron replied, gratefully.

'I have just sent another message to Reglaos notifying them of what we found. The radiation will be an issue for everyone. I think we can assume that structure was the source of the devastation caused to our planet. Damn the Galdorans!' Tocmal was very angry; his eyes were beginning to glow again.

Fifteen minutes later, Junior reached the alternate insertion point for the jump to the Eleventh Realm. Petra initiated the drive, programmed the coordinates and they jumped out of the Tenth Realm.

***

The transit between the two realms would take an hour. The computer was still crunching data and, for the moment, there was little else to do. Aaron and Petra completed their check of the ship and found no damage, other than some loosely stored items that had now been flung around in various spaces.

They stopped at the lounge, brewed both coffee and tea before returning with these to the bridge. Mondrac and Tocmal were grateful for the refreshment and all sat, deep in their own thoughts while they drank.

The silence was broken by the chime from the computer, signalling that the modelling program had finished. Aaron moved the few steps to the console. He stood there, rigid, looking at what the system had compiled, disbelief showing in his expression.

'This is not possible,' he grumbled as he interrogated the system further. 'It can't be!'' He continued to work the keyboard, trying to find an answer.

'What's up?' Petra asked as she reached his side.

"Look at it…the simulation must be wrong…it just can't be here.'

Petra watched as he kept working, Mondrac and Tocmal now standing with her. Aaron used the program to compare the model it had generated with any known objects in the data base. Petra checked the timer; they still had half an hour till reinsertion.

The computer chimed again. Aaron looked at the screen, shaking his head. 'It must be wrong, there's no other explanation.'

"A-Bra-Ham, what is troubling you?' Tocmal asked.

'The results from the data we collected.' He transferred the images to the main screen. 'This is what we saw, plus the additional data from the drone.' An image of the severely damaged structure now appeared on the screen. Aaron worked his pad again, sending new commands to the computer. 'This is the simulation the modelling program came up with. It has taken the data and recompiled it into what is the most probable object.'

The next image showed a completely circular construction, 3,000 metres in diameter. Attached to it were a number of other objects of varying sizes. The outer ring was solid, but inside this was a translucent ring and in the centre, nothing. It was a 2,500 metre hole.

'Aaron, are you sure the data is correct?' Petra asked.

Aaron nodded. 'Yes, I've checked it three times. My friends; what you are looking at is an old exodus gate, or something very much like it. What it's doing here is anybody's guess... it's beyond me.'

Mondrac stood staring at the screen. 'A-Bra-Ham what is the function of the structure?'

'Back when we started to leave Earth, we used the gates to generate and focus a worm hole. In those days, our computing systems weren't good enough to build a ship with displacement drive. The gates were used for a long time, until we perfected the bio/chemical systems. I just don't understand...there is no need for it to be here. You have always had bio computers...you didn't need things like this.'

'Not for normal travel.' Mondrac turned back to the group. 'But consider this...to traverse the Eleventh is a very complex task, full of problematic areas. Even we Eldorans cannot move through the realms without traversing each ... we cannot jump past a realm. But, what would happen if you had these "gates", as you call them, one here and one in your realm, focused on each other. What would that do?'

Aaron saw where his thoughts were going and, although he didn't like the possibility, he had a cold feeling in his gut that Mondrac was right. He set to work again with the modelling software. This time he delved deep into the navigation data the Eldorans had placed in his system. Finally he stood back.

'Now we let it do its job. If I'm correct, the scenario should show where the sister unit will be located in the Twelfth.'

As they stood waiting, the reinsertion alarm sounded and Junior rematerialized in the Eleventh Realm. Petra activated the Eldoran navigation system and the ship changed course. While technically they could jump into the next realm now, it would result in them re-entering nowhere near where they needed to be. It was essential they navigate through this realm till they reached the optimum point to jump, and that was going to take nearly twenty hours.

The computer finished its work and Aaron sent the results to the main screen. Each gate constructed was unique; slight differences in design, small variances in construction—a myriad of things that made them all different.

The program identified this one as EG 132, currently designated as 'functional but not operational.' It was supposed to be in the Dogra system, attached to the Cordova Corporation for transporting the minerals being mined there. The information showed that the operation had ceased twenty years previously and the gate was put into care and maintenance.

'This makes no sense. How did it get here?' Aaron asked.

Mondrac replied. 'A-Bra-Ham, if I may use your computer I may be able to devise a workable hypothesis. It will take time, so I suggest you and Man-Nix retire. Tocmal can monitor the ship while I work. We will wake you if anything changes.'

Aaron looked over to Petra. She did look tired and he too was feeling the effects of the last few days, but he still didn't want to leave.

Petra solved his crisis. 'Aaron, we still have eighteen hours before we jump for the Twelfth...the ship is on an automatic flight plan, so there is very little we can do. Let Mondrac work...we both need to rest.' She was right, but he still didn't like it.

'Ok, we'll take a few hours...call me if anything changes,' he said as they left the bridge.

Aaron's quarters were very well appointed, as was the rest of the ship. They consisted of a lounge area, a dining area, bedroom, bathroom and a kitchen.

'First a shower...then a meal and then bed,' Petra groaned as she walked through the room.

'You can have a shower, but I am hanging for a long soak.'

'You have a tub?'

Aaron smiled as he opened the bathroom door. 'You could call it that.' He reached to a panel on the wall, entered a code and part of the floor started moving.

Petra moved past him and there before her eyes was a spa, large enough to hold two people. She turned and gave him an evil smile. 'I bet this could tell some stories if it could talk.'

Aaron walked past her with a smirk, opened the control console and started filling the tub.

'I can't believe this! What about the water?' Water, the most precious and essential commodity on a space ship was never wasted. To use so much to take a bath seemed extremely decadent. 'I've never heard of anything like this on any other ship. And you have one on your yacht?'

'Yes and an even bigger one on Condor. The water isn't wasted...it's continuously recycled. Most cabins have a bath as well as a shower...depends on crew preference...but as far as I'm concerned ion showers, while being much more cost effective, just don't feel right.' He was very forthright in his defence.

'Hey, don't get defensive, I think it's great.' Petra laughed, throwing up her hands before her face in mock defence. 'It's just I've never seen all this before. Most traders supply the bare minimum. It's no wonder you can attract the best people; you treat them like family.'

'Well to me, that's what they are. Trading is a solitary business...trips can take years and I believe a few creature comforts make it more bearable. If others do it differently, that's their business, but anyone who works with me deserves the same as I do.'

Petra moved to Aaron, reached up and kissed him. 'No more talk, I'm dying to get in.' She moved away and removed her clothes; Aaron stood back enjoying the view. She bent to check the water temperature and then turned to see Aaron standing naked just watching. "Enjoying the show?' she asked. 'Silly question...I can see you are,' she teased as she gazed at his hardening penis. She came back to him, reached out and began to caress him.

'Don't mind him...he has a mind of his own. The rest of me is interested, just too bloody tired. Try again after a few hours' sleep.'

Petra gave him a wicked look and dropped to her knees. 'What if I don't want to wait?' She guided him into her mouth and Aaron's groans told her he was enjoying her attention. Suddenly she stopped.' You're right...we both really need sleep.'

She stepped into the tub and reluctantly, Aaron climbed in after her. They reclined in the bubbling water allowing it to soothe away the tensions of the last few days. After a few minutes Petra moved over to Aaron.

'Well, do you feel refreshed enough now?'

He reached to her, pulled her close and answered her with a kiss. Petra straddled him, slowly lowering herself onto him, engulfing him. They held each other tightly and made love slowly in the spa.

15

*T*ocmal was having difficulty with the command chair until he discovered the recline function.

With the chair laid back, and a couple of cushions he found in one of the cabins, he was able to fashion an acceptable imitation of a Reglaon seat. The entire transit was preprogramed into the nav system so now he was able to monitor the ship's systems in relative comfort while the others had some welcome down time.

Mondrac hadn't looked up from the screen for nearly three hours, so engrossed in his work that time had no meaning. Maybe it was time to divert his attention?

'Mondrac,' Tocmal asked tentatively, 'would you like a coffee?' No answer. He spoke again, this time louder. 'Mondrac, 'would you like a coffee?'

This time an answer came. 'Yes, please.'

Tocmal chuckled. 'I would too but I actually don't know how to make it. Can you assist?'

Mondrac looked up from the console and smiled. 'You are correct, my friend. I need a break, thank you.'

Together they left the bridge and went back to the dining area. Mondrac busied himself making coffee, putting several spoons of sugar into Tocmal's—he'd developed quite a taste for sweet, strong coffee. They sat in silence while they drank. When they finished, Tocmal took their mugs, put them in the sanitiser and followed Mondrac back to the bridge. With his work with the computer completed they now had a few possible locations for a second gate in the Twelfth Realm and, based on these assumptions, the possible location of others in the Tenth.

'Why did you need to do that? Our ships will destroy what's left of the portal in our realm.'

'You may destroy that one, but what if there is a second? Suppose there was an accident on the one we found? The explosion would solve the mystery of where all that energy came from. But I don't think it is the only option. Zarof was far too arrogant, and Nefaris is far too cautious for that. No, Tocmal, I don't think the threat is over yet. We need to find the portal in the Twelfth Realm and destroy it also.' Mondrac's voice was filled with conviction. Tocmal realised that for an Eldoran to propose such violent action the situation was dire.

Ten hours after they retired, Petra and Aaron returned to the bridge. Mondrac had left to rest and Tocmal was working on the computer, so absorbed he didn't see them enter.

Aaron checked the clock on the main viewer. 'Good morning Tocmal.'

Tocmal was startled by the figure at his side. 'Yes, you are correct...good morning.'

'Anything interesting?'

'Yes, Mondrac suggested it. While we can all understand each other, what happens when we reach Earth? Are you going to translate for us? Not very practical, I think. Mondrac suggested I work with your computer; it does have a basic translation capability.'

This amused Aaron. Humans had made such a fuss about their universal translator and here was the first real alien they had encountered dismissing it.'

Tocmal continued. 'The parameters in your standard system are very narrow so I have modified the program to allow it to work more efficiently. All we need to do is transmit this new routine to any receiving station...another ship for example. If it is equipped with even the most basic of translation capability the new routine will automatically upgrade it. For all other situations, where I will be talking in person, I have a simple translator system that can be worn by each person...everyone will be able to communicate normally.'

Aaron studied the schematics on the console screen; the design was simple, elegant and easily fabricated.

'Tocmal, when we reach our realm, I would like to send these to a facility where they can be manufactured. Hopefully when we reach Earth, there should be enough to supply those who need it. I would also like to send any details of your particular requirements...chair and bed design, for example.'

'An excellent idea. While I have made do on your bridge it is not the most comfortable arrangement.' Tocmal worked his personal data pad and transferred the relevant files to Junior's data bank. 'There...all is now available. A-Bra-Ham, I have also placed all the technical detail from our engineers, the repairs to your ship, and all the data on the upgrade.

'The resin is one of our most closely guarded secrets. It is one of our main tactical advantages, but we would be open to trading it with you. To assist in this our engineers have placed a quantity in your hold. It is not a great amount, but enough for a thorough evaluation. I have placed the application details in your data base. We ask that you use it wisely and then we can negotiate on trade.'

'I understand,' replied Aaron. 'Rest assured, we will evaluate it and then we can negotiate a mutually beneficial agreement.'

Tocmal stood and stretched, he too was feeling the strain. Aaron went with him to one of the rooms where they improvised a sleeping arrangement so he could rest comfortably, then returned to the bridge. As the door slid open he heard the chime of the computer indicating that an analysis program had just finished. Aaron went straight to the console, brought up the results but had no idea what they meant. Whatever Mondrac was working on, it would have to wait.

'What time is it?' Aaron asked Petra. 'Zero nine hundred, Earth time. Why?' 'I'm hungry. Care for some breakfast?'

'Yes, but it's *my* turn. You take over here, while I go and play in your kitchen.' Petra stood and offered the command chair to Aaron.

Twenty minutes later, Petra returned with two plates and a pot of tea. On each plate was a sandwich with Poragan ham, egg and hollandaise dressing, on a lightly toasted bread roll. 'I couldn't believe it when I saw you had Poragan ham in your stasis larder...it's so hard to come by. I used generous slices...I hope that's ok?'

Aaron laughed. 'Just the way I like it...thick! We have a contract with the major producer on Poraga...we transport all their smallgoods.' He took a bite and smiled. 'Damn good...looks like we'll have fun in the kitchen.' He winked as he took another bite.

They finished their breakfast in silence. 'We will reinsert in about twenty minutes,' Aaron commented as she rose and left with the empty plates.

Petra returned just as the ship re-materialised back into the Eleventh Realm, changed course and proceeded on the new heading toward their last worm hole insertion point in this realm. Another three hours, then they would jump back to the Twelfth Realm. Six hours from now they should be in the Solar System, and close to Earth. Petra had just sat in the pilot seat when an alarm started to scream.

'Proximity alarm...there is something ahead of us!' She started to interrogate the system. 'It's a ship, just off line to port with a very low energy reading. Either it doesn't want to be seen or it's in trouble!'

'Wake the others up...we may need their help,' Aaron commanded as he resumed manual control. One golden rule he always obeyed: never leave a ship stranded. If he could assist he would. Petra complied as she brought the shields and weapons on line.

'Shields at full strength, weapons at standby...remember, we only have half a dozen torpedos left,' Petra reported as Mondrac and Tocmal hurried back onto the bridge.

'A-Bra-Ham, do we have trouble?' Tocmal asked.

'I'm not sure, we seem to have a ship ahead...no power signature...no motion.' Aaron had altered course and was now on an intercept trajectory. 'Distance to target one hundred thousand kilometres.' He continued to decelerate, 'time to intercept...ten minutes.'

The time dragged by, the Bubble indicating they were closing on the mystery ship. It felt like an eternity as the distance slowly decreased. Mondrac manned the sensor console, watching for any tell-tale that might indicate some sort of treachery. Closer now—only 50,000 kilometres separated them.

'Mondrac, can you give us a visual?' Aaron asked.

The Eldoran worked the console and a hazy image appeared.

'Not close enough...what's the radiation reading?'

'Nothing's registering, just normal background for this sector.' Mondrac continued his sensor probes. Junior edged closer, Petra keeping a solid target lock on the other vessel.

At 20,000 kilometres, Aaron slowed Junior even more. Mondrac, as if reading his mind, spoke at once. 'Nothing showing on long range scans. We seem to be alone...except for our friend. I still cannot determine any life signs.'

'What do you mean by *determine*?'

'I have been getting very faint, intermittent readings, human life signs. But the reading is not reliable. I will keep trying.'

Aaron urged Junior ahead, slowly closing the gap—10,000 kilometres—5,000. The image on the screen cleared, the ship was now clearly defined. Petra started the recognition program, searching Junior's data base for the identity of the ship.

Aaron decided to close and orbit the ship at the same time, giving them a full 360 degree view of the mystery vessel. As they passed the rear of the ship, its fate became evident. A huge hole had been blasted through what should have been the engineering section. It was all gone.

'Mondrac, are you still getting power readings?' Aaron called.

'Yes, very low output and only in one section of the ship.' He used his console and the view of the ship changed. They were still circling it, recording all they saw, but now the screen showed what the sensors were detecting. The design looked familiar to Aaron; a long ovoid shape, flatter on the underside and steeply domed on top, the square rear had been blasted away, exposing the entrails of the ship.

Two tubular protrusions either side of the hull were also heavily damaged, these would have housed the main reactors, generators and drive systems. Now they were just blasted wreckage. The view changed as Mondrac superimposed his power readings and life signs onto the screen. They could all clearly see the problem; just at the rear of the bridge section, there appeared to be a small power source and, more importantly, two life signs.

Mondrac spoke quietly. 'Two very weak life signs...both Human. I have deduced that they are in some sort of life preserving area but their power is quickly depleting. A-Bra-Ham, they only have a matter of minutes of power left.' As he spoke, the screen changed. Aaron now had "Junior" sitting above the derelict vessel, and only 75 kilometres away.

'Now we know who they are,' he said as he enhanced the insignia emblazoned across the front of the hull—the "skull and T" of Tragarian Raiders. 'The mystery of the bodies back on Reglaos is solved, but we have a new one. How in fucking hell did these clowns get here?' he said as he left the command chair.

'Number one, you have the con. Mondrac, Tocmal...I'm going over there. I can't just leave them to die, but I'll need a Second...any volunteers?'

'While Tocmal might be more appropriate, I don't think you have any extra vehicular suits for him, which makes me the only option.' Mondrac said, following Aaron as they left the bridge. Directly below the accommodation deck was a small docking bay. Inside, they quickly donned two suits made of a flexible Acrilan material. It not only protected them from the cold and radiation of space, it could also withstand quite a large number of impacts from debris, making it like a suit of flexible armour. They each selected a helmet, connected the small life support module and were ready.

Aaron opened a cupboard, took out a belt with two blasters attached and buckled it on. He offered one to Mondrac, who declined. Aaron just shrugged, checked the charge of his weapons and re-holstered them. He moved toward the rear of the room, opened another door and beckoned Mondrac to follow him. While Junior was classed as a pleasure boat, Aaron had made sure the design was capable of holding one of the units now before them, a small shuttle, ten metres long and three wide and high. It had a standard gravitron drive, but no reactor, with all the power it needed stored in the two nacelles on its underside.

'Range is limited, but it can hold up to six people. We should be able to get over there and back pretty quick,' he said with pride. A section of the side of the pod moved away from the body and slid rearwards, leaving an entry port for them. Inside were seats for the pilot, co-pilot and four more for passengers. Aaron took the right hand seat and contacted Petra. 'Number one, we are in the pod. The door is now closed and sealed, commence depressurising the chamber.' They watched the indicator on the wall outside the pod; it changed from red to green. 'Now open the doors please.'

They felt the machinery of the door opening beneath them; Aaron powered the pod's systems as this happened. 'Ok Junior, pod ready, releasing clamps.' He tapped an icon on the control panel and the little pod shuddered slightly as the docking clamps released. 'Commence ejection procedure.' As Aaron said this, a blast of compressed CO_2 shot the small craft out of the docking bay. He started the drive, setting course directly to the other ship.

'This is an interesting vessel A-Bra-Ham...what is its purpose?'

'Originally, it was designed as a maintenance support pod,' Aaron replied. 'It can carry six, has a small one-man airlock at the rear and various grabs and implements to help with any repairs the crew needs to do. We manufacture them on Argos and sell them right across our galaxy. I just liked them, and this little guy is the most I can fit in Junior. One problem

I hope we don't regret...no weapons just tools.'

He smiled as he concentrated on the ship; now only a few thousand metres ahead. Deftly he moved the pod to the front of the ship, looking for an entry point. 'I think this is a Tellurian vessel. If so, we should be able to access the emergency hatch just to the right of the bridge.' Aaron moved the ship closer. Having located the best place to enter, he accelerated towards it. 'Junior, what's the status of those two life signs?'

Not good, you need to hurry...one seems to be fading faster.

Aaron didn't need any more convincing. He turned the pod through 180 degrees and lined the rear airlock up with the emergency hatch.

A-Bra-Ham, according to your computer, those two only have about three minutes left. Tocmal's voice echoed in the pod.

'Shit, this is going to be close!' Aaron worked faster, lining the pod up. 'They tell me these little pods are very tough... we're about to find out. No time for a soft lock, we're going in hard.' To attach the pod to the hatch would normally take about five minutes; for a true soft lock, they only had three—total. Lock on, get to the survivors and revive them—just three minutes.

Captain, I'm transmitting a schematic of the ship to you, Petra called. Junior's computer had confirmed the mystery ship's identity and supplied the schematics for it. Mondrac received it and transferred it to a data pad. There was a loud *Bang* and the pod came to a stand-still. Aaron checked all the readings and leapt out of his seat.

'Mondrac...in that cupboard...extra oxygen tanks...grab a couple,' he called as he worked the airlock internal controls. 'This can only take one at a time. I'll go first...cycle time is only about ten seconds so we should be ok. I'll let you know when I'm inside.' The internal door opened and Aaron stepped through. He pressed the cycle control and the airlock tried to connect to the hatch controls—no luck. The hatch control wasn't compatible.

Quickly, Aaron started the manual cycle, dumping the air in the lock back into the pod's tanks. A tell-tale light changed from green to red, indicating that all the air had been transferred—the outer door would open. It slid across easily, exposing the hatch manual control. He opened the control box—manual override was still operational. He interrogated the system; there was no atmosphere in the ship. 'Mondrac, on the rear panel beside the airlock door, there's a control panel. Can you see it?'

'Yes, I see it.'

'Good, open it. Make sure your helmet is closed and your oxygen is feeding.'

'I have done this A-Bra-Ham.'

'Good, there is a yellow button on the lower right part of the panel.'

'I have it.'

'OK, that will depressurise the cabin...just press it. All the air in the cabin will be drained into the tanks.'

'Yes, I have pressed it.'

'When the light on the top of the panel turns red, all the air has drained and you can open the door.'

'Yes,' Mondrac replied as the door opened. 'I have done this A-Bra-Ham.'

As Mondrac stepped through, Aaron moved aside and let him into the ship's airlock. Aaron stepped back into the pod, opened a storage locker and took out two cylinders. 'Collapsible stretchers, we may need them.' Together they raced toward the nearest emergency passage, looking for a way down the three levels to where the victims were.

'Here!' Aaron cried as he wrenched a door open. Mondrac consulted his data pad and agreed. Inside the door was a stairwell, thankfully not an emergency ladder. Even with the greatly diminished gravity on the ship, Aaron didn't like the idea of having to haul two dead weights up a ladder; stairs would be bad enough. The lower gravity might be a help on the return journey but trying to go down was a real pain.

Aaron suddenly had an idea—he climbed over the stair rail and pushed himself down with all his strength. *Three floors in three seconds,* he thought as he grabbed the railing on the floor he wanted. Mondrac joined him moments later. Next, they forced the emergency door open, taking precious seconds looking for something to prop it open, a fire extinguisher finally doing the trick.

Again Mondrac looked at the pad; three doors down the corridor and on their right should find their target; a small chamber at the rear of the bridge.

I don't like being the bearer of bad news but I think you should hurry, Petra's voice sounded inside their helmets. *We just detected three vessels heading this way, at extreme sensor range, but they seem to be moving quickly.*

'It never rains...' Aaron grumbled to himself as they reached the door. He stopped, looked at Mondrac and drew one of his blasters. 'Just in case,' he explained and kicked the door in. Unconscious on the floor were the two survivors. Aaron grabbed the med-kit he had strapped to his thigh and took out the sensor unit, powering it up as Mondrac connected a new oxygen tank to each survivor. He quickly ran the sensor head over them.

'Not good,' he said to himself, 'severe oxygen depletion, hypothermia...life signs are very weak...they're both in comas. We're going to have to carry them back.' He took one of the canisters he had brought, opened it and lay out the contents, Mondrac doing the same with the other. The two stretchers were quickly assembled and, to Aaron's relief both had small anti-grav units in the kit. Once each victim was securely fastened to a stretcher, Aaron activated the anti-gravs and the stretchers both floated off the floor.

'Mondrac, can you get these two back to the pod?'

'Yes, A-Bra-Ham but what are you going to do?'

'The bridge... if I can access their data core, we could get a few more answers.'

Mondrac could see the reasoning. 'Time may be the issue.'

Aaron nodded and called the ship. 'Junior, how far out are our visitors?'

Tocmal answered. *Fifteen of your minutes...we have identified them...Galdorans.* Aaron could almost feel the anger in Tocmal.

'This is going to be real tight. Mondrac, we better get going.'

Mondrac nodded and started to push the two stretchers out of the room. Aaron turned in the opposite direction; ten metres further down the corridor was the entrance to the bridge. As he reached the doorway, he saw the faint red glow of the emergency lighting indicating the door was open. He turned just in time to see Mondrac disappear up the stair well then he stepped onto the bridge.

The story in here was different: five bodies lay sprawled, still strapped in at their stations. Aaron felt a cold shiver run down his spine; he had only ever needed to board a dead ship once before and that memory still haunted him. He shook his head to clear his thoughts, turned to the main computer access control and tapped the power button. He was in luck—the backup power supply still had a little life in it. He quickly searched the system for the data core and found it attached to the base of the command chair.

Aaron moved to the chair, unbuckled the captain's body and moved it aside, his mind screaming for him to get out, as the body floated away. He resisted the fear; *I've got to get the core*. He lifted the cushion from the seat. There was a code pad, still powered but, without the code, he couldn't access the core. 'How long, Junior?'

Eight minutes until they are in firing range...get moving! Petra said, her tone conveying the urgency.

He stood, trying to figure out a way to break the code but there would be over ten million possible combinations. *Two minutes gone...*Aaron thought, as he drew one of his blasters...*no time for finesse, brute strength is all I've got.* He set the weapon to a very fine beam and started cutting the seat off the base; it fell away, exposing the core and its connections.

Aaron grabbed the main connector, ripped it out and used the blaster to cut away the four bolts securing the core to the base. It floated slightly, free of its enclosure. He grabbed it and started for the door knowing he was racing against time. He tore up the stairs, leaping from one landing to the next, the weight of the core negligible in the near-zero gravity. As he reached the last floor, Tocmal's voice entered his helmet, his tone cold and impassive.

A-Bra-Ham, I have a passive lock on all three Galdoran ships. Do I have your permission to fire?

'Not yet...how long?'

Two minutes.

'As soon as the pod leaves, they'll see it but Junior will still be invisible. Have they powered their weapons?'

In truth I do not know; we are only using passive sensors but their output seems to indicate they have. They haven't raised their shields yet though.

Aaron stopped to think...*no shields...why have weapons powered and not shields?* Then it hit him, 'Tocmal, how long before they reach optimum effective range?'

Another six minutes, why?

'Ok, that gives us what...eight minutes? They're here to destroy the evidence, and I'll bet they won't waste energy firing from extreme range. They'll need to make sure, so I believe they'll wait until their weapons will have the most effect and they won't need shields to protect from debris.' Aaron started walking towards the airlock. 'The instant we fire up the pod, we'll be visible, and a sitting duck. No, we'll wait until they reach their firing point, then we'll detach from the ship. At that time you have permission to fire, agreed?'

Agreed, Tocmal replied, a little too enthusiastically.

Aaron walked the last few metres to the pod, secured the ship's door and cycled the pod's airlock. He placed the core into a storage cupboard behind the passenger seats, and moved to the control panel, re-established the pods atmosphere and waited for the tell-tale to change. He moved to the two patients, running the instruments over them again.

"Still in comas but their oxygen levels are climbing, I think they'll make it.' Aaron dialled the oxygen concentration back and took his seat at the controls, Mondrac taking the one beside him. 'You heard?'

'Yes, A-Bra-Ham...unfortunately, I see no other solution and we will be the aggressors in this encounter.'

'Yeah an encounter in a dead realm with an adversary who isn't supposed to have the technology to get here. An adversary with no valid reason to destroy that ship, and that ship is from our realm and should have no way to reach here either. I think we can leave it to history to sort that out. All I want to do is get out of here in one piece.'

A-Bra-Ham, Tocmal was almost whispering in anticipation, *one minute until they reach their optimum firing point.*

'Thanks, we're ready,' Aaron replied. To Mondrac he added with an amused grimace. 'Sounds like the little guy is enjoying this, a little too much.'

Mondrac nodded. 'Reglaons are very passionate creatures.'

Aaron disengaged the docking clamps and let the small craft slowly drift away from the derelict, hoping they looked like a piece of wreckage. He slowly turned onto a heading for Junior and stabilised the pod's attitude.

He looked back to Junior; it was moving slowly. Petra was giving Tocmal the best firing solution she could. Aaron checked the time again: thirty seconds.

Aaron started his mental count down. It was as if he'd choreographed the whole thing. As his mind reached zero, Junior opened fire. The Galdoran ships opened fire and Aaron pushed the little pod's throttle to maximum. It accelerated quickly.

So too did the torpedos from the Galdoran ships.

The pod may have been sturdy but it had no shields, only forward and lateral deflectors which weren't designed to withstand the onslaught about to rain down on it. The pod also didn't have much of a sensor array so Aaron was flying blind; he couldn't track the progress of the Galdoran weapons. He cut propulsion and turned the ship through 180 degrees, to face the Tellurian derelict.

Now, to his far right, he could see the track of the weapons. He increased power to the deflectors and watched. Two seconds later, twelve torpedos slammed into the hulk in a spectacular explosion. Debris flew out in all directions, scattering any evidence over a huge area, some of it heading toward the pod.

'Here it comes...brace yourself!' Aaron shouted.

A large amount of wreckage was on course to hit them.

'There's too much debris, and it's coming faster than we can run!' Aaron cried, desperately trying to manoeuvre out of the way.

Suddenly the pod shuddered to a standstill. Aaron switched to the rear view screen, frantically searching for what they had hit; nothing.

Somehow, they were now dead—just hanging in space. Then a shadow moved over them.

Petra manoeuvred Junior between the pod and the oncoming debris cloud, the shields taking the brunt of the impact. The small amount that broke through was deflected by the new resin compound from Reglaos.

Aaron saw the pod bay hatch open. He quickly moved the pod into position and the docking grapple that Petra had used to catch them pulled them into the bay. Once the atmospheric conditions were matched, he opened the pod door just as Petra entered the bay.

She walked up to him, threw her arms around him and kissed him, a long desperate kiss. She broke free and punched him in the chest.

'What's that for?'

"For scaring the shit out of me; next time you decide to play hero, don't!' she said and kissed him again.

'Who's on the bridge?'

Petra smiled. 'Gunner Tocmal; he's scanning for more

Galdorans and his eyes are doing that red thing again.'

Aaron just shrugged. 'At least he's enjoying himself.'

They moved back to the pod, retrieved the two patients and took them to the med bay, Aaron now grateful that Henry had over-ordered equipment. Both stasis pods were connected to the med bay systems for the trip back to Earth, keeping the occupants sedated and nourished for the duration.

As Aaron resumed his position in the command chair, Tocmal reported. 'I moved the ship to a safe distance, and cannot find any additional Galdorans.' The ships he had fired on were now only three glowing debris clouds on the screen.

'Now can we go home?' Petra asked as she re-initiated the nav program and turned the ship back on the correct course for their last jump co-ordinates. Three hours later, the jump drive powered up and FTS Condor Junior quietly left the Eleventh Realm.